"**W**hen word reached us that a self-styled writer was engaged in a muckraking campaign that could besmirch the reputation of the finest secondary school west of the Mississippi, we naturally became concerned," said Mr. Gillis. "So we took steps to learn more about him."

"So we could scare him off."

"Oh, we doubted extreme measures would be necessary. Had he been the person he claimed to be, of course."

"Of course."

"But our inquiries revealed that you are not a historian at all, popular or otherwise, you are a private eye. What are you up to, Mr. Tanner?"

I shrugged. "I'm undertaking an investigation for hire— that's almost always what I'm up to."

"There are a great many persons of influence in this community who do not take kindly to seeing the institution they cherish above all others being slandered by a . . . man such as yourself."

"If there're no skeletons in the Sebastian closets, you don't have anything to worry about."

"Sebastian is not immune to unfounded rumor, Mr. Tanner. In these days of media zealotry, few institutions are."

"I'll try to be discreet."

"I'm afraid that's not satisfactory."

"What is?"

"That you desist your prying immediately."

I smiled my friendly smile. "I'm afraid that's impossible. I'm like a bulldog, Mr. Gillis—only the client can call me off. And that's not a nuance, it's a rule."

BOOK CASE

A JOHN MARSHALL TANNER MYSTERY

BOOK CASE

STEPHEN
GREENLEAF

BANTAM BOOKS
NEW YORK · TORONTO · LONDON · SYDNEY · AUCKLAND

This edition contains the complete text
of the original hardcover edition.
NOT ONE WORD HAS BEEN OMITTED.

BOOK CASE

A Bantam Crime Line Book / published by arrangement with
William Morrow and Company

PRINTING HISTORY
Morrow edition published 1991
Bantam edition / January 1992

ISBN 0-553-29061-4

Published simultaneously in the United States and Canada

PRINTED IN THE UNITED STATES OF AMERICA

RAD   0 9 8 7 6 5 4 3 2

again, for Aaron

God is a guerrilla.

HOMAGE TO HAMMURABI, p. 9

Chapter
1

I'm not certain whether the affliction originates in genetic disinclination or environmentally induced aversion, but I've always been more a recluse than a celebrant. Most of my lies have been uttered to evade the sticky dangle of a social occasion, and most of my alcoholic intake has been consumed to ease me through those festivities I've been too timid or unimaginative to avoid. As a result, parties and I pretty much parted company early in the last decade, when staying home with Malamud or Mahler or Montana began to seem preferable to most of the alternatives that came my way—cocooning, I believe they call it now that the taste-makers have followed my lead. So it was distinctly out of the ordinary for me to be parading my hard-won nonchalance on the fringes of a handsomely refurbished loft on the trendiest corner south of Market, with something called the Sunday Punch sloshing over the rim of the plastic glass that had been foisted on me the moment I arrived, as I waited for my host to find time to tell me why I'd been invited to spend an evening with half a hundred guests who were far too young to have been confronted by life's more vicious vicissitudes, at least not the sort that made my own little ledge of the world a precarious perch.

As out of place as a parent at a prom, all I knew as I looked for something sufficiently potent to wash away the lingering sweetness of my drink was that Bryce Chatterton had been a friend for twenty years, and all I guessed was that, given the nature of my business, he was in some kind of trouble. If that was the case, I would do anything I could to help, within reason or without. A dozen years ago, Bryce had ushered me across a nasty wrinkle in my life, when my failure to become either professionally consequential or personally connubial had spawned a depression that only Bryce's relentless applications of common sense and good cheer had lured me out of. As a result, I had owed him a debt for a long time. As with all my debts, I would feel better once it was paid off.

The name on the building read PERIWINKLE PRESS, broadcasting its presence to the ever-less-literate nation by a block of off-white neon featuring an appropriately leafy logo that entwined itself among the blinking letters and garlanded them with blossoms of literally electric blue. Bryce Chatterton was the founder, president, and sole surviving editor of the enterprise. Ostensibly, the purpose of the party was to announce Periwinkle's publication of a collection of poetry by the young woman who was now backed into the far corner of the room by the press of her gushing admirers, her smile just slightly less dazzling than the head she had shaved to her scalp in honor of the occasion. All of which was further proof that I must have been present for some other reason—I haven't read a poem since the day Walt Kelly died and took Pogo and Albert with him.

Since in attitude, age and attire I was easily branded alien, my tour of the room was unimpeded by fellowship. I was not entirely bored, however—there's a hot new parlor game making the rounds in San Francisco these days. It's called Earthquake, and the object is to relate the most terrifying, heartwarming, scandalous, or apocalyptic experience that has at least a tenuous connection to the October tremor or its aftermath. The winner, of course, usually tells a tale that combines at least three of those attributes while suggesting he somehow managed to experience the event while at Candlestick Park, on the Bay Bridge, in the Marina, near the Nimitz, and under the bay in a BART tube, in an amazing feat of simultaneity. But the best this party could come up with was some suburbanites' competitive comparison of how much water the quake had sloshed out of their in-ground pools.

Thankfully, the evening was not without its other charms, most of which consisted of the literary snippets that wafted my way as I trailed my host around the room:

"I hear they only printed two hundred copies; that's barely enough to supply her ex-husbands. Of course nowadays what with computerized typesetting they can go back to press in a minute. I think Doubleday printed my book on Lapland life-styles one at a time. . . ."

"He got a five-figure advance from Harper for a coffee-table book about owls. Who knew owls were going to be big, for God's sake?"

"I heard the film rights went for a million, then when Redford decided to do Beanfield instead they just stuck it on the shelf. But why should she care, right? I mean, she can make her own movie for that kind of money, as long as she doesn't have to pick up the cocaine tab. . . ."

"He told me Mailer read it and loved it but Random's list is full till ninety-two and Meredith's not taking on anyone new. I was going to send it to Pynchon, but only his agent seems to know where he is and she's not telling. I guess I'll write a romance in the meantime, just to tide me over. I mean how hard could it be—a mansion, two rapes, and a seduction and they sail off into the setting sun. . . ."

"He told me I didn't really want to write, I only wanted to 'be a writer.' Can you believe it? And to think I was actually going in on a condo with the creep. . . ."

"I'm almost thirty pages into it. Candace says it's the best thing I've ever done, but she thinks it should be a play because my dialogue's so today it totally overwhelms the narrative. At least that's what Candace says. So I was wondering if you'd take a look and tell me what you think. . . ."

"Her editor moved to New Zealand to herd sheep or something and the manuscript disappeared in the process, only Hortense didn't know it for six months. In the meantime, she started seeing a channeler in Emeryville who convinced her that novels were spiritually irrelevant, so when she finally got it back she fed all nine hundred pages

*into the barbecue and cooked a Cornish game hen over
them. She always was an Anglophile, you know. . . ."*

*"The only intelligent thing he ever said to me about
writing fiction was, 'Just because it happened, doesn't
mean it's good.' "*

I continued my misanthropic drift, avoiding the few
people who seemed inclined to talk about something other
than themselves, trying to keep the punch within the
rhomboid confines of the plastic glass, keeping one weary
eye on my host. Weaving his way like an eel through the
gaggle of distaff groupies, Bryce Chatterton was a dervish
of wit and hospitality, keeping glasses topped up, fingers
filled with food, and people whose propinquity was solely
geographical apprised of each other's deliciously eclectic
life-style. Whenever our eyes met, Bryce invariably sig-
naled that he'd be with me in a minute, he had just one more
thing to take care of, he hoped I understood, but somehow
that minute never came. As at every party I'd ever attended,
no matter where you had come from or where you wanted
to go, time stopped well short of satisfaction.

Meanwhile, Bryce's wife occupied a companionably
overstuffed chair in the corner of the room opposite the
guest of honor, her eyes buried in a book she was careful to
demonstrate was *not* the volume being feted that evening.
Normally, such outré behavior would be chastised by a
self-appointed social arbiter, but since Margaret Chatterton's money had underwritten the entire decade of Periwinkle's perilous existence, no one chose to take umbrage at
such aggressive aloofness. Not out loud, at any rate.

The next time I looked her way, I caught Margaret
watching me, a furrow in her brow and a purse to her lips.
But instead of acknowledging my glance, she lowered her
eyes to her book and pretended neither our senses nor our
sightlines had never tangled, a reaction only too indicative
of the state of our mutual regard.

I'd first met her husband back in his bachelor days,
when we began to run into each other at various clubs
around the city in pursuit of our mutual passion for the
bebop trumpet. Periodic encounters at Basin Street West
and El Matador eventually evolved into the bar-ballgame-
bullshit triumvirate that was the cornerstone of male friend-

ship in the days before estimations of present and prospective wealth became the exclusive subject of discussion in the city.

When we met, Bryce had only recently abandoned the literary aspirations that had been fueled by his idolization of Scott Fitzgerald and his Stegner fellowship in Stanford's famous writing program. A clerk in a Post Street used bookstore—an *antiquarian bookshop,* its owner dubbed it in order to justify the markup—Bryce was barely earning enough to stay afloat in the increasingly precious nectar that was post-sixties San Francisco. But because even more than jazz, books were his major passion, he was content to be a minor player in the minor minuet that passed for the city's literary scene.

Eventually, Bryce began to appear with less and less frequency at our haunts. Since both the quantity and quality of American jazz had already begun its steep decline, I thought that might be the reason for his absence. But what I hoped was that, in contrast to my quarter century of failure in that regard, Bryce had found a woman he liked well enough to marry.

Most men are by nature unskilled in the things that matter. Indeed, it is often the very size of their ineptitude that makes them marriageable, in need of a complementary union to function at anything resembling their best. Because Bryce Chatterton was less able than anyone I knew at the mechanics of existence—Bryce couldn't fry an egg, for example, or fill out a deposit slip—I was cheered when I learned his rescue had been realized.

Margaret had seemed in the nature of a coup for Bryce, someone who both shared his love for books and possessed a net worth that could afford him a regular diet of the pricey first editions that were locked away in the long glass case at the rear of his employer's musty establishment. Though the outward signs were thus encouraging, and I wished the two of them nothing but the best, the downside was that our friendship failed to survive the marriage. Partly because such friendships rarely do, partly because Periwinkle was founded shortly thereafter and immediately knotted the loose ends in Bryce's days and evenings, and partly because Margaret clearly felt that private investigators occupied a slot in the social strata somewhere below men's room attendants, an opinion that seemed to slip a notch after she was introduced to me.

Nonetheless, I was pleased when Bryce began to ascend through the local literary stratosphere and when his bon mots began to appear in the city's most prominent gossip column almost as frequently as Strange de Jim's. He would telephone me periodically to bemoan the premature demise of one of our musical idols, or rhapsodize over the discovery of his latest genius, and we would exchange heartfelt pledges to get together soon, for baseball or for lunch. But except for a handful of rather rote occasions and an all-too-recent disaster during a party at my apartment, we seldom followed through. Suddenly ten years had passed, and when I received an invitation to the publication party it was out of a blue as blue as a periwinkle's tiny bloom.

When Bryce swept past me yet another time and tried to give me something resembling a mollusk pursuing a sunburn on a Ritz, I asked him how long he thought it would be before we could talk. Bryce is both thoroughly polite and relentlessly optimistic, which tends to overload his expression with a guileless mix of astonishment and glee. In answer to my question, his eyes blazed so brightly behind their steel-rimmed glasses it seemed certain he intended the next book on Periwinkle's list to be entitled *Talks with Tanner*.

"Soon, Marsh," he promised. "I'm going to shoo them off to the Café Roma in ten minutes. I've arranged something special for Matilda tonight—they're pouring a new drink in her honor, named after the new book. Cointreau, cinnamon, and clotted cream; I think she'll be pleased, don't you?"

I glanced at Matilda. Her pate was glistening from the warmth of her reception and she was clutching her book to her side as though its gossamer imagery would fly away if her grip loosened even slightly. The poems were about traffic, I'd heard someone say—cars and trucks and what happens when you ride around in them. The collection was entitled *Gridlock*, and the jacket photograph featured Matilda in a bikini and a chaise longue, recumbent on an endangered species—an empty parking space within a mile of Union Square.

As one of Matilda's more unctuous friends began extolling her talent at the expense of Amy Clampitt, Bryce glanced furtively at his watch. "I'll meet you in my office at nine, Marsh; you can go on back, if you like. There's scotch in the credenza, lower left—I know that's more your style. But first I've got to try to convince a young postmodern to send her new collection to Periwinkle. She's clearly ready to break out—with the right promotion and some suitably bizarre behavior on her part, I think I can make her the next Kathy Acker."

With a flip of his hand, Bryce went off to foist the Ritz on an impressively outlandish young woman who seemed more insulted than thrilled by the attention, which no doubt made her personality congruent with her prose. When Bryce was well into his spray of flattery, I surveyed my surroundings more closely, since it was my first visit to Periwinkle's inner sanctum.

The party was corrupting what was normally the conference room. Darkly handsome, it was furnished in the timeless style of an English men's club, with ponderous leather chairs and heavily tufted chesterfields. Beneath the gleaming brass reading lamps suitably esoteric tomes were displayed on deeply oiled occasional tables. The wall at my back was entirely a bookshelf and its opposite was mostly glass, beyond which a leather bar and a fabricating plant mocked us from the ungentrified side of the street.

On the wall to my right, precisely paneled squares bore framed and spotlighted covers from Periwinkle's meager backlist, matted in a brilliant blue. Although I read my share of reviews and spent more than a few of my Saturday mornings browsing through the Recent Acquisitions section of my neighborhood library branch, few of the titles were familiar to me. Which might have explained why Margaret Chatterton had a scowl on her face when I looked her way a second time.

When I bowed toward what looked like the standard edition of her disdain, she unexpectedly motioned for me to join her. Margaret was one of those women who demands a fealty that exceeds my understanding and is thus beyond my power to confer, which makes me feel vaguely culpable. I obeyed her summons immediately.

"It's been a long time, Marsh," she said, the makings of mischief in her eye. "Are you enjoying your wallow among the literati?"

I looked down at the gray-streaked hair, the narrow nose, the vertically striated neck, the reluctant breasts that barely disturbed the drape of her cashmere dress. "About as much as you are, I'd say."

Her smile turned snide. "Now you know how I felt at your Super Bowl party."

"I wouldn't have been offended if you'd stayed home, Margaret."

"I wouldn't have hesitated to offend *you;* it was Bryce I was worried about. I had to make sure he didn't make any more of those ridiculous wagers."

"Well, you got the job done. As I recall, no one did anything *remotely* ridiculous that day."

She looked up at me as she fiddled with the jewel that was suspended at her throat like a drop of her husband's blood. "I did put a damper on the whole affair, didn't I?"

By the time the 49ers had launched their winning drive, I had been the only one left in the room, the rest of my guests having retired to the Caffé Sport to escape Margaret's running commentary, which made Howard Cosell's sound like the Reverend Schuler's. "That about covers it," I admitted.

She closed her book with the snap of a steel trap. "So what. Football is sadistic and its trappings are sexist. It ought to be banned." With that burst of intellectual fascism, Margaret turned toward the crowd that continued to buzz with pleasure at nothing more apparent than its self-regard. "It's hardly encouraging, is it, to know that the majority of people in this room think literature begins with Erica Jong and ends with Tama Janowitz."

Her words buckled with a contempt so vast it must necessarily have encompassed herself. Since there wasn't anything else to do, and since if Bryce did plan to engage me professionally it would probably be Margaret who paid the bill, I tried to jar her out of it. "You'd prefer they were discussing Jane Austen, I take it. Or maybe Ayn Rand."

She scoffed. "Actually, my disposition is more a matter of money than poetics." She gestured toward the guest of honor. "Would you like to know how much it cost me to publish Matilda's little exercise in blank-verse egoism?"

"How much?"

She licked her lips. "Well, let's see. With a standard trim size like *Gridlock*'s, a small page number and small printing, the figures run something like this—three thousand for the cover design plus another three for the jacket; twenty dollars per page in plate costs, times a hundred pages equals another two thousand; plus a dollar ten per unit in PP and B, plus—"

"What's PP and B?"

"Paper, print, and binding. Which is another twenty-two hundred. Plus a dollar for every book we estimate we'll sell for promotion, which is two thousand more. Plus the royalty to the author, which is ten percent of the cover price, which in this case means a dollar a book. Which gives us . . . what?"

"Something over fourteen thousand dollars."

"Right. And that's just hard cost, not fully allocated—I haven't even *hinted* at overhead yet, which, given the size of our mortgage, is a horror I won't bore you with." Margaret glanced morosely at the wall across from us. "Suffice it to say, all those precious little poems and precocious little novels have cost more than two million dollars to immortalize. Net loss to me, needless to say." She chuckled without a trace of mirth. "That's exclusive of the cost of the stimulants necessary to revive the poor souls who decided to read them."

"That's a lot of money."

Margaret looked at me with a glint of triumph, as though she suspected I had given Bryce the first book he'd ever read and was therefore to blame for his addiction. "Do you sense a little desperation in the air, tonight?" she asked abruptly.

I frowned. "Not particularly. Why?"

"This is his swan song," Margaret said, the final words a spondee of satisfaction. "I've warned Bryce that at the end of the fiscal year I'm pulling the financial plug. When I do,

I'm afraid his lovely little Periwinkle will rapidly begin to wilt."

"I'm sorry to hear that," I said truthfully.

"Why?"

I thought of the hours I'd spent in the presence of nothing but a book, beginning at about age six with a boys' biography of Kit Carson. Laid end to end, the hours would encompass years. The best years of my life, arguably. "Because books are nice things to make, I guess," I muttered with an odd embarrassment. "And because Bryce enjoys his work more than anyone I know."

Margaret pointed toward the wall. "How did you like *Thin Wind*? That was our best-seller: eighteen hundred copies."

"I, ah . . ."

"I'm sure Bryce sent you a galley. What was your favorite part? The celebrated blizzard scene?"

"I guess so. Sure."

Her laugh was the comeuppance I deserved. "*Thin Wind* is set on a banana plantation in Costa Rica; there is no blizzard. That is, if you discount the blizzard of adjectives that is that particular novelist's most egregious affectation."

There was nothing I could say that would take us anywhere I wanted to go, but in a mysterious shift of mood, Margaret looked up at me with uncharacteristic contrition. "Don't be embarrassed, Marsh; actually, I'm flattered that you cared enough to lie to me. And I didn't intend to be mean—I've told you this so you'll help if Bryce starts behaving childishly after I've taken his toy away. I do care for him, you know," she added as though she knew that among more than a few of her husband's friends it was a subject of debate.

In the echo of her final sentiment, I glanced to where Bryce was regaling a bevy of presumably would-be writers with one of the publishing anecdotes he related so irrepressibly, this one having to do with an autograph party at which no one but the author showed up. "He doesn't look too broken up over Periwinkle's imminent demise," I observed carefully.

"Because he doesn't think it's going to happen."

"Does all this have something to do with why I'm here?" I asked when she didn't elaborate.

"Bryce thinks he's found a substitute for me," Margaret muttered, her gaze fixed on her husband, her injured feelings obvious. "Or for my money, at least."

So Bryce has a mistress, I thought. Good for him, I thought next, then wondered why I wasn't ashamed of myself. "An investor, you mean?"

She shook her head. "A book."

I was confused. "What book?"

"A new one. Not yet published. Something Bryce feels could be a true best-seller."

I felt myself redden. "There are already plenty of books about San Francisco private eyes," I demurred insincerely. "Both real ones and imaginary ones."

I expected her to try to convince me otherwise, but Margaret's cockeyed squint meant I was refusing an offer that hadn't been made, which made me redden even further. I had blurted the unnecessary disclaimer because the reference to a mysterious masterpiece had exposed my deepest secret—a secret I'd kept even from my secretary and Bryce Chatterton: some day I wanted to write a novel. Hatched during the reading rampages of my college years, the desire apparently remained so strong some three decades later that it had led me to grasp at an opportunity that wasn't real and indulge myself in images of dust jackets decorated with my photo and book spines resplendent with my name.

Margaret seemed telepathically attuned to my discomfiture. "Bryce doesn't want you to *write* a book; he wants you to *read* one." Her smile turned thuggish. "You do read books, don't you, Marsh?"

"Once in a while," I said, angry at myself for my irrational fantasizing, angry at Margaret for so readily rebuffing me. "But what I get paid for is reading people."

She raised a brow. "Oh? And what do you read in me?"

"A mystery," I said roughly. "Gothic, I'd say."

"Heavens," Margaret Chatterton replied airily, then made as if to probe the assessment further.

But I didn't give her the chance. Before she could question me again, I excused myself and headed for a mood modifier more reliable than punch, put to a pathetic rout by the resurrection of what was at once the most persistent and arrogant of my ambitions.

Before it was summarily stolen from me, I considered teaching the most noble profession of them all. Though now I am in many ways its victim, I still think that: the most noble; and the most treacherous. Perhaps that is nobility's essence, that it cannot exist without peril. Which would explain why, in a society that so maniacally seeks to obviate risk, a champion is so seldom seen.

HOMAGE TO HAMMURABI, p. 31

Chapter
2

The office was much smaller than the conference area, in its relentless clutter and confusion less a room than a cavern carved out of a mountain of books and manuscripts. The only items of decor not related to publishing and Periwinkle were a stack of Bang & Olufsen components in a cabinet behind the desk and an array of photographs of a young woman that was on display in the many nooks and crannies of the room.

After examining the stylized stereo close enough to decipher how to turn it on, I pressed some buttons until I got the tuner locked on KJAZ and the opening bars of a James Moody ballad, then got comfortable in the desk chair, feeling exalted and at home in the cozy room. To pass the time I leafed through a recent *Newsweek*, stopping only to read the cover story on the delectable Michelle Pfeiffer and a review of the new novel by Richard Russo. I put down *Newsweek* and picked up *Publishers Weekly*. An article listing the American media companies now owned by foreign corporations lent further support to a common prognostication—that by the end of the century America will be little more than a satellite of foreign powers, vulnerable to their policies and preferences, significant solely as a market for their wares.

The radio shifted to the Brecker Brothers, and I grew as

restless as their rhythms. After discarding the dregs of the Sunday Punch in a pot of pansies and filling the void with Bryce's Black Label, I left the desk and wandered around the room, pulling books off the shelves as I went, taking the best measure of a man there is next to examining his diary or his tax returns.

Most had been written by well-known Bay Area authors, present and past, from Frank Norris and Dashiell Hammett to Herb Gold and Anne Rice. Almost all were first editions and many were inscribed to Bryce with sentiments ranging from careful courtesy to effusive thanks. After three or four examples of the latter, I found myself taking pleasure in the fact that so many eminent people shared at least one of my opinions—that Bryce Chatterton was a nice guy.

After enjoying an elegantly brief tribute to Bryce from the pen of Alice Walker, I turned my attention to the manuscripts. There was a yard-high pile of them beside the desk. I selected one entitled *Rampage*. The postmark indicated it had been mailed to Periwinkle some three months before, from a man in Hobbs, New Mexico. I thumbed aimlessly through the bright, crisp typescript, wondering if the author rushed to the mailbox each day awaiting word of its fate, wondering if Bryce had become too jaded to marvel any longer at the dreams that lay pressed as hopefully as four-leaf clovers between the pages he so routinely received and presumably, in all but the rarest of cases, dispatched with a rote thumbs down.

I stopped at page 251: "The blood from her breast spurted onto my face like wine from a goatskin, and was thick in my throat as I drank it." For some reason the image made me laugh. Mercifully, the door to the office opened and spared me a further dose of what Faulkner might have become if he'd tried to sell as many books as Stephen King.

Although I was expecting her husband, it was Margaret who succeeded me behind the desk. "Bryce will be in shortly," she informed me as she rummaged through the pile of papers in front of her, her features dense with preoccupation. "The herd has finally been sufficiently fattened and he's driving them toward the exits."

"Good."

When she didn't find whatever it was she was looking for, she looked up. "I want to apologize if I seemed uncharitable in there," she said, looking less apologetic than crafty. "I'm still not certain I'm going to shut Periwinkle down; it all depends on my ex-husband."

"Why him?" I asked without much interest in the answer.

Margaret raised a brow. "I assumed Bryce told you that Marvin's money paid for all this."

I shook my head. "Marvin who?"

"Gillis."

My interest turned real—I knew Gillis a little, less personally than by reputation; I had even done some work for his law firm, though not on the corporate side of which Gillis was top gun, but rather for the lowly litigators.

"I thought everyone knew," Margaret was saying. "Actually, I thought my divorce settlement was in the nature of a scandal."

"I guess I skipped the columns that week."

She bristled in self-defense. "Marvin made lots of money. It was only fair that I was given a share of it."

Margaret had put it mildly. Marvin Gillis specialized in incorporating new ventures and taking a block of stock in return as his fee. Thanks to the law of averages and Marvin's participation in the zoom of high tech down in Silicon Valley, portions of that stock were eventually worth millions. At one point I heard that only Jobs and Wozniak had a bigger bite in Apple than Marvin did, but I didn't know if it was true. I did know that if Margaret Chatterton had been awarded even 10 percent of her ex-husband's rumored accumulation, she had enough to float Periwinkle over the next century.

"Marvin is still being a grouch," Margaret was saying, "even after all this time."

"How?"

"He's overextended himself in the past few years, so he's trying to finesse me out of my holdings, refinancing and reorganizing this company and that, issuing Class C stock and nonsubordinated debentures and other nifty instruments that have the sole purpose of diluting my stake in his companies. My lawyer says he's being fiendishly clever.

If I can't stop him, Periwinkle will go down the drain." She closed her eyes. "But that's not your concern, is it?"

"I don't know."

She didn't hear me. "I'm sure you have more important things to worry about. I know I do."

"Like what?"

She blinked. "It's really none of your business."

I shrugged. "You look the way a lot of my clients look, Margaret—that you need to talk to someone about something."

She tried to smile. With Margaret, that's as good as it gets. When Bryce first introduced us, I kept trying to decide what I'd done to annoy her. I finally realized that it had nothing to do with me, that Margaret simply resented her husband's interest in anything other than herself.

"Perhaps I should try idle conversation at this point," she said glumly. "I've tried everything else." She paused for effect. "I'm worried about my daughter."

"Jane Ann?"

She nodded.

I recalled the snapshots of his brand-new stepdaughter Bryce had brought by the office several years before. After I'd approved in spades, he'd presented me with a cigar in honor of the occasion. Cuban, in fact. The next day I gave it to Charley Sleet. He said it was the best he ever smoked. Since Charley's a cop, he also said they were illegal.

I gestured to the photo on the corner of Bryce's desk, which was the oldest version of the rest of them. "Is that her?"

"Yes."

"She's all grown up."

"In some ways, yes; Jane Ann's very precocious. But in other ways she's frighteningly . . . regressive."

The modification hinted at complex psychology, in both Margaret and her daughter. "Why are you so worried about her? I mean except for the ways parents usually worry about their kids?"

Margaret closed her eyes, as though better to picture her distress. "Marvin and I divorced when she was nine. For reasons that seemed important at the time, I chose to let Jane Ann grow up with her father. So . . ." Her shrug was massive enough to encompass her daughter's infancy and adolescence. "Still, she survived, for which I'm thankful—so many don't these days. But it wasn't easy, for any of us. When she was seventeen she rebelled against Marvin's strictures, his conventional values, his excessive expectations. She dropped out of high school just before graduation, refused to go to college even though she'd been admitted to one of the finest in the country, and began to associate with peers who were even less responsible than she was. And now she . . ."

"What?"

She sighed heavily. "That just it. What *does* she do? I haven't the faintest idea. She is talented in art and takes lessons twice a week but she never seems to actually *paint* anything. She has no job, yet cruises the city in an expensive convertible, lives in a chic apartment, carouses to all hours. She's had one abortion that I know of; she was arrested for possession of drugs when she was eighteen, though thankfully the case was weak and Marvin got it thrown out on a technicality. Her driver's license is suspended, though that doesn't seem to slow her down. I just . . . don't know what to do." A tear appeared in a corner of her eye. "She has always craved excitement. She *lived* on the roller coaster at Santa Cruz one summer; she adores those horrid slaughter films; she wanders the most frightening areas of the city without a thought for her safety. I'm afraid she . . ."

"What?" I prompted again.

Margaret struggled for the words. "I guess I'm afraid she's gotten herself involved in something dangerous. And quite possibly criminal."

"Like what?"

She opened herself to me for the first time, her bleak and bloodshot eyes a pink patina above a desperate plea for help. "Who knows? These days young people don't seem to experience pleasure unless they're committing an antisocial act."

There was some truth to that, particularly with regard to the children of the very poor and the very rich, but I decided not to point it out. "You don't have any clue at all to what she might be mixed up in?"

Margaret shook her head. "Just that she seems so edgy lately. She lives like she's on the run—changing phone numbers frequently, spending lots of money with nothing to show for it, showing up here late at night in the company of a young man who looks more like a bodyguard than a boyfriend. I just . . ." The enormity of the puzzle silenced her.

"How long has this been going on?"

"It's gotten worse in the past month, but she's been a problem for years." Margaret looked away from me, to one of the photos of her daughter, this one showing Jane Ann waving happily from the back of a horse. In the one next to it she was several years older and on crutches, as though the years of adolescence had crippled her. "I have to tell you that it's not impossible that Jane Ann has used some of the money her father and I have given her over the years to finance an illegal enterprise," Margaret concluded grimly, "and that somehow it's gone bad."

"If it's drugs, she could be in serious trouble. The nuances of the social register don't mean much to the Colombians."

She nodded timidly. "That's why I was wondering if you could look into the situation for me." Her expression congealed and became beseeching. "I know you think I'm a hard woman. And I am, in many ways. I've had to be. But I love my daughter very much. I neglected her for a long time, under the illusion that I wasn't competent to rear her. I couldn't bear it if anything happened to her now that I'm in a position to prevent it. Could you help me, Marsh? Please?"

Because it was in such contrast to her usual demeanor, I found the entreaty moving. But nevertheless I shook my head. "Bryce called first, Margaret. I have to see what he wants me to do. If it's something I think I can handle, I have to give that priority."

"I see."

"Your problems with Jane Ann sound like they need someone full-time. I'd be happy to recommend an investigator for you to talk to. A woman, if you think that would be preferable."

"What if I persuade Bryce to use someone else?"

"I'm afraid the answer's still no."

"But why?"

"I don't mix friendship and business."

"You're willing to work for Bryce."

"Bryce is different; Bryce is balancing the books."

"What about when the business pays twice your normal rate?"

Flush with the profitable resolution of my most recent undertaking, I allowed myself a righteous smile. "Friendship pays better. In the long run."

"When you get to be my age, the long run is not a viable option." Her lips curled bitterly. "Look at me. No *wonder* Bryce spends his every waking hour in here with these stupid books. Who'd want a woman whose flesh drips off her bones like this?"

She held up an arm for me to inspect. It wasn't by any means a teen's, but it wasn't as wattled as her rhetoric suggested. It was just a badge like the badges that all of us over forty carry around, badges worn within and without, badges we tear at when our lives go wrong.

I sighed. Despite our disputatious history there was something pitiable in Margaret's candor. Her inner demons seemed no more blameworthy, nor more governable, than my own. So, since she was fishing for a compliment, I gave her one.

"You're still an attractive woman, Maggie," I exaggerated easily.

Her smile was almost real. "Maggie. You're the only one in the world who calls me that. I must admit I like it."

Somewhere between us, something softened. As it did, Margaret looked out the window, at the towers of light rising out of the financial district, at the fortress of wealth they defined, at the implication that those of us outside that electric forest were doomed to insignificance.

After what looked like regretful reverie, Margaret looked back to whatever she saw as our relationship, her aspect firm and businesslike. "Bryce is certain the job he wants you to do for him will be his salvation. And Periwinkle's. I wouldn't want you to think I'm standing in the way of that. I love him, too, after all," she added, as though I'd expressed some doubt.

While I stayed silent, she framed a qualification. "But you should also know that Bryce's dream is nonsense. If you don't want to see him hurt, you should not encourage him to indulge his fantasies. And if you *truly* care about him, you'll keep me apprised of what you're up to. Otherwise, you may end up doing more harm than good."

With her final caution, Margaret left the room. A moment later the door opened once again. Bryce Chatterton walked to the chair his wife had vacated and sank to a comfortable slant, hands locked behind the sandy hair that crossed his head in tangled wisps, loafers and argyles perched like tropical birds on the corner of his desk. According to his wife, this was Periwinkle's final hour but Bryce looked less like the captain of a sinking ship than an eager mariner who'd just sighted a new world.

"Another legend launched," he said. "I feel like Max Perkins must have felt the day he brought out Thomas Wolfe."

"Congratulations."

"I'm kidding," he said when he saw my look, which let me get comfortable as well—I'm uneasy with people who take themselves too seriously, which means I'm uneasy a lot these days. I sank to the chair across from him, crossed my legs, and took the measure of my old friend, to see what time and his wife had done to him.

As they had been a dozen years before, Bryce's clothes were woolly and professorial, but now they were designed by Ralph Lauren, not assembled from a thrift shop. His body was still rotund and soft, less dissipated than untended, more bearish than porcine. Because his face was amply fleshed, it was sufficiently unmanageable to betray every nuance of his emotions, which had previously been extravagant but now seemed languid and serene. From my inventory, I was prepared to conclude that, more than most people I knew, Bryce Chatterton had thrived during the decade just past. But just as I was awarding him this unspoken accolade, his expression sagged toward melancholy.

As though I'd just admired it, he gestured angrily at the clutter. "It's not as impressive as it looks. By the time a manuscript winds up here, it's already been rejected by every publisher worthy of the name."

"I doubt it," I said, just to be saying something.

"Hell, Marsh, I don't publish books, I publish *authors*. If a manuscript is even remotely promising, I call the writer in to lunch. If I like him—or, more precisely, if I want him to like me—I publish. If not, I don't. Behind the facade, essentially I'm a welfare program. I lavish Margaret's money on souls who have less claim to her bounty than the homeless wretches who camp in Golden Gate Park or the Civic Center Plaza." Bryce groaned heavily in an effort to cast off his sudden depression. "It was a nice party, anyway; Matilda was thrilled. Did you meet anyone interesting?"

I shrugged. "Colt Harrison."

Bryce shook his head. "The eminent critic for the *Chronicle*." The encomium was insincere. "I'm surprised he showed—usually Colt only writes up a collection after it's been reviewed in *American Poetry*, so he'll know what he thinks about it." Bryce worked with the thought, then softened. "Poor Colt. He has his place; the problem is, it's on a soap box, not on the book page. He has no concept of the difference between good verse and bad and lacks the vocabulary to articulate it if he did. All you need to do to get a favorable mention from Colt is parrot his politics—Colt doesn't want to read about the world that is, he wants to read about the world that he thinks *ought* to be. Unfortunately, his politics are somewhere in the shadow of George Will's. It's the shame of my profession that such politics have become *de rigueur*."

"What does *that* mean?"

"If literature couldn't put a stop to a nincompoop like Reagan, or expose the cruelty and corruption of the Visigoths who worshipped him, then what the hell *can* it do?"

"I think that's a job for journalism, not literature."

"Both, Marsh, both. And both have failed us miserably."

Bryce pondered his adjudication for another moment, then reached into his desk, pulled out a cigar, and lit it, as if shrouding himself in toxic gases would shield him from the failings he had just described. When he offered me one, I shook my head.

"What were you talking with Margaret about?" he asked once his stogie was merrily befouling the room.

"Literature, of course. She asked if I'd read the new Danielle Steel; I asked if she'd seen the latest Tom Clancy."

Bryce ignored the burlesque. "She was complaining about money, I'll bet," he speculated glumly.

"Maybe a tad."

He closed his eyes. "She's been saying she's going to close down Periwinkle. It would serve me right, of course—I've treated her more like an underwriter than a spouse for years. Sometimes I think she suspects I'm seeing another woman, even though the only women in my life are those up there."

His finger anointed the books on the shelves that surrounded him, lingering long enough to suggest the relationship was indeed lascivious. As if buoyed by the possibility, his eyes flipped open and his expression brightened. "But if you come through for me, Marsh old buddy, Margaret's funk won't matter."

"Which brings us to why I'm still tasting the Sunday Punch."

Bryce nodded. "I wanted you to come to the party so I could give you a feel for why I care about all this so much. *Gridlock* may be silly—hell, *all* my books may be silly—but the *impulse* behind them isn't silly. The desire to express yourself in the written word, to arrange the language in ways it's never been deployed, to perpetuate what you've *learned* about life—that's the best use of our brain there is."

"Literature's fallen out of favor, hasn't it? People seem more interested in facts these days."

Bryce wrinkled his nose. "What they want is consolation and expiation, and that's all most of the so-called fact books give them. People don't avoid fiction—*good* fiction—because it's false, they avoid it because it's all too true. A great novel is a mirror that shows us who we are; unfortunately, these days that's not something many people want to know."

Bryce's face reddened with ardor. "The *truly* great lives are fictional lives, Marsh: Hamlet, Anna Karenina, Silas Marner, Ahab—even Jesus. The Bible is the best-selling novel of all time, after all. The little monk in Lyon who chose which gospels to include in the New Testament was the world's first great editor."

"That burst of blasphemy could get you tarred and feathered in certain states of the union."

"You know what I mean, Marsh. *These* are the lives that illuminate; these are the lives that suggest who we should aspire to be; these are the *truest* stories." Bryce paused, then cooled to a simmer. "It's stunning how many people want to write, you know. After TV has stolen the time we used to devote to reading, and movies have made us bored by anything but group sex and spatter murders, and politicians have so emasculated the language its glories have become mundane, people *still* want to write novels and stories and poems. How many unsolicited manuscripts do you think I get over the transom each year?"

I shrugged. "A hundred?"

"Five times that. And a big house like Random gets maybe five thousand. None of which they'll publish. Which leaves a lot of leftovers for people like me." Bryce stopped bending a paper clip into the shape of a triangle and looked at me earnestly. "I really don't want to lose Periwinkle, Marsh. You've got to help me keep it."

"I'd like to," I said honestly. "Maybe it's time for you to tell me how."

Bryce nodded, then reached into his jacket pocket, took out a key, and unlocked the bottom left drawer of his desk. When he straightened he was cradling a stack of paper in his hands, a ream of it at least, gazing on it as fondly as if it were his newborn offspring. "This is the Holy Grail for a man like me, Marsh. At least I hope it is."

"What is it?"

"A novel. A good one, maybe even a great one."

Behind his glasses, Bryce's eyes slipped away to the vision of a life of fame and fortune and, since it was Bryce, of the satisfactions that come with the belief that one has added to the small store of truth in the world.

"I still don't understand," I said finally. "What is it you want me to do with it?"

The question tugged him back to the world of schemes and plots, the world of debts and obligations—the world in which I made my living. "I want you to read it."

I laughed. "I have to tell you there aren't a lot of people who buy books based on what I have to say about them. In fact, every time I lend a book I've liked to someone, they invariably hate it. And forget to give it back."

Bryce waved me off. "There are lots of small presses like mine in the Bay Area, Marsh. Dozens. Most of us run on a shoestring, and most of us don't survive more than a few years—the mortality rate for small publishing houses is worse than it is for health clubs. We're competitive with and jealous of each other, but we have one thing in common—we want to make a splash, to make both a reputation and a profit by publishing more and more books by better and better authors. We not only want our lists reviewed in *The New Yorker* and *The New York Times*, we want to discover the next John Irving and Amy Tan."

I enjoyed his extravagance. "Do these dreams ever come true?"

Bryce's eyes glowed like the neon blossoms in the sign outside. "Amazingly enough, occasionally they do. The most recent example is right over in Berkeley. For years the North Point Press was a lot like Periwinkle, publishing mostly stuff by friends and scholars. Then wham. They do Evan Connell's book on General Custer and the memoirs of a hitherto unknown adventuress named Beryl Markham, and all of a sudden they're big-time. Hundreds of thousands of copies sold. *Expensive* copies—hardcover and *trade paper* copies."

Bryce paused for breath, then regarded the loaf of papers in his hand with something close to awe. "The reason I asked you to stop by tonight is, I'm convinced this could make it possible for Periwinkle to do the same." He fondled the manuscript another moment, then thrust it toward me like an alm.

I hesitated, because Bryce's fervor had made me uncertain I was worthy of its custody, because his wife's caution had made me leery. But when Bryce didn't withdraw the offer, I took the pile of paper from his hands and put it in my lap. Bound with twine and rubber bands, it was weighty and oddly soft.

I read the title—*Homage to Hammurabi*—then looked

at Bryce. "I still don't understand what you want me to *do* with it."

"That's easy." Bryce's smile was tinged with a desperation I had seen most recently in the eyes of his wife. "First, I want you to read it. And then I want you to find out who *wrote* the goddamned thing."

They are called the children of privilege—by this apparently is meant that they bear the burdensome privilege of wealth. They came to me possessing the grossest opulence along with perspectives more limited than an urchin's. Never nudged beyond the narrow focus of their time and class, most were satisfied to remain as secure and stunted as the day they arrived at St. Stephen's. But for the few who were eager and able to sample the fullness of the world in which they lived, particularly the inner world of people far different from themselves, it was my pleasure—indeed, it was the highest achievement of my life—to open doors.

My tools were books—Sometimes a Great Notion, Manchild in the Promised Land, The Winter People, them. *And for the handful ready to face the full foulness of the truth, I offered* Child of God, Last Exit to Brooklyn, A Garden of Sand.

Some were never the same thereafter.

Which was of course my purpose.

> *HOMAGE TO HAMMURABI,* p. 47

Chapter
3

By the time I fully appreciated what Bryce Chatterton was asking me to do, there was a smile on his face as broad as his belly.

"You're telling me you've got the greatest thing since *Gone With the Wind* on your hands," I said, still feeling for the scope of my undertaking, "but you don't know who *wrote* it?"

Bryce clasped his hands in front of him. "That's right."

"In other words, you've got the book but you don't have a contract to publish it."

"Right again."

"How did you get it? Through the mail?"

Bryce shook his head. "It just showed up one day. Bound just like it is now—with twine, not even a wrapper around it."

"When?"

"About a month ago. Someone evidently came in when the receptionist was off to the ladies' room and left it on her desk. For all I know, twenty other publishers got copies the same day. That's one of the reasons I want you to get on this right away."

Bryce leaned forward in his chair. The freckles at play above his brow seemed to contract into a solid sphere. "I know I've let things slide between us, Marsh. I know I

should have kept in touch more than I have, and that it's
shitty to call you only when I need help. But . . ." His
excuse was encompassed in the slow cycle of a sigh. "I'm
just trying to say that I'll understand if you don't want to get
mixed up in this."

Bryce was right—he should have kept in touch—but,
paradoxically, the token nature of our recent contacts made
it easier for me to work for him. As I told his wife, I hate
to mix business with friendship, but whatever Bryce and I
were now, it spawned fewer conflicting loyalties than that.

I looked at the manuscript, then rubbed the top sheet
between my fingers. "This doesn't feel like a photocopy; I
think this is the original."

Bryce seemed relieved at my shift to a professional
perspective. "I think so, too."

"Which means you may be the only one who has it."

"Maybe's not good enough, Marsh. I've got to have the
exclusive right to publish the book in this country."

"And the author has to have some money."

The reminder of the reciprocity of contracts seemed
jarring to him. "Yes. Of course."

"How much?"

Bryce fidgeted, more uneasy than uncertain. "What do
you mean?"

"How much would you pay to publish *Homage to
Hammurabi* if the author walked in the door right now?"

Bryce plucked a letter opener off the edge of his desk
and wielded it so menacingly I was glad I wasn't a fledgling
novelist trying to negotiate a deal with him. "If Periwinkle
was the only house in the game," he speculated finally, "I'd
offer an advance of five thousand dollars upon signing the
contract."

"Pretty piddling, isn't it?"

"I know, but that's about average for first novels these
days."

"You mean that's all he gets?"

"No, that amount would be an advance against the usual
author's royalty of ten percent of the cover price, escalating
to fifteen percent for each copy of more than ten thousand
sold. I'd keep an even split of paperback and book club

money, and twenty-five percent of the money from foreign sales, all such rights to be sold by me."

"An author only gets ten percent of the price of a book?"

"Right."

"That makes it about as profitable as farming."

Bryce nodded. "For most writers that's exactly the way it is. The Authors' Guild did a study a few years back—the average annual writing income earned by its membership was less than six thousand dollars."

"What about movies and TV?"

"Those rights would remain with him."

"Or her, as the case may be."

Bryce shook his head. "It's a him. No question."

"You mean you think you can tell if a book was written by a man or a woman?"

"Sure. Can't you?"

"I never thought about it before."

"It's pretty easy to do these days, since neither gender seems to care if the other reads its stuff or not. Sexual politics is fiction's biggest problem, I think—both sides suffer because of it. You'd think they'd want to reach *out* to the other sex. To enlighten them, if nothing else. But all they seem to want is applause from their gendermates."

Bryce gave me a chance to add something. When I didn't, he went back to business. "I suppose I might pay a second five thousand upon submission of a completed manuscript as an incentive of sorts. Though in my experience, to a writer of this quality, money is seldom the prime motivator."

I held up the stack of papers resting in my lap. "You mean this isn't the whole thing?"

Bryce shook his head. "You'll see when you read it—I'm sure there's a final section to be added. Before committing to publish, I'd want to see the conclusion, to be sure it delivered on the promise of the first two sections."

I nodded, then asked a question motivated as much by my own interest in the subject as by the requirements of my job. "What if other publishers started bidding? That's the way it happens sometimes, right?"

"Occasionally. If the author's lucky."

"So how high would you go?"

Bryce gazed once again at the books that surrounded him. The placid look on his face indicated that over the years they had offered him the only security he had ever found.

"I'm like the gambler who's down to his last chip, Marsh—it's make or break time. Which means I'd give him all I've got."

"How much is that?"

He shrugged. "A quarter of a million, maybe."

"You're kidding."

"Not at all. The big writers command lots more than that these days—Michener, Clavell, Irving; Tom Wolfe just signed with Farrar, Straus for an advance of six or seven million for a novel that isn't written yet, and that wasn't even the highest bid."

"Do the publishers make money on those books?"

"Who knows?"

"Then why do they pay so much?"

"Because they think they have to, because the big-name books are the only ones stocked in the chain stores, which means they're the only books most people read. That's why the little literary novel doesn't have much of a chance these days. Even if it's published, it's almost impossible to find an outlet that will stock it."

"What about *The Joy Luck Club*, and books like that? They seem to do pretty well."

"Yes, but no one knows why. That's the problem—no one knows how to make that kind of performance *happen*. Sometimes it does, to be sure, but not often enough to change the assumptions and priorities of the business."

I held up the manuscript he'd given me. "Yet you think this one will beat the odds."

Bryce nodded morosely. "But I won't get it if it goes to auction. The only way I could even come up with a quarter million is if I sold some things—my best first editions, the manuscripts I've collected over the years. I have the original typescript of *The Glass Key*, did you know that? It's worth thousands. It would be like surgery for me to part with it. But to save Periwinkle, I would." He made the prospect sound as barbaric as selling children.

"How about Margaret? Won't she back you on this?"

Bryce shook his head. "Margaret's out of the picture."

"Maybe you should let her read the book. If it's as good as you say, she might change her mind."

"It would be a waste of time. Did she tell you about this wrangle she's into with her ex-husband?"

I nodded.

"Well, that's absorbing all her time. She's becoming a financial wizard trying to figure out how to stop him. Until it gets cleared up, she couldn't finance me even if she wanted to. Periwinkle's my baby now, Marsh. For better or worse."

I looked down at the pages in my lap. "How many people have handled this since it got here?"

"Just two, as far as I know. The receptionist and me. After I read it and realized its potential, I locked it up."

"Do you read everything that comes in the door?"

Bryce shook his head. "I pay a pittance to a grad student over at Berkeley to screen submissions for me. But this one gave off vibrations, maybe because of the way it looks, all tattered and torn, as though the author wrestled with it for years. Or maybe it was the way it just materialized one day, like a supernatural phenomenon." His eyes glazed over, as though the possibility was real and not absurd. "In any event, for some reason I thought *Hammurabi* might be special, and after reading the first few pages, I knew I was right. You can tell after a page or two, you know, whether you're dealing with a real writer or a hack."

I listened to the high whine of his excited breaths. "You really think this is hot stuff, don't you?"

His nod was fervent. "It's amazing, Marsh. The story isn't all that new—hell, there are only a dozen plots in the world, anyway; everything's basically a variation. But the depth, the symbolism, the unconscious levels of meaning. I was enthralled the whole time I read it. And the proof of its greatness is, when I read it a second time, it seemed to speak to me in an entirely new voice."

Bryce drew a deep breath. "I really want to publish *Hammurabi*, Marsh, and not just for financial reasons. Think of the stories that will be coming out of Eastern Europe now that the lid is off. For every Kundera who left, there must be a dozen like Havel who stayed behind. Maybe not as brave as Havel, or as talented, but nonetheless with stories to tell of struggling to maintain some level of spiritual and intellectual integrity in a brutally repressive society. They could be thrilling testaments, Marsh; I'd kill to publish them. I'm so certain *Hammurabi* could make that possible, even if you don't find the author for me, I may publish it anyway."

I raised a brow. "That's risky, isn't it? I mean, there are laws against that, as I recall from the course in copyright I took in law school."

Bryce grimaced. "What are they going to do, shoot me? If I lose Periwinkle, I'll be as good as dead anyway."

For the merest moment I envisioned Bryce still and silent in a casket, in a freshly fashioned grave beneath a granite stone that was etched with tiny flowers.

I shook the vision from my head. "Do you have a Xerox machine around here?"

"Of course."

I held up the manuscript again. "Could someone photo-copy the first five pages of this for me?"

"Sure. I'll do it myself."

I untied the twine and gave Bryce the sheets off the top and he disappeared through the door behind me. I put the remainder of the manuscript on the floor and helped myself to a second jigger of Black Label. The photograph on the corner of the desk—a young girl in a sweater with a large letter S on the front—watched me with a censorious frown, implying I'd already had enough.

I downed half the scotch in spite of the tacit temperance lecture and was about to return to the bookcase to browse some more, when I heard a noise, low and grating, so out of place in the customary quiet of the library that it took me a second to conclude there must be a private elevator to the office from the street below and that someone must be using it. A moment later, the chugging stopped. After a glitch of silence, a door in the corner of the room slid open and two people entered the office.

The young woman looked enough like her pictures to identify her as Bryce's stepdaughter. But the resemblance to the fresh-faced youngster in the snapshots was at best tenuous. Live, her expression was dour and sunless, fiercely guarded, without a trace of the eagerness of youth. Her hair, formerly neat and pertly coiffed, was a clump of frizzy, fuzzy blonde brush, as though each strand had been set with a live wire. Her peasant blouse and short black jerkin topped a miniskirt of acid-washed denim. The black stockings that swathed her legs disappeared into black ankle boots that were fringed and tipped with silver—appropriate were she sitting on the back of a horse. The shine in her eyes was of the sort that used to indicate panic or passion but now can indicate anything from a dalliance with drugs to a new pair of contact lenses.

Her mate was even taller, so thin as to seem fleshless, also blond, also with silver tips on his shoes, which wouldn't have been appropriate anywhere I had ever been. His long black coat covered everything between the silver-tipped shoes and the wrap of a red knit scarf that, in the crepuscular light of the office, allowed me to think for a moment that his throat had just been slashed. Still and silent, he remained by the elevator, toying with a curl that fell in a perfect drip of insolence across his blue right eye. The other eye was on me.

For her part, Jane Ann floated toward me like a ghost, her skin colorless, almost albino, an effect I hoped was a triumph of sunscreen or Elizabeth Arden rather than symptomatic of disease. The shadows in the room allowed her to be sitting behind the desk and reaching for a lower drawer before she even noticed me. And even then it took a word from her friend to warn her.

"Chill out," he said, the meaning obvious, at least to the girl.

Her hand froze in midair as her eyes met mine. "Oh. I didn't . . . Who the hell are you?"

I told her.

"I . . . are you supposed to *be* here? Bryce has some valuable stuff around; I don't know if—"

"He was just here," I interrupted. "He went to copy some things for me. We were taking a meeting."

My show-biz slang and my claim to legitimacy left her flustered. "Sorry I barged in; I didn't think anyone . . ." She gestured meekly in my direction.

"No problem." To give her time to calm down, I glanced from her bemused countenance to the photograph on the desk and back again. "You're Jane Ann, aren't you?"

"Do we know each other?"

"Not since you were about this size." I held my hand at waist level.

She frowned. "Tanner. I remember. You're the *detective*. You had a grimy little office on an alley near the Pyramid and you bounced me on your knee."

"Yep."

"And gave me all those licorice whips."

"That's me."

"Bryce used to talk about you all the time. He'd tell my father to be sure to let him know if I ever ran away, so he could hire you to bring me back."

Jane Ann laughed at a joke known only to herself while I enjoyed her secondhand tribute to my tracking skills. Then, in a sudden twist of mood, Jane Ann's countenance turned grave. "Is he in some kind of trouble?"

"Bryce?"

She nodded.

"What makes you think so?"

I'd reversed our roles and she resented it. "How should I know?" she countered brusquely, then sensed her tone was inappropriate and quickly softened it. "It's just . . . he's seemed sort of strung out lately is all. He and Mom tiptoe around each other like they were afraid of catching herpes or something. It's gotten pretty weird around here. Which makes it weird squared." She paused, then glanced toward the young man, who seemed to belie the notion that humans can't sleep standing up. "And now there's a private eye in his office," she added when no instructions had been forthcoming. "*That's* pretty weird in itself."

"As far as I know, your dad's not in any trouble. Not that I—"

"He's not my dad," Jane Ann corrected quickly. "He's my *step*-dad."

"Right. Lucky for you, Bryce doesn't seem to feel that's an important distinction."

The ensuing silence embarrassed both of us. Jane Ann bristled from what she concluded was an insult as I tried to manufacture an apology for an implication I neither intended nor understood.

"So what are you doing these days, Jane Ann?" I managed finally.

She shrugged. "This and that. Taking some art courses, fixing up a loft on Jefferson Street, living with a pit bull and a saxophone player." She glanced to the sentinel by the elevator once again, as though to be sure she hadn't gone too far. Reassured by something invisible to me, she met my eyes. "Trying to keep from growing up is how my mother puts it."

I smiled. "How do you put it back?"

"That as far as I can see, growing up doesn't make you anything but drab. But *you* look pretty fresh. What do you do for giggles? I haven't seen you around the SoMa clubs, I don't think."

I shook my head. "I doubt if we patronize the same establishments."

"So where do you hang out?"

"Mostly where it's quiet."

"Sounds terminal."

"I suppose it depends on the company."

"Yeah? For instance? A significant other? Herb Caen? Huey Lewis? Who?"

"Mostly just with me."

She rolled her eyes in obvious disappointment. "I get it. The well-examined life, and all that. Didn't you hear, Mr. Detective—that went out with the seventies. Life's a cabaret again. Glitz and glamour is what it's all about; everything else is a nuisance." She glanced at her companion once more, and this time got a thin grin of agreement.

Jane Ann's smile was more endearing than her sociology. "I'll try to pick up the pace, just for you," I said, hoping Bryce would return and get me out of wherever Jane Ann was trying to put me. "But you'll have to help—is sushi in or out these days?"

"Sushi who?" Jane Ann was saying with a wonderfully supercilious smirk just as her stepfather came back to the office.

"Jane Ann," Bryce gushed when he saw her. "I didn't know you were coming by tonight. You should have gotten here earlier, so you could meet Matilda." His delight in the young woman sitting at his desk was obvious. Jane Ann's feelings were less scrutable.

"You know me, Bryce," Jane Ann was saying wryly, her expression controlled and calibrated. "A veritable woodsprite, popping up here and there, bringing joy wherever I go. Is Matilda the bald one?"

Bryce nodded. "A fashion victim, I'm afraid, but she could become a gifted poet."

"So could a million nerds with a million word processors."

Suddenly the young man made a speech. "I got to take a leak and make a call. Meet you in the Jag." He punched a button and was gone.

Bryce was still digesting his brief presence when Jane Ann asked a question. "Mom around?"

"In the conference room. Why?"

"My beemer got stolen."

"When?"

"Last week some time. I left it on Folsom for a few days."

"Why on earth did you do that?"

Jane Ann shrugged casually. "Some guy offered me a ride in a Farrari."

Bryce glanced at the groaning elevator. "Does that mean you and Lloyd are through?"

Jane Ann waited till he looked at her. "It means Lloyd doesn't have a Ferrari."

Bryce seemed less pained by the implication of promiscuity than by the news that Lloyd was still in her life. "Did you report the theft?" he managed.

"That's what I'm doing now," Jane Ann said, and flounced out of the room in search of some reinsurance from her mother.

Bryce looked at me with the parent's familiar stew—a mixture of pride and pain. "She's a wonderful girl—bright, talented, articulate—and I love her very much. But I'll always be the ugly step-father, I'm afraid. Which is too bad, since she's going through a rough time right now, trying to decide who she is and what to do with her life. Wild parties, lots of drugs I'm quite certain, living with that young man—he calls himself a musician but he doesn't seem to own an instrument." Bryce smiled bleakly and shook his head. "They always think they can put a stop to it before it gets out of hand, don't they? But sometimes they can't. Right, Marsh? Sometimes they just get lost in the hubbub."

I decided not to mention Margaret's similar concern. "A pretty common situation," I said instead.

"I just wish I could be more of an influence. Her father has always lavished far too much money on her—at some point he became afraid to say no to anything Jane Ann asked of him, I suppose because she always threw such tantrums when she didn't get her way. So she got the impression early on that money and the things it buys would solve all her problems. But it obviously hasn't, because beneath that outrageous exterior Jane Ann's essentially insecure. Perhaps even frightened. And Margaret's response to the situation has been to keep doing more and more of what's already been done, because she feels guilty about not being close to Jane Ann in her early years." Bryce shook her head sadly. "Both of her parents act as though a ton of money will keep Jane Ann out of trouble, when in my opinion the opposite is more likely to occur."

"If you're so worried, why don't you do something about it?"

Bryce shook his head. "Whenever I try to interfere, one of them makes reference to Periwinkle's latest balance sheet, which calls into question my competence and effectively shuts me up. But someone needs to do something— Jane Ann seems to be becoming increasingly manic and self-destructive. But as long as she sees me as little more than a leech upon her mother's assets, I won't have any influence for the better."

His expression became the frame for a heartfelt plea. "Which is why this book is so important to me, Marsh. It could save my business, and maybe Jane Ann, too."

He handed me the photocopies. My thoughts more on Jane Ann than on his manuscript, I gathered the papers in my lap and left Bryce Chatterton to the potent devices of his wife and stepdaughter and the ominous lad named Lloyd.

Oblivion is delivered by a variety of servants—booze and drugs, music and madness, quite often by theology. Since I first read *Robinson Crusoe* and *The Deerslayer*, my own assistant has been fiction—I'm more familiar with the sleeping streets of Gibbsville and the teeming fields of Yoknapatawpha than I am with the grandeur of Pacific Heights or the raucous blocks of Mission Street, though I've never been out of California.

But in the circumstances in which I find myself, to be oblivious is to die.

HOMAGE TO HAMMURABI, p. 88

Chapter
4

After dodging a transient in search of a doorway to inhabit for the night, I found a phone booth two blocks down. Luckily, I came up with enough quarters to establish the occurrence of a minor miracle—Charley Sleet, Detective Lieutenant, SFPD, wasn't doing paperwork at the Central Station or gulping espresso at the Bohemian Cigar Store or patrolling the greasy streets of the Tenderloin; Charley was at home. Because his normal nocturnal behavior is to roam the most disreputable areas of the city till well into early morning, alert for pleas for help both audible and otherwise, I knew he wouldn't stay home long, so I angled over to Market and drove up the eastern slope of Twin Peaks as fast as the perpetual state of street construction would allow.

Back in the early seventies, Charley and his wife had finally fulfilled a promise they had been making to each other since they'd risked her father's wrath and run to Reno to be married some twenty years before—they bought a house. It was a tidy little stucco place just off Upper Market, five rooms and a single bath, postage-stamp yard in front, the lump of Twin Peaks a sobering presence out the back. They'd paid just under fifty thousand for it, and Charley had had heart palpitations for the next six months worrying how he was going to keep current with the deed of trust. But the payments had been made on time—Charley would have auctioned off a vital organ rather than default on an obligation—and Flora had worked her magic both inside (a cozy sun porch and delicate terrarium) and out (a steeply terraced rock garden that decorated the plunging hillside). Thanks to the improvements and the fifteen years of feeding frenzy that went under the name of the Bay Area's real estate boom, the house is worth eight times that today. Not that Charley cares, though, because Flora is dead and Charley maintains the house less as a home than as her memorial. Which means it's too painful for him to bear until he's sufficiently exhausted to make sleep a certainty.

I parked in front of the house, grabbed the five sheets of manuscript pages I'd had Bryce copy for me, and rang the bell. Charley must have been on his way out, because when he opened the door he had his jacket on, tie askew, shoulder holster strapped in place, and a look on his face that said this better not be nonsense, like borrowing a lawn mower or suggesting that he spend an hour discussing how badly God wants us to consult the Book of Mormon.

When he saw who it was, Charley's scowl began to fade. For my part, when I saw what was blocking the light in the doorway I was hurtled back in time—Charley was wearing a houndstooth sportcoat he'd purchased off the rack at Cable Car Clothiers twenty years before, to commemorate the conjunction of his promotion to detective and the day Neil Armstrong set foot on the moon. I'd been with him when he got it, his unpaid sartorial consultant: the blind leading the blind. One of the things I'm most thankful for is that neither Charley nor men's fashions have changed much in the interim. Nor has the moon, for that matter.

Charley would have been bald even if he hadn't cut his hair with a straight razor and big even if he didn't put away half a fifth of Bushmills a day. Blessed with the genetic makeup of a hunk of concrete block, he was a bastion of honor in a department that was, in the rampant racism and penchant for brutality of too many of its members, increasingly an embarrassment to a city that had remained willfully deaf and blissfully blind to its police problems for years.

As I was remembering our ancient shopping spree, Charley shook his head with feigned disgust. "That'll teach me to get home before midnight; there's all kinds of riffraff afoot out here in the evenings."

I sniffed at a peculiar scent that had made the air as itchy as wool and gestured toward the house. "Toilet back up on you?"

Charley shook his head. "One of the Lord's more neglected children barfed on me while I was trying to get him to a shelter before the detox boys threw a net over him. I been in the shower for twenty minutes and I *still* reek."

"That's putting it mildly," I said as I took a step back. "Homer, I assume."

"Right."

Among other things, Homer's the guy Charley invites over at Thanksgiving every year, then deposits back in the Tenderloin when the last piece of pie is gone. Homer's been living in the alley next to the dumpster behind the Clift Hotel since seventy-six—he lost his job to a binge to celebrate the Bicentennial is how he explained it to Charley. I'm not sure why he picked Homer as a surrogate for the thousands of men in the city just like him—probably Charley doesn't either—but there's no doubt in my mind that Homer is as important to Charley as I am.

Charley muttered a curse. "It's too rough for him out there now. Some young dudes discovered the dumpster, and Homer's been beat on so many times defending his turf he barely knows me. He'll disappear one of these days— they'll tag him as a Doe at the morgue and put him in a pauper's grave in Colma." Charley glared at the stars that were peeking at him over my left shoulder. "I just hope wherever he goes there's someone paying more attention than there is down here."

Charley's expression darkened to match the night, and I stayed silent while he contemplated an afterlife that, according to Charley's old-time orthodoxy, necessarily included several of his colleagues as well as the woman he'd worshiped for forty years, the last five after she'd been interred.

"You have much quake damage?" I asked, gesturing toward the house.

Charley shook his head. "A few cracks in the plaster— needed a spray coat anyway."

"Jim Gibson's piano flipped over."

"Yeah?"

"Baby grand. Quake flipped it over on its back."

"Jesus." Charley took time to envision an acrobatic Steinway, then sniffed the air as though that would tell him if he was needed anywhere. Apparently the answer was no. "You want a beer, or you just here to get me to sign your petition?" He gestured at the papers I was holding. "What is it, another plan to prod the mayor into building a new ballpark? Or some AIDS thing?"

"I'll take the beer if you've got anything better than that rotgut you usually drink," I said. "And it isn't a petition, it's the first five pages of a novel."

Charley looked at me as though I'd grown a horn. "Decided to do the full Hammett, have we? The exciting careers of private eye and detective novelist wrapped up into one?" He bowed elaborately. "John Marshall Tanner, San Francisco's newest Knight of the Mean Streets. How may I serve you, sir?—by relating some incidents of suitably grisly realism drawn from my years of experience with such matters?"

I shook my head, oddly self-conscious once again, this time at the implication that I possessed an ego sufficient to deem myself an author without ever having written a word. "You're confusing your writers," I said gruffly. "It was Chandler who called them mean, not Hammett. And Hammett had left the Pinkertons before he began to write. And anyway, they're not mine," I added quickly, holding up the pages.

"So what do you want *me* to do with them?" Charley asked. "I haven't read a novel since they made *Tropic of Cancer* legal."

Some people read novels and some don't. Normally I prefer the company of the former, since they're more likely to come to their own conclusions about life than parrot the best-selling pablum some slicker is promoting that month, but in this as in a lot of ways, Charley was an exception to my rules.

"I want you to check the pages for fingerprints," I told him. "If you find any, I want you to ask the cop computer who they belong to."

"This have anything to do with the commission of a crime?" Charley asked skeptically.

"This has to do with Bryce Chatterton."

"If this will bring him back to the poker table, I'll check it out tonight; I miss the fifty bucks a week I used to relieve him of. How's he doing, anyway? Haven't seen him since he married that witch who thinks football should be a felony."

"She says nice things about you, too; I think the term 'Neanderthal' came up."

Charley swore.

"Bryce is okay, I think, but he'll be better if he can find out who these belong to."

I waved the pages under his nose. Charley took them and examined them. "How'd they get so dirty?"

I shrugged.

"This spot here looks interesting." He pointed to a smudge on the title page, then looked up at me. "I guess writers really do sweat blood. Or is there more to this than meets the eye?"

I shook my head. "Not as far as I know. So you'll check it out?"

"That depends," he countered. "Do you owe me, or do I owe you?"

"You owe me," I declared, then made reference to the last time we had a mutual interest in a murder, one whose reach had almost included my secretary, one I had delivered to Charley wrapped in a tidy package, suitable for indictment.

Charley's effort to dredge up a response made him look like Yul Brynner. "How about that tip I gave you last month at the track?"

"Your tip faded down the stretch, whereas *my* tip finished in the money."

"I don't call eight to five a tip, for God's sake."

"Did you cash a ticket on him or not?"

Charley cursed my lineage and led me to the beer, which was rotgut as I'd suspected. But bad beer is like bad art—if you endure enough of it, eventually you forget the alternatives.

Adolescents seek someone to blame for the turmoil biology inflicts on them. Most of them too readily blame their parents; many ultimately blame themselves. For some reason, on a gray November day in 1980, Amanda Keefer decided to blame me.

HOMAGE TO HAMMURABI, p. 59

Chapter
5

I carried the manuscript and a Budweiser buzz up to my apartment and got ready for bed. Normally the approach of midnight and a few beers is all it takes to send me straight to slumberland, at least till three A.M., when more often than not I am jolted awake by the crystal conviction that something in my life has gone substantially awry. It is the peculiar fiendishness of such moments that the dreamed-of debacles are so variable there is no way to catch up, no way to take suitable precautions, no way to fully, finally set things right. I expect to wake up at three A.M. forever.

I stumbled through my evening's routine, casting off my clothes, checking the cable news, making sure the deteriorating furnace and the equally infirm appliances were turned to nonlethal levels, nipping the barest bit of brandy after I was in my pajamas but before I'd brushed my teeth. But this time, after I turned off the light and was curled cozily between my flannel sheets, there was a twine-tied Siren beckoning in the moonlight, aglow on the corner of my desk.

We maintained our standoff for thirty minutes, until my imagination had exhalted the manuscript into something like scripture. I got up, fixed some hot chocolate, opened a pack of Fig Newtons and a bag of M & M's, grabbed the manuscript, brought them all to bed, and began to read.

Such was the allure of the exercise that I didn't stop until the comestibles were gone and the final page had been dropped to the floor and the light in the room came less from the lamp beside the bed than from the re-emergent sun.

Frankly, I was surprised I liked it that much. Bryce Chatterton had projected *Homage to Hammurabi* as a sure best-seller, and I don't usually enjoy novels that attain such heights. To me, the fevered couplings of the rich are mundane and unenlightening, the schemes of terrorists and drug dealers banal and uninvolving, the thump of impending horror essentially laughable except when matched with the age of those who constitute the genre's chief consumers. In the books I prefer, the driving force is not the imminent ignition of an explosive device but the intricate warble of the language. The plot unfolds not in an exotic foreign capital but in a house much like the one across the street, and the characters are not hulking mafiosi or silk-smooth financiers but people I might find in line behind me at the Safeway or in the chair across from my office desk. What was impressive about *Hammurabi* was that while it managed to satisfy these expectations, it would, if my guess and Bryce's were right, meet those of the mass market as well.

The story was a simple one—confessional and ultimately allegorical. A young man named Dennis Worthy—idealistic, altruistic, optimistic—graduates from college and is hired as an English teacher at St. Stephen's, an exclusive private high school in an unnamed city. His work with students is frustrating and challenging, but occasionally rewarding. A few years after taking the position, he falls in love with Sharon, the instructor of fine arts at the school, and a year later they marry. Over the succeeding decade they thrive in the intricate society of the school, dote on their students to the extent the students are receptive, have a child of their own. With the aid of some school alumni, Sharon discovers a market for her endearing portraits of people's pets and leaves teaching to become a modestly successful artist. Dennis begins a novel that even his most cynical associate on the faculty declares to be "promising."

Life is proceeding splendidly, if not munificently. The frustrations of trying to educate the increasing number of unteachables produced by the age of dual incomes and TV are outweighed by Dennis's successes with the small but persistent trickle of talent that comes along each year: One of his students is admitted into the writing program at Iowa, another has a poem published in *Antaeus*, a third becomes an editorial assistant at Simon & Schuster, a fourth writes soap operas for daytime TV. These and others make a special effort to look up Mr. Worthy when they return for class reunions, to tell him how important he was to their futures, that they remember his class with fondness, occasionally that they have found time to reread one of his favorite books.

In the middle of this idyll, a fracture suddenly occurs—the morning after Election Day in 1980, Dennis is called into the headmaster's office and informed that he has been accused of sexually molesting one of his students. In deference to his record, the police are not called and no charge is filed, but an informal inquiry is undertaken by the chairman of the board of trustees. The student—Amanda Keefer—is examined by two physicians and is found to have unquestionably suffered sexual assault. The chairman convenes the entire board for counsel and advises all concerned to keep the matter confidential.

Dennis is confused, frightened, dismayed. Rumors roar through the school, increasingly irrational and unfounded, wounding all the same. Dismissal procedures are updated to include the most recent demands of due process; the girl's parents erupt during a secret session of the board and engage a lawyer of their own to seek civil damages; colleagues pledge unswerving support, but are increasingly engaged in furtive colloquy whenever Dennis joins them in the lounge; anonymous callers accuse him of all varieties of bestiality, some with such specifics they seem necessarily to be speaking from experience. Six female students transfer out of his course in modern lit; the yearbook is assigned a new adviser.

In response to his inquiry, the teachers' union pledges Dennis its support and offers the assistance of its counsel. The ACLU chimes in as well, but Dennis decides to eschew such mercenaries and fight the battle on his own. To calm the tide of suspicion and surmise and allow the school to return to some semblance of its mission, he agrees to a leave of absence, pending the conclusion of the inquiry by the chairman, certain he will be exonerated. The investigation takes two months; at its end, the finger of suspicion still points exclusively at Dennis Worthy.

The power of the opening section of the novel lay in its rendering of the young man's deteriorating psychology. The war he wages with himself as he struggles to find both a mental and moral pathway through the wilderness into which he has been cast by the girl's appalling accusation was so deftly set forth that when Worthy ultimately finds no escape from the charge—when he pleads guilty to a lesser offense and is sentenced to jail for a period of eight years—I absolutely believed his sanity had been so fully shredded.

At the pivotal point in reaching the decision to resist the juggernaut no longer, Dennis Worthy reflects on its origins:

> The best proof of my state of mind—proof that I was no longer among the rational—is that a life in prison began to seem preferable to the life I was living as a supposedly free man. I was propelled to that conclusion, absurd though it now seems, by two events I did not anticipate, events that made me desperate for a refuge, even though the only sanctity available was behind a row of greasy iron bars.
>
> After the accusation had echoed through my life, after my friends began to consult with me in increasingly pessimistic timbres, after the chairman informed me of his findings, after it was found to be better for all concerned that I spend my days at home rather than educating young people at St. Stephen's, I was finally allowed to confront the evidence against me: Not live, to be sure, but in the form of a videotape of the informal deposition of the complaining witness.
>
> Alone in the headmaster's elegantly appointed chamber, the only light the accusatory glow of the TV screen, I dug my fingers into the stiff brocade of a wing chair as Amanda Keefer bravely told her tale—how she'd joined my class because she'd overheard a cheerleader say that I was "mint," how she tried out for the school play because she'd found

my discourse on Macbeth "far-out" and because people always said that with her looks she could make it big in Hollywood, how she hadn't gotten the role (Lady Macbeth) she wanted and even with a minor part she'd had difficulty learning her lines to the point where I'd offered to tutor her privately in a series of evening meetings in my home.

True, all of it, even the claim that Amanda embodied the common conception of the vapid loveliness that has long been the staple of the silver screen. True, that is, up to the point where Amanda looked into the camera—looked straight at what she doubtless had been told would one fine day be me—crossed her arms and said, "All of a sudden he started talking about my breasts—about how nice they were and stuff. I mean, the *guys* talk trash like that all the time, you know, but Mr. Worthy? Get *real*.

"Then he asked if he could *see* them. And I laughed because I thought he was joking, but then he asked again and I could tell he was, like, serious and stuff, so I said no *way*, Mr. *Worthy*. Then he grabbed them. Kind of pinched, you know, and it sort of hurt since I was about to get my period and they get sore when that happens. So anyway, I told him to stop and he just looked at me funny and said, 'I don't think that's *really* what you want, Amanda. What you really want is this.' Then he took hold of my T-shirt and ripped it down the middle, which made me mad because it was my new Liz Claiborne.

"Then he grabbed my breast and kissed it, the left one, real quick, right on the nipple. I told him to stop, but he pushed me back on the couch and pulled down my biking shorts and before I could do anything he put it in me. I mean, I fought back and cried for help and stuff, but he was way too strong, and there was no one around to hear me anyway.

"When he was done, he asked me how I liked it. So I told him it was gross. And he just laughed and said it'd be more fun the next time. Then he asked when I wanted my next lesson because he couldn't make it Wednesday, he had to speak to the Alumni Club about the play. I told him *never,* and when he went to get me a can of diet Sprite I ran out the door and went home.

"He hurt me real bad. I still have bruises. See?"

As she raised her shirt to accuse me with contusions as purple as her curiously affectless assertion, the screen went as dark as the stain that spread across my heart as I realized that, whatever the consequence to me or to my family, I could never allow Amanda Keefer to say such things about me in public, could never allow her to say such things about herself.

A more painful encounter occurred that night. Dazed by what I'd endured in the headmaster's office, confused by the scope and power of the lie being wielded against me, I went to bed at sundown. When Sharon joined me some time later, I was still awake in torment. I reached to her for comfort, reached for what had always been there, reached for who she had always been. But instead of offering me a quick embrace, I felt her pull away. All the sordid stories, all the slimy speculations, all the horrid fates my pessimism had projected, were validated by that single flinch: The woman I loved more than I loved my life believed I was capable of the abomination Amanda had just accused me of.

The next morning I did what that fateful confluence demanded—I called the chairman of the board and told him I was guilty. I left the consequence of my confession in his hands, and I must admit, he handled it quite nicely. If I acquit myself well in this place, I will be released before my forty-seventh birthday.

The second section of the novel—more compelling than the first in some ways—was the account of Worthy's life in jail: the solitude, the boredom, the longing, the pervasive and persuasive dangers, the danse macabre of prisoners, guards, and visitors was made as familiar to me as my own

unremarkable routine. By the time I finished reading, I felt
as though I'd served the time myself.

> I am as despised in this place as I became at St.
> Stephen's, despised by men whose crimes are as
> reprehensible as the one they assume to be my own,
> despised because to them my victim was the child
> they are certain they had been once upon a time
> themselves, before fate or family corrupted them.
>
> But was she? It is a large part of my misery that
> Amanda Keefer—young, uncomplicated, to my
> knowledge previously unsoiled either in body or in
> spirit—must nevertheless be lying.
>
> But why? She was found to have been assaulted;
> presumably the finding is indisputable, so she has
> reason to be outraged. But at whom? Who could
> have raped her, then convinced her to accuse not
> him but me? What kind of power was that, what
> kind of spell over poor Amanda, what kind of fume
> at me?
>
> It is to my shame that at this point in my
> analysis—an analysis I have pursued each day for nine
> years but for the time I spend eating, sleeping, and
> baptizing the dinner dishes in a steam-clean washer—
> that I begin the smear. Back in my cell, amid the
> vulgar clamor of the early evening, I remember Aman-
> da's enticingly molded hair, her artificially exotic
> jewelry, her carelessly fastened blouses, her appall-
> ingly brief skirts, her provocatively phrased lapel pins
> (e.g., I Earn Money the Old-fashioned Way—I'm a
> Whore) and I allow these recollections to convince me
> that she was a tart and got what tarts deserve. There
> was no crime, the condemned man's logic goes;
> therefore, why must I serve the sentence of a criminal?
>
> But of course my crime—thankfully it remains
> my *only* crime—is to allow myself to sink so low as
> to blame Amanda Keefer for my plight.

The manuscript ends as Worthy is released from prison,
vowing to learn what really happened almost a decade
before, swearing to wreak vengeance on those responsible

for his decline and fall, hoping to resurrect the relationship with Sharon, who divorced him a year into his incarceration. The vow is chillingly real—as with most convicts, confinement made Worthy far more murderous than repentant. It was testimony to the author's skill that a part of me wanted to become a companion vigilante and join his quest for justice.

As *Hammurabi*'s final phrase receded into memory, I put aside the pile of pages and looked out the window at the slopes of Russian Hill, brightening in the morning sun. Images from the book kept occupying my mind as I drifted back and forth between my world and the world of the novel. Instincts and emotions urged me to action—Dennis Worthy remained so tangible to me I felt he must be present in the room, must have been telling me his story face-to-face, must have been a friend.

I assembled the pages, tied them back together with the ragged lengths of twine and replaced them on the desk. As I lay back in my bed and tried to decide how to find out where this new friend was, I was thinking all the while how ennobling it would be to have a valid claim to have written the words I'd just been reading.

Because I already stood guilty of a lifetime of venial sin, it was difficult for me to urge my innocence of anything, despite the implication of my silence. I suppose I expected others to take up my sullied banner, but in that as in so many things that transpired that November at St. Stephen's, I was disappointed. It was only after my confinement that I came to realize that humans are inherently insatiable, which makes disappointment the necessary fate of all relationships.

I tried to explain this in a letter to my wife. She responded with a suit for dissolution.

HOMAGE TO HAMMURABI, p. 92

Chapter
6

Had I been versed in the deductive wizardry of psychoan-
alytic criticism, I could have constructed an intimate biography of *Homage to Hammurabi*'s author without even
knowing his name. Lacking such skills, I nevertheless made
the following conclusions: He knew how to write, which
probably though not conclusively meant that he was an
educated man. More specifically, both the labyrinth of
secondary school procedures and the emotional accordion
of family life were so precisely evoked it suggested the
author must be both a teacher and a spouse. And he knew
San Francisco—although the city was never mentioned by
name, its hallmarks were tellingly portrayed: the hills, the
views, the bridges, the incessant jingoism, the luxuriant
summer fog. But there were few hints beyond such non-
specific indicators, which didn't leave me much to go on
unless my early-morning suspicion proved right—that the
entire story was a clue to its creator.

I'd come to that conclusion about halfway through the
manuscript, when Dennis Worthy's life became almost as
baffling and authentic to me as my own. The jolt of the
claim of misconduct seemed too vivid, the shame loosed by
his colleagues' suspicions too credible, the terror of his
incarceration too immediate for *Hammurabi* not to have had
its source in a real life. But although it would make my task

easier ıf what I had read was not fiction but fact, it occurred to me that Bryce Chatterton's job might become more difficult. When it was close enough to noon to call him, I did.

Bryce still pursued a single track. "Have you gotten to *Hammurabi* yet?"

"I just finished it."

"Really? You must have been up all night."

"Close enough."

His enthusiasm made raw noises in the wire. "I told you it was special, didn't I?"

"You did, indeed."

"So what's the plan? How do we go about learning who wrote it?"

Though I was reluctant to dampen his mood, I edged toward the warning I had called to issue. "The easiest way to find out who wrote it is to assume it isn't a novel."

"You mean to assume the story's true."

"Exactly."

He paused to reflect, then seconded my conclusion. "It almost has to be, doesn't it? I mean, no one could make *up* all that agony."

"And even if they could, why would they?"

"Right. So we find out where this frame-up happened— what town, what school, etcetera—and go on from there."

"Something like that."

"Well? Are you free? Can you do it?"

I hesitated. "If you still want me to."

"Why wouldn't I?"

"If *Homage to Hammurabi* is fact, it changes things a little, doesn't it? From your perspective, I mean?"

"How so? Nonfiction crime books sell a ton—Joe MacGinnis, Ann Rule, Shana Alexander . . ."

"Truman Capote."

"Right. Right. In fact, that's what *Hammurabi* sort of reminds me of—*In Cold Blood*. A nonfiction novel: the art of literature grafted onto the resonance of journalism." His voice swelled with pride. "It really is a great story, isn't it?"

"Not yet, it isn't."

"It can use some editing, sure—he overwrites in spots, but—"

"That's not what I mean. It'll only be a great story when you get the rest of the manuscript—when Worthy tells us who framed him, and why. That's *really* why you hired me, right?—to track the author down so you can get him to finish it."

"Sure."

"So what's the limit on your libel insurance policy?"

Bryce reacted as any publisher would at the mention of the word. "Libel? *Hammurabi* is *fiction*. There's nothing even remotely libelous about . . . Oh. I get it. If we publish it as true crime, then we could have libel problems if the author accuses the wrong person of the frame." Bryce hesitated, then spoke with obvious relief. "Well, hell. We'll just call it a novel no matter *what* it is. Complete with the usual disclaimer about any resemblance to persons living or dead being coincidental. That'll get us off the hook."

"I don't think so."

"Why not?"

"I seem to remember some recent court cases, including at least one in California, that say a book can be libelous even though its author and publisher call it fiction."

"You're kidding."

"Nope. Have you got a lawyer?"

"I use Andy Potter once in a while. But only when I have to."

"Maybe you'd better have Andy put one of his associates on this—give you a memo on the latest law in that area."

"Andy Potter's associates charge two hundred bucks an hour; I can't afford that much advice right now."

"It's your decision, Bryce, but if I were you I wouldn't go too far down this road without knowing all the pot-holes."

"I think that's pitfalls."

Bryce paused once again, grasping at straws. As I feared, it turned out that I was one of them. "Your rate's still forty, right?"

"Yep."

"How come you've never raised it?"

"Because my life-style makes me immune to inflation."

"How do you manage that?"

"I never buy anything."

Bryce laughed. "Well, hell. *You* remember how to do legal research, don't you? I mean, it's not the kind of thing you forget, is it? Just bury yourself in those books till you find the right one."

"No way, Bryce," I countered quickly. "They use computer networks and data banks and electronic mail and all kinds of high-tech stuff in law libraries these days. I haven't kept up and I don't want to *catch* up, even at your expense."

"Why not?"

"Too much law nauseates me; I think I'm allergic to it."

"Come on, Marsh. How long could it take, a couple of hours? Where's the nearest law library?"

"The nearest good one is at the Petit office in the Pyramid. The nearest good one I can get into is over at Hastings. But Jesus, Bryce. Back when I was practicing law, the case reporter system took up three rooms in the library. Now they've got that same amount of material on CD-ROMs and you can carry it all in your briefcase. And you know what?"

"What?"

"I haven't the faintest idea how to use a CD-ROM, or even what one is, and I'm going to try like hell to make it to my grave without having to learn. Plus I gave away my briefcase."

"Come on. *All* the libraries can't afford the fancy stuff. Go down to City Hall—I'll bet *they're* still doing it the old way. Take a cab, on me. Check this thing out. Nothing elaborate, just the nuts and bolts of the thing, you know? For your old buddy Bryce."

"I don't have any buddies old enough to get me back to practicing law."

"I'm not talking about that, I'm just saying I need to know what my exposure is on this." He paused. "I'm not sure I *have* any libel insurance," he added nervously.

In keeping with my surprisingly stiff resistance, my voice hardened. "Listen, Bryce. It would be stupid of me to give you advice about your exposure to a lawsuit, and it would be even stupider for you to take it."

"I think it's 'more stupid.'"

"I think you're wrong."

"Come on, Marsh. How hard can it be? You were in the top ten percent of your class, weren't you?"

"No."

"Didn't you write an article for the law review?"

"I wrote it; they didn't publish it."

"Well, you can still . . . can't you?"

That's the trouble with friends, they know more than is good for you sometimes, and Bryce's resurrection of my most egregious failure had made me churlish. "Call Andy Potter, Bryce. Have him put his newest man on it. Maybe he'll give you a rate."

"Lawyers don't know the meaning of the word. Come on, Marsh. What's a couple of hours?"

It was a lot more time than I wanted to spend surrounded by musty law books and scowling law librarians and indecipherable computer terminals, but I sympathized with Bryce's plight the way I sympathize with anyone who has to pay a professional person a fee. Like the businessmen who constitute their meal tickets, most lawyers feel the need to live like kings these days, so the price of advice has become as outrageous as the price of neckties and stealth bombers.

"It is kind of an interesting question," I yielded finally, my aversion to legal research overcome by my interest in the origins of *Hammurabi*. "I guess I could check it out for you. But not as a lawyer, just as an interested party. And only for a few minutes. If it looks like it's going to get complicated, I'm going to quit."

Bryce was plainly cheered. "Sure. No problem. When do you think you can let me know?"

"Later this afternoon."

"Great."

"You want this manuscript back?"

"Keep it. Somewhere safe, it's the only copy. And don't let anyone in the business get a look at it."

"No problem. I'll put it in the drawer that locks, just in case Joyce Carol Oates drops by for some tips on the pathetic fallacy."

"Do you *believe I'm guilty?"* I asked a colleague,
a young woman, next to my wife my closest friend on
the St. Stephen's faculty.

"No," she said. "Never."

"Even though I have admitted it myself?"

"Even then."

"Why not?"

"Because if you needed sex that much you could
have gotten it from me. And you've known it since
the day we met." She started to cry. "And because
you're the only man in this whole damned building
who's read Little Women.

HOMAGE TO HAMMURABI, p. 134

Chapter
7

When I reached Charley Sleet at the Central Station in North Beach, he was about to go out on another gang shooting. Gang activity had taken the city fathers by surprise, apparently because they think San Francisco is immune to antisocial behavior, at least on such a systematic basis. I guess that means they think we're immune to racism, poverty, envy, and despair, though they are conferred on certain elements in society on an equally systematic basis. But despite the easy delusions of its leaders, the city isn't immune to anything.

"I suppose it's too early to ask if you checked the pages for prints yet," I asked after Charley's opening grumble.

"It's too early to ask if I've had breakfast."

"Let's try this. Suppose someone committed a crime in this city some nine years ago."

"Suppose you remember how much I hate playing games."

"Come on, Charley. A guy does a number back in 1980."

"The guy have a name?"

"No."

"What kind of offense?"

"Sexual assault. Maybe statutory rape."

"They don't call it that anymore, they call it unlawful

sexual intercourse. Which you'd know if you ever bothered to read the penal code."

Charley thinks he knows more law than I do, and he's right. "Also suppose he pleaded guilty to aggravated assault as the result of a plea bargain, and served his time in Folsom. You with me so far?"

"Suppose you hurry it along a little; if you don't get on top of these gang bangs right away, the witnesses have a tendency to get nervous about their prospects."

"What I want to know is, how could I find out who this guy was?"

"If he was a sex offender he'd have to register."

"I know. That's probably the reason he bargained to agg assault."

"Is he on parole?"

"Did the full term. Refused to appear before the board, said he wanted to leave a free man or not leave at all."

"Tough guy."

"Or an innocent one."

"Says who?"

"Says him."

Charley laughed. "Along with every other con who ever lived."

"Sometimes they are though, right, Charley?"

"Just because they're not guilty, doesn't mean they're innocent."

"Thirty people in this state have been convicted of murders they didn't commit. That's *murders*, Charley, not just felonies. When Mario Cuomo vetoes the death penalty bill the legislature sends him every year, he reads off the names of eight people who were *executed* in New York before the authorities learned they were innocent."

"Which is why the death penalty is shit," Charley said, a statement I'd heard him make many times before, one that surprised other people when they heard it but didn't surprise me at all. "But if you called a meeting of all the Folsom cons who had never committed a major felony, you could hold it in the trunk of your car."

"Which is apropos of nothing," I said as Charley muttered an aside to someone.

When he came back on the line his attitude was

peremptory. "I got to go, Marsh; there's another turf war warming up in Sunnyside. Look, I could ask the computer to kick out a bunch of names with the MO of the guy you want, but it would be a long list and someone would have to check it out and I can't put the department on it unless it's part of an active file. If I were you I'd find out where the crime was committed and go out there and nose around till you get a name. In other words, make like a cop and put in a little legwork. Once you've got a name, I can probably get a line on him. Or you can sit back and wait. If it went down the way you say, he must have a real mad on for somebody. One way or another, his name's going to pop up again."

Charley hung up before I could remark on the subject of legwork in general and police work in particular. I scribbled a note to my secretary, then grabbed a cab to the Hastings College of Law—I decided to take a chance that there was still something to read down there that didn't come packaged within the rays of a VDT.

Hastings is an urban school, part of the University of California's system but not attached to any of its campuses. Its chief claim to fame is that its faculty is made up of eminent professors who have retired from other institutions and gravitated to Hastings to keep active in an environment in which they're cherished rather than regarded as dead wood. As I entered the library I felt the usual press of claustrophobia, the usual wheeze from the mold, the usual compression inside my skull from anticipating the drudgery that lay ahead of me, and the usual prayer of thanks that I didn't have to do this for a living anymore.

People often ask why I quit being a lawyer. If I think they really want to know, and if I think I want them to, I relate the specific incident that led to my retirement, having to do with the judicial system's persecution unto death of one of my less resilient clients. But there were more general reasons for my withdrawal as well, some having to do with the law and some having to do with me.

As introduced in law school and made familiar in my five years of practice, the law was a decidedly mixed blessing—stimulating intellectually but daunting psychologically; exciting philosophically yet intimidating pedagogically; august in the abstract and slimy in too many of its earthly manifestations. Intellectually capable of digesting and even profiting from my legal education, I nevertheless lacked the temperament—perhaps some would say the courage—to enjoy the incessant hostilities that are endemic to the profession, at least the only aspect of it I was drawn to, which was trial work.

By the time I figured out that I was never going to adapt to its demands, and that my clients were going to suffer more than I was from my inadequacies, I was thirty-five years old and convinced I had wasted the prime of my life. Which was approximately where I'd been when Bryce Chatterton had ridden in to rescue me those many years ago. Now, for good reasons of his own, Bryce had shoved me back from whence I'd come. I hoped I survived the trip.

While I looked in the stacks for the reference set I needed, I prayed for a piece of luck that would save me from slogging through the leaden prose of *Am Jur* and *ALR,* or even the more sprightly accounts in Witkin, looking for a line on the libel case I told Bryce I thought I'd remembered. Luckily, my prayer was sufficiently modest to be answered, in the form of an entry in the *Index to Legal Periodicals* that listed several articles on the subject of libel in fiction. After an hour with the Brooklyn, Santa Clara, and Utah law reviews, and a quick dip into the Supreme Court and California Reporters, I had enough of the nuts and bolts of this peculiar aberration in the law of defamation that I could call them in to Bryce.

"Here's the deal," I said after he came on the line. "Unfortunately, I was right—there's a recent California case in which the court of appeals held that a writer had defamed a person in a novel. It's *Bindrim versus Mitchell,* 1978."

"What was the novel about?"

"A nude encounter group, sort of like Esalen. The way it happened was, the author went to a retreat run by this Bindrim guy, hung around and took the therapy, then went home and wrote a novel about it. The kicker was Bindrim knew who she was beforehand, and the kind of books she wrote, so before he agreed to let her in she had to sign a contract promising she wouldn't write about the program."

"Then it's breach of contract, not libel."

"That's what it was, but that's not the way the court described it."

"So why didn't the author just change the guy's name?"

"She did. She changed his name and the way he looked, changed the name of the therapy and the way it was conducted, and put in a bunch of imaginary characters as well. But the court still found she'd defamed the guy."

"Why?"

"Because the description of the guru wasn't close enough to the way he was in real life, which according to the court meant he was defamed."

Bryce bristled. "Of *course* it wasn't close—it was a *novel*, for crying out loud. That's what novels *do*, they rearrange reality. If they're good ones, they do it in the service of a greater truth."

"The court of appeals didn't see it that way. It also said labeling something fiction isn't decisive, it's just one of the factors to look at to see if the book is 'of and concerning' the person who claims he's been defamed. And the only thing it takes to prove that the book *is* 'of and concerning' someone is for one person to show up in court and say they thought the person portrayed in the novel was the person who claims the libel."

"One person?"

"That's it."

For one of the few times since I'd known him, Bryce Chatterton sounded incensed. "Wait a minute. You mean if I write a novel about a black teenager who's ruining his life as a coke runner, and Dan Quayle can find someone to come to court and say he really thought I was writing about Quayle, then Quayle can sue me for libel because he really *isn't* a coke runner?"

"A jury has to believe the witness, of course, but that's what this court said."

"That's asinine."

"Worse. Luckily, that particular aspect may not be good law anymore. In the case where Jerry Falwell sued *Hustler* for printing a cartoon in which Falwell implied that his first sexual experience was with his mother in an outhouse, the Supreme Court seemed to approve the lower court's dismissal of the libel claim because the implication in the cartoon wasn't reasonably believable. So your Quayle example may not hold up. But the *Falwell* language on libel was dicta—the only claim before the court was the tort of intentional infliction of emotional distress. Plus, Falwell is a public figure, which means the cartoon had political implications, so *Falwell* may not be determinative in a case like *Hammurabi*."

"What if the book *is* 'of and concerning' someone? *Then* what?"

"The jury looks to see if the book harms that person's reputation by making a false statement about him. If it does, the person can collect damages."

"Even if the writer didn't *intend* to say anything bad about him?"

"Apparently the author has to have been negligent, or to have acted in reckless disregard of the truth if the real person is a public figure like your friend Mr. Quayle."

"Isn't that the *definition* of a novelist, Marsh? Someone who recklessly disregards the truth?"

"Not according to the courts. This particular one, at least. Which makes it pretty much a catch-twenty-two, as far as I can see. If you're true to life you should have been false, because you've written about a real person; but if you're false you should have been more accurate, because the bad things you've said about the person weren't true."

Bryce sighed. "Jesus. Why didn't someone appeal this nonsense to the Supreme Court?"

"They did, but the Court wouldn't hear it."

"What about the First Amendment? Doesn't that help us somehow?"

"If it does, you can't tell it from some of the decisions. Robert Bork—you remember him, Reagan wanted him on the Supreme Court—doesn't think a novel is entitled to any First Amendment protection whatsoever."

"Reason number two hundred to be glad Ronnie didn't get the job done." Bryce paused and tried to calm himself. "We're just talking about one case, right?"

"I'm afraid not. *Penthouse* printed a story a few years back that portrayed a fictional Miss Wyoming engaged in a variety of unnatural acts, and the real Miss Wyoming sued for defamation. Guess how much the jury wanted to give her for the mental anguish she claimed she suffered?"

"How much?"

"Twenty-five million dollars. That's how much juries care about the First Amendment."

Bryce sounded frantic. "That didn't hold up, did it?"

"It was reversed in the Tenth Circuit, but only by two to one. And I'll bet it cost *Penthouse* at least a million in attorney's fees to get out from under the judgment. There are some more clinkers out there like that one, too."

"Jesus. I don't know if I could go *through* something like that. I *know* I couldn't."

"You're lucky it's not the sixteenth century. Back then they punished libel by pillory and loss of your ears. But the picture's not entirely bleak. In the *Springer* case in New York, the author used the same first name, the same physical description, and the same personal background of an old girlfriend—same college major, same street address, same taste in jewelry, same ex-boyfriend—then made her a prostitute and a courtesan in his book. Despite all that, the court said there was no libel because the defamatory statements weren't believable. It called the parallels between the real Lisa and the Lisa in the book 'superficial similarities,' and said that because the current circumstances of the real and fictional women were different, no one could reasonably believe they were one and the same, even though their background was similar. It's a particularly strong case for publishers because the libel claim was dismissed by the trial judge, which means the author and publisher saved the expense of a trial."

"Thank God there's at least one court out there with some sense."

"Too bad for you it's not in California—that case isn't precedent out here, Bryce. In this state most of these cases go to the jury, and juries are notoriously unpredictable. I imagine most major publishers settle libel claims for nuisance value if they can. Which can still amount to a lot of money."

Bryce sighed. "What I can't understand is why there's all this *hostility* toward fiction. All it is is storytelling, for crying out loud."

I thought about it. "Partly because people think it's a cheap shot, at least when they think the author is writing about a real person under the cover of a claim of art."

"But let's say the book is a disguised exposure of some form of corruption," Bryce countered, "which the best ones often are. The only reason the book is written in the *first* place is that the person being written about has such command of the popular media he can inundate the world with *his* version of the story while truth gets buried in the hype. A novelist is just fighting back the only way he can."

"I agree, Bryce. Calm down."

"People don't want the truth," Bryce repeated glumly. "What they want is an answer—one thought or deed or creed that will solve all their problems. And God knows there are plenty of charlatans out there who will serve an answer up to them. But no true artist would *ever* make that claim—that there's a single path to glory, one golden idea that will yield eternal bliss—no one writing in this century, at least, because there are too many *failures* out there, too much wreckage from revelations gone wrong. The *true* artist knows the only thing that's real is the never-ending struggle, the painful grasp for salvation that a writer like Flannery O'Connor or Graham Greene illuminates. If only—"

I had to put a stop to it, if only to save wear and tear on my psyche. "Come on, Bryce," I said. "We're not going to restore the glories of literature over the telephone. I need to know what you want me to do."

Bryce paused for a leavening breath. "What you're telling me," he went on after taking enough of them to make his temper return to normal, "is that if *Hammurabi* is a true story, even a fictionalized story based on fact, then publishing it could ruin me."

"I'm just making sure you still want me to go ahead, knowing all the possibilities," I said. "Maybe you should put an end to it right here."

"You mean not publish at all."

"It's an option."

Bryce hesitated long enough for me to know what he was going to say. "There's a principle at stake here. I can't let some misguided judge dictate what I publish."

"I suppose not."

His rhetoric began feeding on itself once more, until his inflection became ecclesiastical. "*Hammurabi* could be an important book, Marsh—the barbarity of the prison system, the ramifications of false accusation, the difficulty of learning the truth when sexual abuse of a minor is at issue. Those are important subjects."

"True."

"Plus, it's time to remind people that no matter how disturbing it is to see criminals get off on technicalities, it's those very technicalities that distinguish us from dictatorships. Like China, for example."

"I agree."

"I mean, isn't it amazing how closely the right wing wants America to look like Stalinist Russia and Communist China? Pretrial detention, prison for impure thoughts, state management of everything from sex to patriotism—the only thing different is that if they get their way we'll have to join a church instead of a political party."

"In this country they're becoming pretty much the same thing."

"All I can say is it's going to be ironic as hell the day Czechoslovakia is freer than South Carolina."

"I think it's already happened."

Exhausted by his geopolitical dissertation, Bryce groaned with gloom. "I want you to go ahead," he murmured after a moment.

"You're sure?"

"Positively. I'm going to publish *Hammurabi* as soon as I can."

"Good for you," I said, and meant it. "But there's one more thing I want you to think about."

"What's that?"

"Assume the book is true. Which makes our author a college grad, an English major, an aspiring novelist even before he got into trouble at the school."

"Okay."

"Now assume the guy I just described actually *does* write a novel. What does he do with it?"

"He sends it to Alfred Knopf and hopes to hell they buy it."

"Okay. So what I want you to think about is, why did *this* particular novelist send his masterpiece to you?"

In some ways it would have been easier to bear had I actually committed the offense with which I was charged. Had that been so, it would have been only me who was inhumane. Since I was not, the entire nation stood guilty of that failing.

HOMAGE TO HAMMURABI, p. 102

Chapter
8

If you're a single man with even a mediocre social life, sooner or later you're going to date a schoolteacher. Mine was named Betty Fontaine, and I met her in the summer of 1982.

Betty and I somehow emerged intact from a blind date arranged by a woman who was at once Betty's friend and my temporary secretary and anyone-who-knew-her's idea of a person who got her way through the exercise of monomania. Despite the chancy nature of our first encounter, Betty and I had gone on to enjoy a pleasant if not spectacular relationship over the next few years, its ambitions never broadcast much beyond the mechanics of the evening's entertainment, its obligations exclusive on neither side, its existence a thing of value nonetheless.

Then Betty met a marriageable man. Since neither of us had ever put me in that category, we parted ways, amicably enough, with best wishes all around. Though San Francisco is in most ways a small town, I never laid eyes on Betty again. Thinking back on it, I couldn't even remember if she had married my more eligible counterpart or not. I decided I hoped not, but for present purposes it was enough that during the time we were dating, Betty had taught Western Civ to an astonishing percentage of the junior class at

Jefferson High, a public school in the city's Outer Richmond District.

I called the number that still languished in my little black book along with dozens of its anachronistic mates, but it was out of service. There was no listing for a B. Fontaine in the phone book, and directory assistance said she was unknown to them as well. As a last resort I called the school. The woman in the office wouldn't give me Betty's number, but she did confirm that Betty was still on staff, not as a teacher but as an administrator with the dizzyingly amorphous title of Second Assistant Vice Principal. After lunching at Zorba's and accomplishing some minor errands about town, I drove out to the avenues that lie like a sergeant major's chevrons along the western half of the city, commemorating its advance on the sea.

For some reason, San Francisco has organized its secondary school system so as to ensure its failure. All of the problems can't be traced to the Board of Education, admittedly—a large portion of the city's middle class is Catholic and its children attend parochial schools, an exodus that extracts from the public sector much of the support for excellent education. But the administrators are responsible for a more debilitating development— skimming the intellectual cream off the top of each of the public high schools and sending it en masse to a single institution, Lowell High, leaving the remaining schools to survive as best they can without the students who constitute the best role models for their peers and the most apt recipients of the teachers' labors. As Betty had often lamented, Jefferson High was one of the victims of the system.

I parked by the door Betty had used back when we were dating and she was struggling to explain the Treaty of Ghent to kids who had never ventured east of Fillmore or south of Market and whose lives had concocted no desire to do so. I was out of the car and weaving my way through a pack of fractious kids—all of them Oriental, most of them speaking in their native tongues, two of them tossing a football back and forth in a leap of epic ethnic dimensions—when I saw Betty come out of the building.

She was talking with a colleague while keeping one eye

on the ball being tossed with sufficient volatility to merit monitoring. After the women parted company, I called Betty's name and watched while a succession of expressions played tag amid the dark and gentle contours of her face. I chose to believe the expression that survived could be interpreted as pleasure.

I smiled as she approached, a tall, handsome woman, strong and self-assured, cynical and smart, an informative companion, a stimulating foil. It occurred to me that maybe I should have married her.

"Good afternoon, Second Assistant Vice Principal Fontaine."

Her smile was wide and unrestrained. "Marsh Tanner. Aren't you a scratch on an itch, as my grandmother used to say."

"I take it you mean Ethel. The one in south Georgia who puts up a hundred quarts of peach preserves each fall."

"The very same." She seemed happy that I had remembered a page of her history.

"So how's it going?"

Betty crossed her arms and glanced at the bleak stretch of playground on which the kids were now trying to master the mechanics of the punt. "About average. Two steps forward, one point nine steps back. That's on the good days."

"You survive the quake okay?"

"The school has some kinks—I figure they'll be repaired some time in the twenty-first century. But I got through it okay. I was on a bus, on the way home. After we figured out what happened, we all began to sing, 'A Mighty Fortress Is Our God.' I'm not a religious person, as you well know, but it seemed hugely appropriate at the time. How about you?"

"The quake? No problem. I just crawled under my desk and rode it out with the help of the pint in the bottom drawer. Congratulations on the promotion, by the way."

Betty's look became inscrutable. "It depends on how you look at it."

"Administration not your bag?"

She sighed. "I wouldn't know; I've yet to administer anything more vital than the roll call."

"I don't know what that means."

She made a face. "Basically, I'm the attendance cop. I spend all day on the phone, asking parents why their kid didn't show up at school today. It's a real uplifting task—half the parents sound like they've forgotten they *have* a kid."

"So why take the job?"

Her lips twisted. "They promised the attendance gig would be temporary, that after a semester I could move up to redesigning the curriculum. Ask me how long ago the promise was made."

"How long?"

"Three years. But it's either this or get out of education completely, and I don't have any place to go. Everyone in San Francisco is so overqualified, a Masters in Education doesn't open doors to anything but the faculty rest rooms."

"Maybe you should go back to school."

Betty gestured to the building behind her. "Go back? I never left. I've been in one school or another, in one *capacity* or another, for over forty years. Which I tend to think is the problem."

As Betty contemplated the scene of her lifelong struggle, I snagged an errant pass with one hand and flipped the ball to a boy who seemed overly impressed by the maneuver. "Hey," he called out. "Are you someone?"

When I shook my head he seemed nearly as disappointed as I was.

In the interval, Betty had shrugged off her mood and took my arm. "So what brings *you* out here? We don't have a career day scheduled till next month."

I smiled. "Investigation isn't something you get into on the way up, it's what you grab on to on the way down."

She gave me a comforting squeeze. "God. Between the two of us we could start an asylum for the terminally disappointed. What's gnawing at you, anyway?"

"A book."

She made a face. "Don't tell me I'm going to be chapter nine in your memoirs."

I shook my head. "Sorry. This one's a novel."

Betty blossomed. "That's *wonderful*. So how far are you? Do you need some editing? Maybe we could—"

"Hold it," I interrupted. "It's not by me."

"Oh. That's too bad. You *should* write a book someday, you know."

"Maybe I will." In the ensuing silence, I warred again with wonder. This time I envisioned myself as a domestic le Carré.

"I still don't get it," Betty said after a moment. "Did someone steal a rare book, or what?" She turned saucy. "And how many chapters will be *in* those memoirs, anyway?"

"No comment; I just need information."

"What kind of information?" She sobered suddenly. "Does it have to do with the drive-by last week?"

"Drive-by?"

"The shooting. One of our kids got killed in a gang thing. It's so sad; she was just an innocent bystander. For some reason, gangs don't seem to shoot very straight anymore."

"That's because their weapons aren't made to shoot straight, they're just made to shoot often. So you've got gang problems out here too."

She nodded. "I've collected enough knives to open a cutlery shop, and the *guns* . . ." Betty shuddered. "Isn't it glorious how the government's policy toward those weapons seems to be based exclusively on the balance of *payments* problem? How did you get mixed up in it, anyway?"

"I'm not."

She looked puzzled. "Then why are we talking about it?"

"Chitchat," I said as I remembered some nights of our old days. "How come when we were going together it seemed so hard to think of something to talk about?"

Betty was game enough to laugh, and I did, too, as we recalled the labors of dating. "Because when you like someone, it's *never* chitchat," Betty concluded.

I motioned toward my car. "Got time for a cup of coffee? Or dinner, if you can."

Betty glanced at her watch. "Why not? I have to be back by seven, though. Big PTA meeting. I'm the A. Lucky for me, most of the time the P and T don't show."

I led the way to my car and opened the door for Betty, then got in the driver's side and aimed it at Clement Street. "I couldn't remember if you married that guy or not," I said as I took a left on Twenty-seventh. "Sam, or whatever his name was."

"I did. Unfortunately. His name was Stan."

"What happened?"

"That smile I thought was so dazzling was really a sign that he was heavily into coke. He almost died at a party one night: cardiac arrest. Luckily I knew CPR. When he got out of intensive care, I told him we were history. That was about a year after I told him I'd cherish him in sickness or in health. So much for a solemn vow." Her laugh was raw and self-critical.

"I don't think that applies to sicknesses that are self-inflicted and curable by an act of will."

She patted my arm. "Let's pretend that's true."

Shades of our dating days, I didn't know what to say at that point, so I just went left on Clement and waited for the light to change at Park Presidio, risking an occasional glance out of the corner of my eye at Betty's thoughtful stare, trying to guess, as I always did when I was with a woman, what the hell she was thinking about.

"It's just that it's so damned hard to tell the good ones from the bad ones anymore," Betty said as we started moving again, as though she'd heard my question. "It's so hard that after a while you start believing there aren't any good ones left. Which means that if you've never been married, but want to be, you find yourself starting to settle for something you shouldn't have to settle for." She brightened. "But only once. At least for me. I kind of like my life these days, all things considered."

"Good."

"I've got a lot of friends, both at school and elsewhere, including a couple of men who value me for more than my bust size. I sing in a madrigal group, hike Muir Woods with the Sierra Club, mother the hell out of a couple of cats, and cultivate a plot of ground about the size of this car. It's all sort of vicarious and displaced, I suppose, but people are living far worse lives than mine out there, let me tell you. I used to live one of them myself."

I pulled to a stop in front of a Russian bakery and we went inside. After we placed our orders, Betty looked at me over the salt and pepper. "How about you, Marsh? What have you been doing for the past six years? You've been shot more than once, I see from the papers." Her eyes narrowed and she offered a sly smile. "I trust it didn't damage any vital organs."

I matched her grin. "I'm okay, I guess, organs included. I'm not so sure about their vitality."

"How's Peggy?"

"Fine."

Betty cocked her head. "You don't make her sound so fine."

"She's not working for me anymore."

"Really? I thought you and Peggy were forever. Actually, I thought Peggy was the reason you and I never went much beyond third base. So what happened?"

"I got involved in a personal problem she had, and basically I screwed it up."

"I think I read about that—a phone freak, wasn't it? So what happened?"

I shrugged. "Instead of blaming the creep who was doing the damage I sort of blamed Peggy for the whole mess, subconsciously at least, which she didn't appreciate, understandably. We caught the guy, mostly thanks to Peggy, so the immediate problem got taken care of, but she decided it would be better if she didn't work for me for a while. And I decided that based on the way I handled her problem, I wasn't the man I thought I was."

"In what way?"

"I don't know how to put it, exactly; being able to be professional no matter how difficult the situation is what it amounts to, I guess. No matter how unbecoming my instincts."

"No one's perfect, Marsh," Betty said softly. "Not even Mrs. Tanner's baby boy."

"That doesn't make it easier."

"Easier to what?"

"Keep doing what I do. When I know it's trivial. When I know other people do it better."

Betty's look became maternal. "Sounds like mid-life crisis number twenty-four."

I shrugged. "That's what age is all about, I'm finding out—eating away the rationales that got me through the first forty years. So I'm trying to find some new ones."

"What have you come up with?"

I smiled. "Settling for less seems to be what it comes down to."

Betty stuck out her tongue. "Thanks a lot."

"You know what I mean. For some reason it helps to remember that I'm one of the species that brought us the holocaust, mud wrestling, and the last presidential campaign—a species only slightly more evolved than the neighbor's dog. From that perspective, all you have to do to keep going is convince yourself that you do less harm than good in the world."

Betty's expression clouded. "You find that easy to do, do you?"

I met her eyes. "Not always."

"Me, either," she muttered.

Though I hadn't sought it, Betty had joined my mood. The silence between us was overwrought, but it contained a bond that led Betty to ruminate on her life as well.

"I really do love teaching, you know? Even after all these years. I'll get back to it, eventually, I hope. But it's *scary* what we've done to our school system, Marsh. It used to be our pride and joy, but now the urban public school is essentially an extension of the ghetto—the voters don't want to pay for it, the rich don't send their kids there, the poor blame it for not solving their problems, and the teachers get burned out trying to make it work. So we end up with what we've got—a system that thinks it's done its job if its graduates can read a bus schedule."

"That's a pretty dismal picture."

"I haven't even gotten to the worse part."

"Which is?"

"That inner-city public school graduates don't have a chance at the most prestigious colleges."

"Why?"

"Because regardless of the propaganda they put out, those schools don't feel a responsibility to disadvantaged kids in ways more meaningful than tokenism. So no matter how hard they try, and no matter how well they overcome obstacles the slick colleges don't even try to fathom, for the majority of poor kids the ticket to the good life stays well out of reach." Betty raised a brow. "You haven't become a father since I saw you last, have you?"

I shook my head.

"Too bad. If you had, you could put your offspring in a school like Jefferson and watch her begin to rot. I'm sure you'd find it fascinating, from a clinical point of view." Betty finished her coffee in a savage gulp. "So why are we here? You said something about a book."

Though I had a morbid fascination for the previous subject, I was thankful for the shift of theme. "What I need is for you to tell me about the private schools here in the city."

Betty cocked her head, as though educational institutions were the last things she expected me to ask her about. "Elementary schools? Middle schools? High schools? What?"

"High schools."

"That narrows the field. Montessori? Waldorf? Parochial?"

I shook my head. "I don't think so. Something more ritzy."

"As far as I know there are only two exceedingly exclusive private high schools in San Francisco."

"What are they?"

"San Francisco Arts and Sebastian."

"Tell me about Sebastian."

She shrugged. "Like I said—expensive, exclusive, originally Episcopal, now nondenominational. Endowed to the hilt by its more illustrious graduates, which include half the moguls in town if you don't count immigrants from the Pacific Rim. And good, unless you feel rich kids ought to be taught something more altruistic than the Pythagorean Theorem. Why? You know someone who's angling for a scholarship?"

I shook my head. "You know anyone who works there?"

Something in my look made Betty careful with her answer. "Maybe. Why?"

"I'm trying to get a line on something I think happened there about nine years ago."

"What was it?"

I hesitated. "Does any scandal come to mind when you think of Sebastian?"

She considered it. "Nope. Should it?"

I hesitated. "This is confidential, okay?"

"Sure."

I summarized the plot of *Hammurabi*, neglecting to mention that so far it was only that and not an extract from the police files. "You ever hear of anything remotely like that happening at Sebastian? Or any other school, for that matter?"

Betty shook her head. "But I'm not that close to the place. And teachers molesting students isn't unique, unfortunately, though in most schools no one does much about it, if it didn't amount to rape and the teacher resigns without a fuss. But a scandal like that would have stirred things up at Sebastian, that's for sure—they guard their reputation like Fort Knox. And they would have moved heaven and earth to keep it quiet."

"Could they have gotten the job done? Covering it up, I mean?"

"Let's put it this way—if any institution in the city could, Sebastian could. They've got graduates in half the board rooms in town, and in most of the city departments, too; the DA's office included."

"I need to talk to someone who was around there back then. Preferably a teacher."

Betty thought a minute. "I used to know a woman, she was the soccer coach, if you can believe it. Kind of intense, even discounting the jockette routine, but a good person. She's not there anymore, though; I think she's a paralegal."

A passage from the book came back to me. "Was she a big fan of *Little Women*?"

Betty laughed. "This is the weirdest conversation I've ever had in my life."

I was not immune to lust, Heaven knows, nor oblivious to the emergent charms of the young women who decorated my classes at St. Stephen's. But I swear to all that I was formerly able to regard as holy that I did not lust for Amanda Keefer. If I felt anything for her it was pity, an urge not commonly regarded as blameworthy, but one that has in my case proved more culpable than lechery.

HOMAGE TO HAMMURABI, p. 145

Chapter
9

After borscht, piroshki, and a dessert of reminiscences, Betty Fontaine gave me directions to the Sebastian School. After dropping her back at Jefferson, I followed the route she described, down California to Divisadero, over the hump of Pacific Heights, eventually into the notch of Cow Hollow, in the shadow of the Presidio Army Base.

Long a San Francisco treasure, the base is slotted to fall victim to the leavings of Reaganomics—in order to reduce its budget without sacrificing its store of hardware, the Department of Defense wants to close it down. The consensus is that transfer to civilian control will occur some time in the next decade unless the budget boys decide it will cost more to close it than to keep it open. The base sits on such prime property that if the transfer really happens, it will be warred over by everyone from tree huggers to condo kings to disarmament utopians for the rest of my lifetime. The battle will no doubt feature the oxymoronic methodology so prominent in Vietnam—they will destroy the property in order to save it.

The Sebastian School was established in 1908, or so the plaque on the gatepost informed me as I glanced at it while circling the block the school occupied as forbiddingly as a Scottish fortress. From outward appearances, school looked permanently out—no students or teachers were in evidence, no bikes or balls had been left behind at recess, no litter or graffiti besmirched the walls or corners. Then I remembered this was a private school, which meant among other things that it could afford to keep itself clean.

I found a parking place on Greenwich, then reconnoitered on foot. As I strolled toward the school, the evening mists began to gather, adding weight to the pulse of aggressive seclusion that emanated from the houses that surrounded me—the healthy pulse of aristocracy—that seemed to want to shove me out of the neighborhood before I got anyone into trouble. I shrugged my jacket higher on my neck and, like Carroway and Gatsby, pressed on against the current.

I was kept from getting closer than twenty yards to the building by a row of wrought iron spears that were sufficiently sharp to disembowel anyone who tried to scale them. Beyond the stiff black fence the grassy carpet and well-tended grounds were like no school yard I had ever seen, indicating the curriculum at Sebastian included everything but high jinks. In furtherance of that impression, the granite blocks that formed the walls seemed mates with those that defined the City Hall and the Hall of Justice and other structures about town that most commonly trafficked in misery.

I spent several minutes alternately looking out for someone who might regard my presence as suspicious and pressing my face through the pickets in the fence, wondering whether the excellence of the education that I readily assumed was conferred within was important enough to offset the sense of superiority and separation that I assumed would be a by-product of that environment. If the past decade has proved anything, it's that money and morality are not congruent, and the blame for that surely lies in part with schools like Sebastian. The last thing I wondered, as the dusk of evening became the sepulcher of night, was whether anyone who labored within that formidably fenced enclosure was inclined to do anything about it.

I abandoned my sociological speculations and started back toward my car when I heard a clank and a squeak from somewhere behind me. I stopped next to a nearby ginkgo, backed against its trunk for camouflage, and waited to see what the odd sounds signified.

A moment later a man appeared at the side door of the school—tall, erect, patrician in manner and carriage, wearing what appeared to be a uniform. He took two steps, glanced up at the fog, then came toward me at a martial pace, the suggestion of a limp in his stride.

As I watched from within my vertical shadow, he proceeded to the gate, unlocked it with a key chosen from a ring of at least a score of them, came out to the sidewalk, relocked the gate behind him, and turned in the direction opposite me and my tree. Up close, I could see the uniform wasn't of the type issued by the army whose headquarters was at my back, but was rather a work suit of some sort, topped with a leather bow tie, black and shiny and snug beneath the proud jut of a well-honed chin. Given the grace with which he made his movements, I was as surprised to discover the man was a janitor as I was that he didn't produce a top hat and cane before setting off down the street. When a suitable distance separated us, I started after him.

We paraded down Filbert to Lyon, the captain of the Fusiliers and his scruffy troop of one, then turned north in the direction of the Presidio's main gate. Because of his bearing, I assumed my man had business on the post, but when he was halfway to the gate he disappeared. When I reached the place I'd seen him last, I was standing outside a tavern that called itself the Mess Hall.

Given its name and proximity to the post, I assumed it catered primarily to the military, and the scene inside confirmed it. The bartender wore a helmet liner, the waitress a jaunty service cap. The patrons had the well-shorn aspect of active troops: many wore fatigues and most displayed a thirst that suggested they'd just come off duty. There was enough weaponry dripping from the walls and ceiling to outfit a platoon. A sign above the bar declared that all the weapons had been captured; it didn't say from whom.

Viewed in the light of the Mess Hall, my man was at

least sixty years of age, making it possible he'd been employed at the school during the period in question. Before he could adjourn to a table, I hurried to the bar and filled the stool that was closest to him.

When the bartender brought my beer, I found a pair of steel-gray eyes in the mirror in which we regarded ourselves, at least if we weren't careful. I raised my glass. "Cheers."

After a dubious moment, he took me up on it. "Up the rebels."

I nodded, then we drank to complete the ceremony. "You work on post?" I asked, eyeing his uniform.

He shook his head.

"No?" I raised a brow to convey surprise. "The reason I asked was, you look like a fighting man to me. Retired, maybe. Signal Corps or Engineers. Got a civilian job now, the motor pool or the PX, the way they do for you if you served your stint and aren't too bad a boozer and maybe earned some valor ribbons along the way."

I paused to let him answer, but he didn't. I pegged him for an honorable man but I also pegged him for a lonely one, one who hadn't been asked to tell his story for many years. I decided to try to become his audience, in the hope that once he started talking he wouldn't stop.

"So I'm wrong, huh?" I continued cheerfully. "Which is surprising, since I specialize in stuff like that."

He met my mirrored glance. "Stuff like what?"

"Guessing what people do, where they're from, who they are. Stuff like that."

He managed a weary smile in response to my forced garrulity. "The battles I fight are private," he said obscurely, then took a pull on his drink that was deep enough to suggest that one of his battles might be with demon rum. "Not that it's a concern of yours."

"But you did do a hitch when you were younger, right?" I persisted. "I can always tell a man who's seen action—there's a look in his eyes, like he sees double or something. Like he's not sure whether the war's really over."

"What you see is luck," the man said bluntly, then motioned for another whiskey.

"So which one was yours?"

"Which what?"

"War."

"Korea."

"What unit?"

"Second Battallion, Fifth RCT."

"The Regimental Combat Team. Hell of an outfit. Put in your twenty?"

He shook his head. "When they started to crank up the next one before the dead were buried from the last, I decided to retire."

"You mean Vietnam."

He nodded. "I saw it coming back in 'fifty-six, when we wouldn't let them pick their leader. Which meant we were going to put in one of our own, which meant sooner or later he'd suck us into a war to bail him out. So I turned in my duffel—I'd done enough fighting Asians on Asian soil; there's no future in it." He took another hefty pull on his drink and the impact made his eyes glaze and his demeanor pensive.

"What the hell, you'd already done your part, right?" I said. "How many wars can they ask a man to fight?"

His smile was wan. "They will ask you every day of your life and make you fight until you die. But at some point you acquire the wisdom to see that wars are hatched by cowards and fought by lunatics. If you're neither, you find someone to take your place." He issued a morose belch. "It's not hard; there are plenty of both around."

I toasted him once again. "Here's to peace on earth."

He shook his head. "Not in this lifetime."

"Why not?"

"War is like communion—it's too good a substitute for the genuine article for men to live without it. Phony piety and bogus courage—that's the diet we have today. God help us. It's the devil's world we live in."

After a stark and unblinking contemplation of his dark assessment, he adjusted the tilt of his tie and regarded me in the mirror once more. "I take it you have been under arms yourself."

I nodded. "Vietnam."

He turned to look at me directly. "Are you one of the mentals from up the hill?" He gestured in the direction of the Letterman Army Hospital, which lurked high on the post behind us.

I shook my head. "I got rid of my stress in a Saigon whorehouse."

"How fortunate. For everyone but the whore."

In face of his sharp censure, I took a drink myself. "What do they call you?" I asked after a minute.

"Arthur O'Shea." He swiveled on his stool and stuck out a hand.

"Marsh Tanner," I said as I took it. "Do they call you Art down at the shop?"

"The shop? Ah. My place of employment. Down there they call me Mr. O'Shea."

I gestured at his uniform. "Must be a strike outfit. You're dressed in style."

He shrugged. "It's a respected institution."

"Do I have to guess or are you going to tell me?"

"I'm a custodial engineer," he said after a moment. "A janitor, if you will."

"Yeah? Who for?"

"The Sebastian School."

"The place down the street?"

He nodded.

"I just passed it; hell of an establishment, it looks like."

"That it is."

"Bunch of rich kids, right?"

"Most of the students are wealthy, yes. A few are on scholarship."

"They give you any trouble?"

"They try, on occasion."

"You're too foxy for them, I suppose."

"Let's just say that after twenty years at the school and eighteen before that in the armed service, there's little devilry I'm not capable of disarming."

Arthur O'Shea drained his beer, the light in his eye indicating the devil and his work were as tangible to him as the bartender who plied his trade in front of us. "And what might your business be, Mr. Tanner?" O'Shea asked, almost affably.

"Call me Marsh," I insisted. "I'm sort of a historian, I guess you could say."

O'Shea regarded me as though I'd declared myself an alchemist. "And who might *your* employer be? Surely not an institution of higher learning."

I shook my head and motioned for another round. "I'm more of a practical type of historian. I write the history people *really* want to know."

"Such as?"

"Celebrity bios is my main gig. You know, dig up dirt on the jocks and the movie stars. People love the shit out of learning which are the perverts and the psychos and the dope fiends. Makes them feel like part of the family."

"So what brings you to this neighborhood?" His smile was arch. "Don't tell me there are celebrities about."

"Wouldn't matter; I'm into something else at the moment." I leaned to a conspiratorial closeness. "I got a big advance to do a book about scandals. You know, the city's most embarrassing moments, from the brothels of Sally Stanford to the murders of the gay councilman and the sexy mayor to the collapse of the savings and loans."

"Savings and loans hardly seem sufficiently titillating for an audience like yours."

"You'd be surprised, pal," I said, my grin stretching to lascivious proportions. "Easy money makes everyone a sinner."

O'Shea's look suggested he agreed with me. "To what end do you stir such embers, sir? Filthy lucre, I presume?"

I shrugged. "It's history. As some guy said, if we didn't have history books we'd have to do everything twice."

O'Shea laughed dryly. "I doubt scandal sheets and celebrity bios were what he had in mind."

"Hey," I said as though it had just occurred to me. "I think there's something in my files on that school of yours. Sebastian. Yeah. Sure there is. Know anything about it?"

O'Shea looked in his drink as though the past was floating in it, its form and content as imperiled as his ice cube. "I'm afraid I don't know what you're talking about."

"You must, if you've been over there for twenty years. Sex, it was—teacher and a kid. A coach, maybe; no, that was somewhere else. Pretty basic stuff, though, except in this case the kid must have been rich and the parents must have been power people. Heads rolled, as I recall. The teacher even did time, am I right?"

O'Shea wrinkled his lips with distaste. "As I say, I know nothing about it."

"I'm trying to think of the guy's name. The one caught with his pants down."

"I'm afraid I can't help you."

"Come on, Art. It's not like you were involved, for Christ's sake. Or were you?"

He bristled. "I most certainly was not."

"So you *do* remember. Don't worry—I won't quote you, if that's what you're worried about. Hell, I don't have to quote anyone—that's the beauty of these deals, no one wants to publicize the stuff even more by denying it or worse by filing a lawsuit. Or we can go the other way, make you a hero. Whichever you want." I chose a whisper fit for my impersonation. "So was it as bad as they say?"

O'Shea stayed silent for a long moment. When he spoke, his voice rattled the glassware on the back of the bar across from us and proved I'd underestimated him. "If you're smart, you'll not disturb the school or its students, Mr. Tanner."

I smiled lazily. "You wouldn't be threatening me, would you, Mr. O'Shea?"

His eyes turned sad and weary, as though he'd been through all this before. "No. But if you persist in your inquiry there are those who will. Believe me."

"Sounds like there were some matters more serious than sex involved. Like what? Money, maybe? Blackmail? Or did someone tap the till?"

"I really can't say."

There was just one thing left to try. "I'm going to write it one way or another, you might as well give it to me straight. If it's as juicy as I think it is, there could be money in it for you. I'd need the publisher's okay, but . . . Just give me a name—teacher, kid, whatever."

"No."

"Come on, it's been ten years, hasn't it? Who could it hurt?"

O'Shea folded his arms and regarded me from within the ice of inner rectitude. "You can't be much of a historian, Mr. Tanner. Otherwise you would know that despite the most persistent imprecations, the O'Sheas have not named names for a thousand years."

When the chairman of the board came to question me, the first thing he asked was whether I knew a student named Amanda Keefer. I admitted it readily. From the expression on his face, I was certain I knew what he was going to say next—that poor Amanda had committed suicide. Then he would ask if I had any idea why a young girl like Amanda would do such a thing. And I would sigh and tell him, "Yes. Of course I do."

But that's not the way it went.

HOMAGE TO HAMMURABI, p. 166

Chapter
10

By the time I knew my approach had failed and Arthur O'Shea had divulged all he was prepared to about past troubles at Sebastian, it was too late to set off in pursuit of the former soccer coach Betty Fontaine had told me about. Since she was my only other lead, I grabbed a cheeseburger at the Lombard Street Clown Alley, then went back to my apartment and accomplished a week's worth of domesticity in about an hour and a half.

When the chores were done I listened to my old records of Benny Goodman's concert at Carnegie Hall, started to re-read a novel of James Crumley's, listened to the CNN news while I nipped a bit of brandy, then climbed in bed. An hour later I was still awake, reprising my past with Betty, wondering what would have happened if I'd done what was necessary for us to stay together, which meant wondering if our marriage would have survived this long, which meant wondering if either of us had any idea how to make that happen—trying, at some level, to come to grips with my mistakes. Which led me to wonder about Bryce Chatterton and the passion he had for publishing and his rhapsodic utterings about the functions of good books. Before drifting off, I resolved to check the price of a word processor in the morning, before setting out after *Homage to Hammurabi*'s elusive creator.

It took me an hour to convince the salesman I wasn't a hacker, wasn't likely to get the computer bug, wasn't interested in spread sheets or computer graphics, that all I wanted was word processing. When he finally believed me, he suggested an IBM clone with 640K of RAM, a hard disc and WordPerfect, and he was good enough at his trade to make the package sound essential for writing anything more elaborate than a Post-it note. I was close to making the deal, until I remembered that Tolstoy had never heard of IBM and no novelist before Mark Twain had used anything as marvelous as a typewriter. So I did what I do best—I procrastinated, under the guise of waiting to see if my energies or abilities proved needful of a step I generally take care to avoid: a tango with technology.

With his commissionless grumbles still rattling in my ear, I got in the car and headed west. Betty Fontaine had told me her friend the coach was now a paralegal. I knew several paralegals from my work for various law firms around town, and I only had to call three of them to get a line on Betty's friend. Her name was Emma Drayer and her current employer was the law office of Gillis and Hook-straten, a firm that occasionally employed me. Her job, it turned out, was not paralegal but office manager. A more interesting fact was that the firm was headed by Margaret Chatterton's ex-husband, with whom Margaret was still locked in battle over the terms of their property settlement.

Although it was Saturday morning and Emma's number was not in the book, that didn't keep me from tracking her down. The current state of the law is such that the big firms never close—twenty-four hours a day, seven days a week, the law factories churn out briefs and contracts, leases and petitions, writs and warrants, making the world more complex and lawyers as essential as oxygen. Once in a while it comes in handy.

When I called her office, there was a long pause until the receptionist came on the line to tell me what I knew already—Ms. Drayer wasn't answering her phone. When I asked for her home number, the receptionist was reluctant to provide the information, but when I indicated I had a line on an experienced legal secretary who had expressed a desire to work for a particular lawyer in that particular firm, she relented. Any lawyer I've ever met would suspend the Bill of Rights for a competent secretary, and every firm I've ever worked with had instructed its office manager to conduct a constant search for them. In a gush of helpfulness, the receptionist allowed as how I might reach Ms. Drayer at her apartment, which was in the Sunset District, on Twenty-eighth just off Noriega. When I called the number she gave me, I was told by the woman who answered that Emma was out but would probably be back shortly. I decided to believe her and drove there in my Buick.

No one answered my first three knocks, but as I was about to try the adjacent unit the door opened without a cautious preamble. The woman in the doorway looked at me with what was clearly disappointment from behind a basket of dirty laundry and a bright blue bottle of Bold. She was blonde and bright-eyed, so vibrant her muscles seemed to be twitching to protest their inertia. Her baby-blue headband and yellow running outfit suggested that for her, doing the laundry was akin to aerobics.

"I thought you were the guy who was going to tell me when his whites hit the spin cycle," was the way she introduced herself.

"Sorry. I'm the guy who called about Emma Drayer."

"She's not back yet." She examined me more closely. "You can wait, I guess, but I've got to be in Sausalito by one, so . . . Who are you?" The question was easy and unconcerned. "One of the dads?"

"The dads?"

"You know, of one of Emma's teamers."

"Teamers?"

"That's what I call them. The Toe Jammers is their official title, I think."

"I still don't get it."

She blinked in exasperation. "The *soccer* kids. That's where Emma is, over at the park, coaching her soccer team."

"Ah."

"You must not know her very well—except for Häagen-Dazs, soccer's what she lives for."

"I see."

At this point, the nonverbal dynamics of the encounter caused us both to take stock. While we thought it over, she crossed her arms across her shirt, but not before I read its message—What Do You Think I Am? I wasn't sure I got that, either.

"You must not be a dad," she decided finally, "otherwise you'd be watching your pride and joy run up and down the field."

"I'm sure I would," I agreed. "But my pride and joy wouldn't be playing soccer." -

She raised a brow. "Why not?"

"I'm of the baseball generation. We view any activity that forbids the use of your hands as counter-evolutionary."

She waited to see if my entendre was double; I wasn't sure I knew myself.

When I didn't drool or leer, she shrugged. "Guys and their spectator sports. I will never understand it till the day I die." She looked down at her laundry, then back at me, as though debating which of us would offer a more enduring stimulus. "So what are you if you're not a dad?"

Time was wasting, so I cut to the quick. "I'm a private eye."

"You're kidding," she said, but didn't seem as surprised as most at my most common confession. "And people say nothing's happening out here in the Sunset." She tried to suppress a laugh but succeeded only partially. "So what did she do? Assassinate one of the parents?"

I shook my head. "She taught at the Sebastian School."

She frowned. "I know that's a chore, but is it a crime?"

"Not that I know of."

"So why is it important?"

I unbuttoned my jacket. "Could I come in and sit down? My feet don't like being used like this."

She looked down at my Rockports. "How are they supposed to be used?"

"To get me from the couch to the refrigerator."

I had finally earned a smile. "You should join a club; my trainer could firm you up in no time."

"I'm already in a club."

"Yeah? Which one?"

"The Fruit-of-the Month. So how about it? Have you got a stool I can rent for ten minutes?"

For some reason, the request fully activated the protective devices women have to use these days in order to keep from becoming crime statistics. "Have you got a license of some sort?"

I showed it to her.

"Tanner," she read off the license. "I've heard of you, I think. In fact, I think my firm *uses* you from time to time."

"What firm is that?"

"Gillis and Hookstratten."

I nodded. "I know it well. So you and Emma work at the same place."

"Cozy, right?"

"What are you, a paralegal?"

Her curse was generic and justified. "I happen to be a lawyer—they're starting to let a few of us do that nowadays, I guess you hadn't heard. It's a controlled experiment; they're hoping it'll be as big as Retin-A."

"Sorry," I said, and meant it, having endured enough lampoons of my own profession to willfully inflict them on others.

"I won't say it's all right, because it isn't," she countered. "But at least you didn't assume I was a secretary."

I seized the opening gladly. "Not that there's anything wrong with being a secretary."

"Of course not." She colored, then matched my grin. "Some of my best friends are secretaries." She gestured toward the apartment at her back. "Come on in. I'd make coffee, but I've got to get these in the Maytag as soon as it's free."

"All I need is a chair," I said, so she found me one.

"Maybe I should know your name," I said as we both got comfortable, sitting across from each other in a colorful room that contained enough flowers to suggest a maternity ward or a mortuary.

"Christine White."

"And you live here with Ms. Drayer?"

She nodded. "We were sorority sisters at Oregon. We kept in touch, and when we both ended up in the city, we decided to see if two could live cheaper than one plus one. Then she got a job at Gill and Hook, and when I decided to leave the city attorney's office, she convinced them to take me on."

"What time does Emma get back from soccering?"

She looked at a watch the size of a jar lid. "Could be anytime, but it might be hours. I just remembered— sometimes she plays referee after she plays coach." She curled her legs beneath her, making interesting bulges and attractive creases. "So what does Gill and Hook have you do for the good of the cause?"

I shrugged. "Mostly the messy stuff."

"You mean litigation."

I nodded. "That's usually where the mud gets thrown. How about you?"

"Trusts and estates. The only things thrown at me are crutches and safe-deposit keys."

"I have to confess I always thought probate would get pretty boring pretty fast."

Christine White stretched her back like a cat and luxuriated in the crushed velour. Her contortions allowed me to believe that our relationship might be moving to a different plane. When I checked, I discovered that I hoped so.

"It would be boring if they didn't give me a hundred and twenty thousand a year to keep it interesting," she commented with the offhand tone that is always meant to convey its opposite. "If I keep a lid on expenses, and if my defined benefit plan is any good, I'll have enough to retire by the time I'm fifty."

"A real comet, huh? Slave night and day for twenty years, then flame out."

She seemed unembarrassed by the metaphorization of her life plan. "That's about it."

"How long have you been at it?"

"Eleven years. How long have you been a detective?"

"Fifteen. What will you do when you retire?"

She met my look. "I'm going to run around the world."

I looked to make sure I heard right. "Literally, you mean."

"You're damned right."

"I want to do some traveling, too, someday. Maybe we'll run into each other. I'll be the one in the rickshaw."

She regarded me with a lawyer's eye. "Since you come so highly recommended, I might have some use for you myself."

"Tracking down a missing heir?"

She shook her head. "Dinner. Tonight. At Speedo. I made a reservation for a business thing, but the client canceled." She reddened. "Actually, the client died. In my business they have a tendency to do that." She couldn't suppress a laugh and I couldn't keep myself from joining her. In the right company, death easily becomes hilarious.

"So how about it?" she asked when we had finished.

I hesitated, then shook my head.

"Why not?"

"I don't have anything to wear."

She frowned. "Isn't that supposed to be *my* line?"

I nodded. "But you already used mine up."

She crossed her arms again, this time to keep from throwing something. "Can't come to grips with the modern woman, huh, Mr. Private Detective?"

I matched her obstinacy. "I can if I want to."

"What would make you want to?"

"A modern woman who lets a man be old-fashioned."

She looked at me for what seemed like a hour, then grew self-conscious and eyed the basket of laundry that lay like a sixth continent between us. "You wouldn't happen to know how to get a red wine stain out of a white blouse, would you?" she asked, suddenly blasé, looking out the window at a stretch of houses that seemed like cookies cut from the same cutter.

"Cotton?" I asked.

She nodded.

"Stretch it over a bowl, put salt on the stain, and pour boiling water on it from a height of three feet."

Her eyes ballooned. "You're kidding, right?"

I shook my head. "Not unless my grandmother was. And she didn't seem the type."

"Your grandmother drank wine?"

"She made it."

"Napa?"

"Council Bluffs."

"Out of what? Corn?"

"Apricots and Concord grapes."

"Was it any good?"

"It was back in 1957," I said. "But then so were Chevrolets."

Just then there was a knock at the door. Before Christine had a chance to move, it was opened by a young man wearing red Jockey shorts and nothing else. "Yo, Crissy. Go for it, babe."

The young man disappeared. Crissy looked at me. "That's my cue. Once a month Roger washes everything he owns," she added when she saw my look.

She reached for her laundry basket with her foot. "Good luck getting Emma to give you the straight dope on the Hell Hole."

"What's that?"

She pulled the basket to her and put it on her lap. "It's what she used to call that school."

"Why?"

"She had some problems down there."

"What kind of problems?"

She shrugged. "I don't know—first she was winning all her games and getting raises and taking kids to soccer camps in Europe with all expenses paid, then all of a sudden she got canned. Actually, I think it started with the Balboa game."

"What happened?"

"Balboa played rough. One of the Sebastian sweethearts got a tooth knocked out and another broke an ankle, so the headmaster ordered Emma not to schedule any more matches with the public schools, except with Lowell, of course. Emma refused, so she got fired. And that's all I know about Emma and Sebastian."

Christine White picked up the laundry basket, stood up and waited for me to join her, then headed for the door. When I offered to carry her load, she shook her head. "The modern woman, remember?"

She reached for the doorknob but I opened it for her. "The throwback, remember?"

We smiled at each other. "Sorry about dinner," I went

on, "but I have a thing about spending more on a meal than I spend on rent. Maybe we could do something next week. Somewhere in North Beach."

She raised a brow. "You know where to reach me if it still seems like a good idea the next time you're hungry." Then she lowered it. "But I don't do anyone's laundry except my own."

My task is literally death-defying. All I have to do to prove that I was framed is survive incarceration among men who are stunningly able and eerily willing to kill me, then persuade a person who may well be equally in fear of her life to tell someone—anyone—the truth.

HOMAGE TO HAMMURABI, p. 156

Chapter
11

The soccer fields were at the far end of Golden Gate Park, nestled between the windmills, only a high hedge away from the Great Highway in one direction and the sewage treatment plant in another. Luckily for the kids who were swarming over the fields like ants on their way to a second bite of bologna, the summer fog had remained in its offshore bed that morning—the sun gave the grasses the gleam of shredded emeralds and made the eager athletes glow like diminutive golden gods.

I guessed the age of the participants as immediately preteen, and guessed the adult observers along the sidelines to be their hyperactive parents. From the fringe of the middle field, I tried to figure out which of the women cheering the kids on might be Emma Drayer, but I soon gave up such Holmesian speculation and reverted to type.

My fifth interrogatee was an excitable young man who thrilled at every kick the Blue Team let fly, whether it struck the elusive ball or not. After a portly youngster missed an easy header, then dispatched the ball beyond the boundary in mostly melodramatic frustration, the man calmed down long enough for me to ask if he knew where I could find Emma Drayer, or if he knew which team was called the Toe Jammers.

After taking a moment to consider my right to question

him, the man pointed in the direction of a stout and resolute young woman whose cleated shoes, knee socks, and satin shorts were topped by the vertical stripes of a referee's blouse. "Tell her the Jammers play too rough," the man muttered when I thanked him for the information. "Tell her to teach those little bastards some sportsmanship."

I successfully suppressed a laugh.

When the teams had assembled for the inbounds pass, the referee started to hand the ball to one of the players in red, then suddenly drew back and blew a blast on her whistle. "Listen up," she shouted. "Red team, come to attention. Come on, Red, move! That's it. Now, Blue team, do the same. Quickly! Good. Now. Both teams. *Look at your feet!*"

In an instant, all heads were bowed, as though Emma Drayer were not a referee but an archangel just in with instructions.

"Okay, troops," she continued, "if you need to tie your shoes . . . *tie your shoes!*" She crossed her arms and waited. "Quickly, teamers, quickly. Good. Okay, straighten up. Red ball, in bounds." The ball was handed over, the whistle blew, and again the game was on—shoes tied tightly, worshipers and worshiped both earthly once again.

The final score was eighteen to thirteen, an exuberant if not a skillful contest. When each team had given a pro forma cheer for its opponent and congratulated or consoled itself, the players trooped off, leaving me to wait while the referee supervised the collection of the balls and the removal of the goal nets. I lay in wait for her as she came off the field, but before she got close enough for me to introduce myself she was waylaid by the man I had questioned earlier.

His gripe seemed to be that his pride and joy should have been awarded a free kick somewhere along the line. The referee's response—"That wasn't a foul, that was a fuckup"—seemed to take care of the matter as far as she was concerned.

When she reached my side I interrupted the man's rebuttal. "Ms. Drayer? My name's Tanner. I wonder if I could talk to you for a minute."

The disgruntled dad looked me over. He was a foot shorter and a decade younger than I was, two characteristics that often encourage their possessors to take a chance on fisticuffs, but this one decided not to risk it. After leaving us, he skulked to the side of the biggish boy who had booted the ball out of bounds and began berating him in the manner he had used on the referee.

Emma Drayer watched him for a moment, then muttered, "Prick," to no one in particular. "I love these guys who never had the guts to take the field themselves but try to make their kid another Pelé." She looked me over as we continued toward the parking lot. "If you've got a complaint about the way I worked the game, take it up with the league."

"I don't waste complaints on games."

That slowed her down, though not to a stop. "You have a child on the Toe Jammers?" she asked as she brushed a drop of sweat off the tip of her nose.

"Nope."

"I didn't think I'd seen you at the organizational meetings. So what do you want to talk about?"

"The Sebastian School," I said as we reached the edge of the lot.

That stopped her cold. Her face, formerly flushed and full from its exertions and exhortations, tightened into a knot of caution. "Why would you think I know anything about the Sebastian School?"

"Because you used to teach there."

"No, I didn't."

"Coach, then."

She hesitated. "What if I did?"

I looked at the set of stripes around her torso. "You're acting like I'm accusing you of being an ex con, Ms. Drayer."

She looked for a clue to my purpose, then looked past me to see if anyone was poised to overhear. "Are you a cop?" she asked carefully.

I shook my head.

"If you're not a cop, I don't have to answer your questions."

The statement seemed more hopeful than constitution-

ally secure. "True enough," I said, "except that when
people don't want to talk to me about subjects that seem
innocuous, I tend to get interested in why that is."

"So?"

"I've been a private detective for fifteen years. One of
the reasons I've lasted that long is that when I get interested
in a question, I poke around until I find the answer."

"Haven't you worked for the firm before? Gillis and
Hookstraten?"

I nodded.

"I thought the name was familiar. You work for Ken
Bolling."

"Right."

She hugged herself as though the fog had just tumbled
out of bed and rolled on top of us. "Are you investigating
the school? Is that it? Has the state board brought charges
against it?"

I tried to disguise my ignorance as pretext. "Why do
you suppose the state would do that?"

She looked at me closely. Although I tried my best to
fool her, she reached the right conclusion. "Shit. You don't
have any idea what you're getting into, do you?"

She started to walk off, but I grabbed her arm. "I know
enough to ask more questions."

She shook her head and pulled away. "I don't have
anything to say on the subject of the Sebastian School."

"I've got a feeling this thing is going to get complicated,
Ms. Drayer. Which means I'll get back to you. Which
means the next time we meet it might not be in the middle
of a pretty park and out of earshot of anyone who matters."

She wrinkled her brow and considered her options. "We
can't talk here," she said finally.

"There are some places on Clement we can—"

She shook her head. "Too many people I know shop
Clement. The Zim's on California Street. I'll meet you in
fifteen minutes. If you beat me there, order me a waffle."
She caught my look. "I coach because I like to help kids be
kids, not because I want to live forever."

I hesitated. "I guess this is where I should give you a
warning."

She stiffened. "What kind of warning?"

"If you don't show up at Zim's, I'll come after you, Ms. Drayer." I waited until I knew she knew I was serious. "But only after I've eaten your waffle."

She turned on a cleated heel and walked toward the cluster of vehicles still parked in the tiny lot. Hers was a dented and dusty Econoline, with a bumper sticker that said MY OTHER CAR IS A CAR. As she drove away I noted the license number in my book, then got in my dented and dusty Buick, drove east on Kennedy Drive, and took Thirty-sixth Avenue north to California.

I lived for an eternity on a diet of self-pity. Then I went to jail. Finally possessed of grounds, I no longer made use of them.

HOMAGE TO HAMMURABI, p. 133

Chapter
12

A Spanish omelette and a Belgian waffle were languishing in front of me when Emma Drayer slipped into the other side of the booth. She'd found a place to splash water on her face and exchange her stripes for a sweatshirt, and elapsed time and the costume change had made her more confident of her ability to parry whatever my thrust might be, so much so that I mentally kicked myself. I'd had her on the ropes and let her off—a bad idea in both boxing and interrogation.

"I should have had you order juice," she said as she surveyed the limited repast, then motioned for the waitress. "Got to keep the electrolytes up." She glanced around the restaurant to be sure what she was about to say would remain private. "How did you find me, anyway?"

I explained about the receptionist and the fictitious secretary.

"Do you know who Marvin Gillis is?" she asked as the juice arrived.

"Of course I know who he is."

"Do you know how much trouble he can bring down on you for what you're doing?"

"Why would he want to?"

Exasperated by such ignorance, she shook her head. "Gillis is the chairman of the board of trustees of the Sebastian School. Rufus Finner's the headmaster, and has been for forty years, but Gillis really runs the place. From a policy point of view, I mean. Marvin lives and dies for that school. He thinks it's more important than Harvard. And to San Francisco, it probably is." She cocked her head. "That's news to you, isn't it?"

I admitted it.

"Which must mean you're not."

"Not what?"

"Looking for dirt on Sebastian."

"I didn't say I was."

"I guess you didn't. Not exactly." Her tone was a mysterious mix of relief and disappointment. For my part, I was content to let her assumption go uncorrected.

"What would I come up with if I *did* do that kind of digging?" I asked after a moment.

Unconcerned now that I was no longer a threat, Emma Drayer shrugged casually. "All kinds of things—sexism, tokenism, elitism, despotism—to name a few."

"In other words, a typical private school."

She smiled for the first time since she had blown the whistle to end the game. "I suppose that's true."

"Sounds like you still haven't gotten over it," I said suddenly, to keep the focus on Sebastian, maybe to jar something loose that I could use.

The comment startled her. "Gotten over what?"

"The Balboa game."

She squirmed. "How did you know about that?"

"Your roommate told me."

"When did you talk to her?"

"An hour before I talked to you."

"What did she tell you?"

"Not much. Mostly about the game and the reason you got fired."

"What else?"

"That's about it."

She hesitated, as though she was rehearsing my earlier representations. "The Balboa game." Her look was arid. "Who knew such a little thing could haunt me for a decade?"

"Haunt you how?"

It took a long while for her to decide to tell me. "You know what I do at the law firm, right?"

I nodded. "Office manager."

"A glorified bookkeeper, is what it amounts to. You know why I do it? You know why I'm not teaching or coaching anymore?"

"Why?"

"Because I've been blacklisted at every school in the Bay Area."

I looked for a sign of hyperbole but found only a marbled eye that demanded I believe her. "What makes you think you were blacklisted?"

"Because when I knew I was going to be fired at Sebastian, I sent off forty-two job applications. Coaching, teaching history or civics, administrating—I've done them all, and done them well." She paused and readjusted. "Except maybe the administrating—I'm too impatient for that."

"But you didn't get a job."

"Right."

"Teaching jobs are hard to get in the city, aren't they?"

"Sure, but not getting the job wasn't the point. The point was, I got all my rejections back within two weeks."

"So?"

Her words were harsh. "They were *waiting* for me, the bastards; they'd been warned about me and told to head me off."

"All because you played a rough team in a *soccer* game?"

She looked into the distance, beyond the cars that were streaming past, beyond the disheveled street. When she spoke, her voice was thick with memory. "Marvin Gillis decided I was a threat to him and he wasn't about to put up with it. So he made an example of me—he took away my job, the thing I loved most in the world, and he made it clear he could do the same to anyone *else* in the school who might go up against him."

She made it sound like the stuff of tragedy, and perhaps for Emma it was. "Gillis has that much power?" I asked. "Even in the public schools?"

She nodded wearily. "What he has power over is money. Ever since Proposition Thirteen put a lid on property taxes in this state, the public schools have gone to hell. The dropout rate is soaring—sixty-eight percent of the tenth graders leave school before graduation. That's two out of three, if your math is rusty. Plus, class size is enormous; discipline is a joke; and the quality of new teachers is pathetic, particularly in the cities."

"What does that have to do with Gillis?"

"The chief impact of the budget cuts is extracurricular—sports, art, music, debate—there's no *money* for those things anymore. But those things are important, particularly to parents, so schools look for other sources of funding. Things are better now, what with the lottery and Prop. 98, but back then where the schools looked for some extra money were the foundations. Pools of private bucks, established by rich people on their deathbeds, doled out afterward by their lawyers or their heirs."

"And Gillis has sway with the foundations."

Her eyes widened. "Sway? Marvin Gillis can deliver any foundation in the city. If he wants to."

"How?"

"Because of that *school*. Chances are good that a majority of the board members of the foundation went to Sebastian once upon a time and chances are even better that their kids *are* going or *will* go there. They don't want to cross Gillis because they don't want the school to take it out on their kids."

"There can't be *that* many foundation people with kids in Sebastian."

"It only takes a few. Foundations get all kinds of requests for funds, far more than they can approve. If someone comes up with a reason for denying an application, the easiest thing is to move along to the next item, without debate."

"One less decision that has to be made."

"Exactly." She gulped her juice. "God, this is depressing. I had all this bottled up, and you come along and pull the cork. Pardon me if I don't thank you. And you can pay for the goddamned waffle."

She made as if to go, so I reached out a hand to stop her. "I haven't gotten to my questions yet."

She looked at her watch.

"It'll only take a minute. Actually, I am digging up some dirt."

The revelation made her angry. "In other words, you lied to me."

I shook my head. "I just let you live with your assumptions for a while."

Her breaths quickened. "What are you trying to do? What are you trying to find out?"

"I'm interested in a sex scandal at Sebastian—I think it happened about nine years ago."

She stayed where she was, then returned my words to me: "You *think?*"

"My information is hazy," I admitted. "It may not have been sex, it may have been something else. But what I *think* happened is that a female student accused a teacher of molesting her. He may have been an English teacher. I think he went to jail for it." When I looked closely at her I thought I saw a fresh intensity and even a trace of panic. "So how about it? Does anything salacious come to mind about the old days at Sebastian?"

She wouldn't meet my eye. "Why do you want to know about this?"

"I can't tell you."

"My God, don't they feel six years is *enough?*"

I sighed and leaned back against the booth. "So it did happen."

Pained, she bowed her head and closed her eyes. "Yes."

"As I described?"

"Pretty much. Except not that long ago. It was 1983."

"Who was the girl?"

She raised her head and shook it. "I won't tell you. Not without knowing more."

"More what?"

"About what you're going to do with the information."

"That's no concern of yours, is it?"

She looked at me with the severity of a schoolmarm on detention detail. "I don't know if it is or not. I do know there's been a lot of pain involved in this already and I don't want to add to it." Her next question was so hopeful she seemed a different woman. "He's out of prison, isn't he?"

"I think so, but I'm not sure."

"Do you know where he is?"

I shook my head. "I wasn't even sure he existed, till now."

"Then I don't understand what you're doing."

"And I don't understand why you're so protective of him."

She turned away and sighed, attuned to images from half a dozen years before. "I've never seen a more pathetic creature than he was after the rumors started." She shook her head sadly. "I was afraid he was going to kill himself; I'm a little surprised he didn't."

"What did you think when you first heard about it?"

"I couldn't believe it. Not of . . . him."

"So you thought he was innocent?"

She shrugged. "At first."

"Do you think so now?"

She was tentative with her answer. "I want to, even though I don't know why he would have let them lock him up if he'd been innocent." She met my eye. "What I *do* know is that you should let him alone. No one will be helped by resurrecting all this."

I decided not to tell her about the book. "Why are you so sure? Maybe if you help me, we might learn what really happened back then."

I'd stretched my undertaking further than it would legitimately go, but not so far that I couldn't live with it. "All you have to do is tell me his name, Ms. Drayer," I said when she didn't respond.

What she wanted was to feel that if she helped me I would make things better for all concerned, but she couldn't make herself believe it. "A possibility isn't enough. I won't talk to you unless he tells me it's all right. He's suffered too much already; I won't add to his burden. Not inadvertently." The speck she wiped from her eye looked like a murky tear.

"I can't find him to tell him to give you the authorization to talk to me unless you give me his name."

She shook her head firmly. "That's your problem. I'm sorry. He was the only one who was decent to me while I was at that school. I can't betray him now." She stood up and fished in her bag for a card. "This is my number, home and office, in case you find him and he wants to talk to me about it. Otherwise, I'd appreciate it if you wouldn't bother me again."

And she was gone, leaving the restaurant with the strong stride of an athlete, leaving me with the echo of her resistance and a limp and soggy waffle.

As I lingered over my third cup of coffee, I reviewed what Emma Drayer had just told me, then remembered as much of *Homage to Hammurabi* as I could, which was enough to give me an idea. After I found a pay phone I dialed a number that was staring back at me from Emma's card. "Ms. White? This is Marsh Tanner. I was over there a couple of hours ago."

Her tone was sour. "I remember. Believe me."

"I thought you were off to Sausalito."

"I was just going out the door."

"Did you keep your date with the spin cycle?"

"I'm in the folding phase, thanks for asking." She softened. "If you've changed your mind about Speedo, I have to tell you I already filled your slot."

"Actually, I was wondering about that painting on your wall."

"Which one?"

"The carrots."

"*That* thing," she scoffed. "What about it?"

"I was wondering if you could tell me who painted it."

"Are you a collector, Mr. Tanner? Somehow you don't seem the type."

"Let's just say I know what I like, and what I like is carrots."

"Descended from a long line of bunnies, are we? Well, that one's Emma's; I forget the name of the artist, just a minute . . ." Noises left the telephone, then returned. "Her name is Lily Lucerne. The painting's called *Carrot and a Stick*. The stick is Wrigley's Spearmint, I don't know if you noticed."

I thanked Christine for the information, made a statement about seeing her again sometime that sounded more ambivalent than I intended it to be, then returned to the booth and finished my coffee. At some point I began to wonder why, if Marvin Gillis had gone to such lengths to blackball Emma Drayer at Sebastian, he'd ended up by giving her a job.

The mystery novels that I used to devour late at night suggested that motive is the key to crime. Certainly my own was so eagerly presumed, it eased the assumption of my guilt. But what of the motive of the true perpetrators of the outrage? Why would someone go to such extremes to remove me from both school and society? The only power I wielded was the assessment of performance in the most elemental of academic disciplines. Also, I acknowledge, I was for a few young women the focus of an adolescent crush. Hardly unprecedented, hardly ominous, hardly the stuff of conspiracy and vengeance.

Yet here I sit.

HOMAGE TO HAMMURABI, p. 188

Chapter
13

I drop by the Museum of Modern Art from time to time, when someone like Kline or Hoffmann is being featured or when I'm in the neighborhood anyway, waiting to testify across the street in City Hall. And on the rare occasions when someone in my family comes to town, I'll shepherd them to the de Young or the Legion of Honor, just to prove that San Francisco is different from the places in Iowa and Kansas they will return to in a week, though deep down I know the difference is mostly superficial. But I don't keep up with the art world as a matter of course, so when I got back to the office I phoned someone who tracked it for a living.

Darryl Dromedy had been measuring and interpreting the visual arts for the *Examiner* for over twenty years. Iconoclastic and bombastic, perverse and puckish, his Sunday survey pieces were a pleasure to read even if you didn't know the Impressionists from Ingres or Dada from David. Inveighing against fads, champion of the unknown, debunker of the overpraised, Darryl had boosted more than one minor figure to a place of national prominence and, in the process, had made both himself and certain favored collectors wealthy beyond their dreams.

Normally, I don't travel in Darryl's circles, but some years back I'd gotten a call when a self-described "organic ornamentalist" had decided Darryl had demeaned him in the review of his retrospective. Inspired by the "turd birds" he'd seen for sale while on an NEA–aided trip to Nebraska in search of egalitarian inspiration, the sculptor had abandoned his normal metier, which featured the tensile properties of soda cans, and begun to work in dung. The finished products of the new direction were lumpy pieces of dinnerware and food molded from a variety of wastes produced by everything from elephants to rats, the only additives being a dollop of clay for bonding and a layer of glaze to preserve the stuff incarnate.

When Darryl had opined in print that this was the clearest case in history of an artist devaluing his materials—i.e., the dung was no longer suitable for fertilizer—the sculptor had threatened Darryl with bodily harm. While persuading the ornamentalist to reconsider, I was forced to use one of his cow pie casseroles as a cudgel. Among other things, the experience led me to avoid any artwork more avant-garde than the comics page for well over a year.

Whoever answered the phone at the *Examiner* told me that Darryl had just come in for the day and was roaming the room in search of a bagel. While I waited for him to come on the line, I glanced at the clock. It was four-fifteen.

"Long time, no seascapes," Darryl began—among other things, Darryl fancies himself a wit. "Did you buy that little Thiebaud I told you about?"

"I'm afraid Thiebaud's out of my league."

"It was a steal at that price, Marsh—the guy didn't know what he had. You'd have quadrupled your money overnight."

"I don't doubt it."

"Your loss is some speculator's gain, you know. He'll scarf up that lovely little canvas and stick it in a chilly old vault and wait for the appreciation. No one else will be able to enjoy it for fifty years."

"It's unconscionable, I agree, but I don't have that kind of money."

As he is wont to do, Darryl began to scold. "If you'd forgo your *athletic* indulgences, you could enjoy a more *permanent* aesthetic, you know."

"You mean trade my season ticket for a still life?"

"Precisely."

"I'll give it some thought."

"Good. In the meantime, Survival Research Laboratories is staging another techno-allegory tonight—I hear this one might bring out the bomb squad. Of course you'll have to sign a release before they let you in."

"Why?"

"They commit all *kinds* of mayhem at SRL performances—machines assaulting other machines, underground explosions, computers run amok, electronics going haywire. It's *delicious*. The *last* time they gave us goggles and *ear*plugs. Want to be my date?"

"No, but it sure sounds fun."

Darryl giggled with the abandon of one who thrives on the risks of others. "It's art, ain't it?"

"You tell me."

"Of *course* it is. It *bothers* people. That's enough to make it art in *my* book."

"Which makes Tiny Tim the greatest artist who ever lived."

Darryl giggled again, then shouted something to someone who must have needed a battery in his Beltone. When he got back to me he had calmed a bit. "So why'd you call, Marsh?—you got a nephew who thinks he's the new Schnabel?" He stopped abruptly. "*Please* don't tell me the *dung* master's back in town."

"Nothing like that," I said, hastening to disabuse him. "Ever hear of an artist named Lily Lucerne?"

Darryl audibly relaxed. "Sure. Photo-realist. Protégé of Bechtle, studied with him at State. Very big with the objectivist crowd."

"Know anything about her personal life?"

"Not really. Married to a business type, I think. She doesn't hang out with the trendettes, that's for sure; sort of a recluse; in fact."

"Ever hear anything scandalous about her?"

Darryl scoffed. "It's pretty tough to be scandalous in *this* town, Marsh. Of course if she could document it, being a virgin would make her a *sensation*."

"This is more along the lines of her husband spending some time in jail. Her ex-husband, I mean."

Darryl perked up. "I never heard anything like that. Is it true? What for?"

"I don't know yet."

I could hear the calculator begin to click. "Well, it would certainly raise her prices if it was—collectors love the *hell* out of scandals. I know a man in Sausalito who collects inmates' art exclusively."

"We're talking about Lily Lucerne," I reminded him. "You wouldn't happen to know where she lives, would you?"

"No idea."

"Do you know which gallery shows her?"

"Let me think. The Grasshopper, I believe," Darryl said after a moment. "That's on Post, just east of Union Square."

"Do you know anyone who works there?"

"Only the owner," he sniffed royally. "Will *she* do?"

"Which is who?"

"Giselle."

"Giselle who?"

"Just Giselle. She came over as an Air France stewardess, then married some *hotel* money and decided to do something with it more uplifting than a lifetime of plastic surgery."

"Do you suppose she'd tell you how to get in touch with Lucerne?"

Darryl snorted impatiently. "I gave their last show a minor *rave*. The question is, why should I ask?"

"Because sooner or later you're going to piss off another macho Michelangelo and he's going to come after you with his chisel."

Darryl got off his high horse. "I'll get back to you. The Survival Research opening is at seven, if you change your mind."

I pressed the button to free myself from Darryl, then dialed the Central Station.

"I was just about to call you," Charley said when they tracked him down. "The lab found prints on those pages you gave me."

I voiced my guess. "Some of them belong to a guy named Lucerne."

Charley hesitated long enough for me to know my hunch was wrong. "Who's Lucerne?" he asked carefully.

"Just a shot in the dark. I guess she uses a nom de brush."

"Am I supposed to understand this?"

"No, you're supposed to tell me whose prints they are."

"There were several prints but only one that we could ID. Female."

"You sure?"

"The lab boys seem to be, but maybe you'd like to discuss it with them. I'm sure they enjoy being double-checked by an amateur."

"Sorry, Charley. Which female?"

"Someone named Gillis."

"Margaret?"

"Wrong again."

"Jane Ann?"

"That's the one. Good thing it was Twenty Questions." I swore. "That's the only one they matched?"

"That's it. Just a minute, I've got an address for her somewhere."

"That's all right, I know how to find her. Why did she pop up on your computer?"

"Juvenile thing. The court record's expunged, but the prints are still in the machine. You know her?"

"She's Bryce's stepdaughter."

Charley's interest was confined to a grunt. "I still don't understand it, but I promise I'll buy the book you write the minute it comes out in paperback."

The phone rang six seconds after Charley had hung up in the middle of my disclaimer.

"You're in luck," Darryl Dromedy gushed. "Lily Lucerne is meeting a prospective buyer at the Grasshopper tonight at six. Japanese, of course—needs something to perk up his homes in Maui and Gstaad."

"So do I just show up?"

"I've paved the way with Giselle, but you're on your own with Lucerne. From what I hear, she's a tough cookie."

"Cookies crumble," I said, then walked up to the Caffé Trieste. Along the way I thought about what Charley had said about me writing a book about the Chatterton case. By the time I had finished dinner I had my notebook out and was making an outline of the week's events, under the heading Chapter One.

Last night while I was sleeping, my cell mate set fire to my hair. When he assured the guard it was an accident, he was routinely believed.

HOMAGE TO HAMMURABI, p. 192

Chapter
14

Although the sun was about to stage its exit, a swarm of conventioneers still littered the environs of Union Square, thronging to Macy's, massing in the Neiman Marcus rotunda, exclaiming over the fabulous new Nordstrom, marveling at a thousand kinds of perfume and a hundred makes of shoes, loading up on merchandise they could buy for half the price in Des Moines or Columbus, wondering how to get a cable car from there to Fisherman's Wharf, telling themselves it had to get warmer tomorrow, all under the life-numbed stares of two score ladies and gentlemen whose annual incomes wouldn't have covered the cost of the contents of a single shopping bag in sight.

Outside the Grasshopper Gallery, a crowd of tourists eddied among and around each other, angling for a better view. Since the object of the exercise was intriguing to me as well, I decided to join the throng.

The entire front of the gallery was open to the street, an expanse as wide as a double garage, the heat lamps in the ceiling the only concession to the out-of-doors. But it was the interior of the space that caused all of us to gape the way kids used to gape at the sight of Mantle and Mays before TV made even heroes common.

A triumph of trompe l'oeil, nothing inside the gallery existed in more than two dimensions—the window looking out into the verdant garden, the rubber plant rising out of the colorful ceramic pot, the lighted EXIT over the rear door, the neon coals in the fireplace, even the fire *extinguisher*—all were products of objectivist art, rendered more real than reality on a series of floor-to-ceiling canvases that ringed the room without a break. Even the woman in the back— seated demurely at a writing desk, smiling expectantly at those of us who dared peer gingerly into her superreal domain—would maintain both her pose and her poise forever.

There must have been a sensor of some kind wired into the doorway, because when I walked beneath the heat lamps and crossed the slate-black threshold, a hidden door in a wall painted to look like a bookcase opened at the rear of the showroom and a young woman hurried out to greet me.

"May I help you, sir?" Beneath the wild outpouring of her hair and above the pulpy pomegranate of her lips, her eyes were exactly as expectant as those of the acrylic woman who remained seated at her desk.

I dredged both a posture and accent from the latitudes of my youth. "This here gallery is quite a place, young lady," I enthused. "You sure had *me* fooled, especially that there mirror."

I pointed to the canvas to my left, the one that so precisely duplicated the opposite wall it seemed to contain a real reflection. "A man could get real discombobulated around here, especially if he was likkered up. What do you *call* these doodads, anyhow?"

The woman smiled, though less spectacularly than before she'd encountered my drawl. "Photo-realism. It's breathtaking, isn't it?"

"I never seen nothing like it, though I've seen a billboard or two that made me look a second time."

She remained saleswoman enough to smile. "Are you a collector, by any chance?" From her tone, I would more likely be a monk.

I shook my head. "Not yet, anyways. What I am is a trucker."

Her regard for me, moderate at best, plunged to zero. "I see. Well, you're welcome to look around. If we can be of assistance, please let us know."

She started to turn away. "How much is that one?" I asked quickly. I pointed to the rubber plant.

"That's one of our best buys. Only four thousand."

"Dollars?"

"I'm afraid so."

"No wonder folks take up this line of work, making pictures of things that are already there. Me, I prefer the squiggly ones, the pictures of things that can't be seen."

The ripe lips pursed. "Expressionism is nice, but there's room for other points of view as well," she commented frostily. "Many of us feel expressionism is too . . . *sauvage* for the eighties."

"Sure. I can see that. Folks like to know what's what. Not many chances being taken these days."

"That's one way of looking at it, I suppose. If you're in the market for something more in your price range, there's a printshop down the street that—"

"What's your name, young lady?" I interrupted.

Unaccustomed to assertion, for the first time she seemed off-balance. She touched her neckline and her hair to make sure her allies were still in place. "Joy," she said.

"That's a real pretty name. It suits you."

"Thank you."

"Well, Joy, when I said I was a trucker I believe you took me to say I *drove* 'em. But what I meant to say was that I *own* 'em. Thirty-four rigs as of this morning. Tanner Trucking, out of Fresno. Hell, if you've ever shipped any pictures from here to L.A., we probably hauled 'em for you."

Joy had become considerably more attuned. "We do *lots* of business in Los Angeles—the film community is a *particularly* important market in our business—so perhaps you have indeed 'hauled' some for us."

As amazing as evolution itself, her hand crawled forth and found a purchase on my arm. "You know, Mr. . . . Hammer, was it?"

"Tanner."

"You know, Mr. Tanner, the most amazing thing has just occurred to me."

I rolled my eyes in a lascivious whirl. "What might that be, young lady?"

"Do you know what some of the very first canvases we carried in the gallery depicted?"

"What's that?"

"Trucks!"

"You're joshing."

"I'm not," she countered happily. "May I show them to you?"

"Well, I don't know if—"

"It'll just take a minute. You'll be stunned, I'm convinced."

"But—"

She held up a hand to silence me, then hurried behind a folding screen and plucked a white phone off the wall, dialed a number, and spoke softly and urgently. A second later she was at my side. "Juan will bring a sample for you momentarily."

This wasn't where I wanted us to be. "What kind of truck is it?" I asked dubiously. "Mack? Pete? Kenny? What?"

Joy frowned. "Why . . . I'm not sure. I didn't know there was that much . . . *selection* in trucks."

"Young lady, there's as much different between trucks as there is between that little black dress you're wearing and a set of Osh-Kosh B'gosh with a full bib."

With that, Joy found a need to search the gallery for another customer. It was only when she didn't find one that she turned her blue eyes back to me. "Isn't that fascinating."

"Listen," I said quickly. "While we're jawing, I wonder if you've got something that Wanda June might like in the way of art."

"And who might she be?" Joy seemed leery of the possibilities.

"My dearly beloved, of course. Whenever I take a trip to the big city, I always bring something back for Wanda June. Kind of a tradition, if you know what I mean—I get a new eighteen-wheeler, she gets a new stove. Or whatever. That's what brought me in here in the first place, to be honest about it."

Joy pretended she was giving it some thought. "Well,

let's see now. What are her interests? Maybe that would help us decide what's best."

I grinned. "Not trucks, that's for sure." I paused to think. "The only thing Wanda June likes more than spending money is tending her garden. She *lives* out in her potato patch, which is what I call it, from sunup to noon, all summer long. I've et more zucchinis than Iacocca's got cars."

Joy was nodding excitedly. "I think we have something she'll love. One of our very best artists specializes in portraits of fruits and vegetables. Her accuracy and enhancement is amazing. And her palette, well, they look fresh from the garden. It's uncanny."

"Sounds like just the ticket," I said, trying to match Joy's level of commercial ecstasy. "Forget the trucks; let's see *those* puppies. Have old Juan haul 'em out here."

Joy hurried to the white phone and issued rapid-fire instructions. As she did so, the door in the bookcase opened and a young Chicano came into the gallery carrying a canvas the size of a beach towel. Schooled in the Grasshopper's sales techniques, he propped the canvas on the floor but kept its back to me, so I couldn't see the art quite yet. Only when Joy joined us did Juan unveil the masterpiece.

With a practiced twist of his wrists, the huge painting pivoted on a corner, and there it was. Twice true size, even more daunting than in real life, the front grill and fenders of a big Mack diesel, fire-engine red and trimmed in brilliant chrome, shimmered like a mutant jewel in the artist's reproduction of the noonday sun. Joy could not have been more pleased had we been gazing on a Rembrandt.

"It's a truck all right," I said dubiously.

Joy's glow quickly faded. "What's the trouble, Mr. Tanner?"

"Well, it's not that it's bad, honey. Not at all. In fact that's the best picture of a truck I've about ever seen, except for the ones that come with naked ladies hanging off 'em."

"Then what's the trouble?"

"To be quick about it, it's the wrong truck, honey. See, I run Freightliner. And I tell my drivers I run 'em because dollar for dollar they're the best rig on the road. So it would hardly do to set there with a big grin on my face beneath a pregnant version of one of the competition, just like nothing odd was going on."

Joy had wilted. "I see."

"Now, if this here truck artist would happen to have one of a custom Freightliner with the Cummins forty-four, we might be in business." I took another look at the canvas. "But maybe not as big."

"Well, I can certainly find out if he has one. Or perhaps he could do something on commission. If I could have the name of the hotel where you're staying, perhaps I can get back—"

"I never spend the night, doll—Wanda June don't like to climb in the four-poster without me there to warm it up." I looked at my watch. "How about them fruits and such, honey? I got to get a move on."

Joy glanced back at the bookcase, then nodded to Juan. "He'll bring them right out."

Juan departed with the Day-Glo Mack, and Joy and I found things to look at besides each other. In the next minute Juan was back.

"Here they are," Joy enthused again.

And there they were indeed, a set of three paintings, tasteful and congenial arrangements of pears and apples, squash and peppers, cauliflower and tomatoes. The latter were particularly impressive—sliced, arranged in a circle on a gaily painted plate, they were so red and juicy I expected the canvas to start dripping momentarily.

"Now that's more like it," I said. "How much?"

Joy met my eye. "We can offer these at six thousand."

"Each?"

"Each."

"Hmmm. Those tomaters sure look good. Almost as good as Wanda June's."

"Don't they?"

"So who did it?"

"What?"

"The artist. What's his name?"

"It's a she. Lily Lucerne. A lovely woman. And so obviously talented."

I raised a brow. "She around?"

Joy frowned. "You mean in the city?"

"I mean in the building."

"Well, I . . . why?"

"Like to talk to her."

"But why?"

"I like to look eyeball-to-eyeball at the people I do business with. Habit of mine. Took me a long way in the trucking business."

Joy glanced back at the telephone. "This is most unusual. Generally, we—"

"Come on, Joyous. A minute of her time for twenty-four Gs? Not bad wages where I come from."

"But she's a very private person. I don't know if she—"

"I'll treat her like I would a pickup with a bad valve. Come on, honey. No artist, no art."

Joy's lips pursed, then spread with the élan of salvation. "As luck would have it, Ms. Lucerne was in the building only moments ago. If you'll give me a second, I'll see if she's available."

Joy nodded to Juan and both of them disappeared through the disguised door. A moment later I followed them and found myself in a warren of offices and storerooms that opened off a central corridor.

Juan had disappeared. The other people in sight were all gathered at the end of the hall beneath a sign that read EXIT, a real one this time. There were three women and a man, and one of the women was Joy.

The man was Oriental, presumably the businessman out of Maui and Gstaad. He was holding the hand of an even smaller woman who was dressed in black slacks and turtleneck, with eyes and hair to match. The man bowed, said something I couldn't hear, smiled, and bowed again. At that point I made a noise, and all of them turned my way.

"Mr. Tanner," Joy said quickly. "You were supposed to wait in the exhibit hall."

"No time, Joy. Got to wrap this up and hit the road to Fresno."

"But—"

"Who *is* this?" the third woman interrupted. Her accent made her Giselle of the hotel money.

I started to answer but Joy spoke for me. "This is Mr.

Tanner, Giselle. A trucking magnate from Fresno. He's very interested in four of Ms. Lucerne's pieces."

"I see." Giselle seemed incompletely mollified. "We are concluding some business here, monsieur. If you will excuse us, I will see you in the gallery *tout de suite.*"

"Like I said, sister, no time. This the artist?"

I shouldered my way toward the small dark woman, hand extended, my most friendly aspect making my face a sunflower. "Happy to meet you, little lady. You sure know how to paint yourself a picture, I'll tell you that. All them tomaters need is a little salt."

When I was as close to her as I was going to get, I lowered my voice. "I need to speak with you privately. About your husband."

I had hoped to keep it between the two of us, but Giselle had decided to attend to me. "What *is* this? Who are you, anyway? I must ask you to leave, *immediately.*" Both the charm and the accent had disappeared.

Despite Giselle's harangue, my eyes were on the artist. At my approach, she had begun to edge away, and when I whispered my request to speak with her she pressed her back against the door as though the building had just caught fire. "Is it Paul?" she asked as I looked at her. "Has something happened to *Paul?*"

"This is absurd," Giselle interrupted, grasping my arm, trying to pull me away from her client. "Pay no attention to this gentleman, Lily. Mr. Takahara, please come this way; I'll show you out the front. Joy, if this man hasn't left the premises in twenty seconds, call Juan. Better yet, call the police. I'll be right back, Lily. Don't worry about a thing."

The customer bowed again, this time including me in the gesture, then allowed Giselle to lead him down the hall and through the door to the main gallery. In their wake, Joy was nonplussed by her assignment; the artist was irritated at being sacrificed to the needs of a monied patron; and I was grasping for an effective gambit.

"Please, Mr. Tanner," Joy said. "You must leave the gallery. Giselle will—"

"Just give me one minute, then I'm out of here." I turned toward the woman still pressed against the door. "I'm a private detective. I used a ruse to see you because

I'm looking for your husband. It's important to a lot of people that I find him. If you could—"

"He's at home, isn't he? I just left there. If he *isn't*, then—"

I shook my head. "Your *former* husband. The one who went to jail."

I was still feeling my way, but the splay of worry across her face suggested I was on track. "The information I have is that your husband has just been released from prison," I continued rapidly. "I was wondering if you'd heard from him, or have an idea where he might be."

Although she had begun shaking her head when I was halfway through my spiel, I kept going. "That's all I need to know. This doesn't have anything to do with your life now. If I can get a line on your ex-husband, I'll be out of your way."

"But I know nothing," she murmured. "Leave me alone. Please."

"He hasn't tried to contact you?"

As she shook her head I heard the door open at my back. "The police have been called," Giselle said as she marched toward me.

I gave Lily Lucerne one last look. "Then give me his name."

She was rigid with fear. I reached for a business card and held it in front of her. "Please call me. Especially if you hear from him."

Striking from behind me, Giselle slapped the card from my hand. I turned on her and snarled. "If you make another mistake like that, I'll tell Darryl Dromedy you're still pushing pictures of trucks."

When I turned to make a final plea to the skittish artist, I was talking to the black hole of an open doorway.

"*Let me tell you precisely where I am,*" I wrote in the first letter I was brave enough to mail. "*I am where Charles Manson is.*"

HOMAGE TO HAMMURABI, p. 211

Chapter
15

By the time I was free of the clutches of Joy and Giselle and out the rear door of the Grasshopper and into the narrow alley of Campton Place, there was no one in sight, at least not a tiny artist in a baggy black turtleneck with an expression of abject terror on her face. I cursed myself for bungling it when I had gotten close enough to speak to her—like a politician, I'd spent too much time running the race and not enough thinking about what would happen if I won.

I trotted to the front of the gallery on the chance Lily Lucerne might have parked in the vicinity, but there was no luck there either, not even when I ran to the Stockton corner and looked in every direction but up. Defeated all around, I headed for my car, which was buried in Union Square in the garage that was sunk like a burial vault beneath it.

I was walking down the ramp toward the elevators, fishing in my pocket for the claim check while trying to remember what level I was on and whether I was carrying enough cash to cover the toll, when the fates took unaccustomed pity—Lily Lucerne was sitting behind the wheel of a trim Toyota, waiting for her change at the pay booth, urging the attendant to hurry with every ounce of psychic energy at her disposal. For the first time in my life, I was grateful that the city possessed such limited parking options.

She was still frightened, strangely so, looking to her left and right in quick spasms of panic, so desperate to get on her way she must have been convinced my powers were such that I could materialize at will in any place and time. Little did she know. I backed out of her line of vision, then tried to creep up on her from the rear as she was busy getting her change from the attendant, not certain of what I was going to do if I penetrated her defenses.

When I was five feet away I spooked her. She had gotten her change and was putting it in her purse, but in the process she glanced in the rearview mirror. And there I was, as unwelcome in the glass as a trooper with his lights flashing.

With a cry of alarm she tossed the change on the seat, grasped the wheel like a life preserver, then stomped on the accelerator. With a squeal of rubber I would have thought impossible given a Toyota's torque, the car careened up the ramp and out of the lot, leaving the toll attendant shaking his head and two tourists shaking their fists at the boxy blue missile that had just threatened to dismember them and me chugging and puffing up the ramp in a pursuit that was futile before it began. Left in the dust, all I could think to do was write the Toyota's license number in my little black book, then go back the way I'd come.

A few months ago, a young television actress was murdered in Los Angeles by a fan whose idolatry had evolved into a homicidal mania. The fan tracked the victim to her home by getting the license number off her car and employing one of the services that will for a fee obtain the DMV registration records of any given license number, home address of the owner included. As a result of that incident, legislation has been passed that restricts access to such data. I still have a mole in the department, but she has to be careful not to spark the suspicions of the aroused bureaucracy, so when I need fast action these days I rely on Charley Sleet.

I used the phone on the wall of the garage and tracked Charley down for what seemed like the hundredth time that week. It must have seemed that way to Charley, too. "I'm busy," he grumbled when he came on the line.

"DMV check."

He swore. "You're pushing it, pal."

"I'll buy you a meal."

"The Balboa."

"Capp's."

"Wine included."

"No older than 'eighty-six. No dessert more exotic than pie."

"When?"

"Whenever."

Charley mellowed. "What's the number?"

I read off the Toyota's plate. "Name and address, please."

"This have anything to do with those book pages you gave me?"

"Yep."

"This something I should get up to speed on?"

"Not yet, I don't think."

Charley hesitated. "I'm not as solid since the shake-up after the Dolores Huerta mess."

"I know that, Charley."

The reference was to the department's latest scandal, the beating administered by crowd-control cops to a longtime farmworkers' activist during a protest during the last election campaign. As a result of the overreaction of the police and the plodding pace of the internal investigation, the mayor had made several adjustments in the police command structure. Apparently some of Charley's mentors had taken a hit in the process.

"It wouldn't do either of us any good if I got pushed into an early retirement," Charley was saying. "So don't do anything dumb."

"That's my new motto. I'm having it engraved on my card: 'John Marshall Tanner—Private Eye: He Won't Do Anything Dumb.'"

Charley only grumbled. "Speaking of your less-than-brilliant behavior, how's your secretary?"

"Last I heard, she was in Vancouver with her daughter. Her place in the Marina got wiped out in the quake."

"She okay?"

"She's fine."

"I hear it's nice in Vancouver."

"I wouldn't know. That was almost a month ago," I calculated, more for myself than for Charley.

"Still like that, huh."

"Pretty much."

"When she gets back, send her some flowers. Flora always forgave me if I brought home flowers."

I sighed. "I already did that, Charley."

"What happened?"

"She sent them back."

"How?"

"How what?"

"How'd she send them?"

"What difference does *that* make?"

"I don't know; I just wondered."

"Bike messenger."

"Sparky? Jesus."

"All that was left was the thorns."

I hung up before Charley could commiserate any further, then found my car. Although it was late, it was time to check in with my client—all of a sudden, the shape of the case was starting to look more like a circle than a straight line.

The place I found to park was uncomfortably close to the building at Sixth and Bluxsome that had crumbled in the quake and killed six people in the cars that got buried in brick. It was so uncomfortable, in fact, that after getting out and locking up, I immediately got back in the Buick and moved it a block away. It occurred to me that despite Charley's warning I was being dumb—the best thing that could happen to my transportation situation was for the Buick to become a total loss.

Periwinkle's main entrance was closed, but there were both lights and music leaking into the evening from up above. When I pressed the after-hours bell and spoke my name at the intercom, someone eventually buzzed me in. The someone turned out to be Margaret, and she was waiting for me at the top of the stairs.

After we exchanged a well-modulated greeting, she ushered me into the conference room—stately without Matilda and the revelers—and sat me down directly across from her, virtually nose to nose. "What have you found out?" she demanded.

I bowed my head. "It's nice to see you, too, Margaret. I'm fine, thanks for asking."

She shook her head impatiently. "There's no time for pleasantries—things are happening and I don't know why."

"What things?"

"*These* things."

She took a newspaper off the table beside her and thrust it at me. It was the afternoon *Examiner,* opened to the gossip column. "Fourth paragraph," Margaret instructed.

I read it: "Local literary lions are all agrowl with the rumor that Bryce Chatterton's Periwinkle Press is about to launch a steamy new novel that insiders insist is a thinly disguised exposé that will blow the lid off some of Cow Hollow's sexiest secrets. When asked for comment, the publisher would say only, 'Mum's the word at this point.' The author's name and the price Bryce paid for the book are among the many mysteries that surround the much-anticipated event, so stay tuned."

When I finished I looked up. "Well?" Margaret demanded. "Is it true?"

I shrugged. "I don't know. What does Bryce say about it?"

" 'Mum's the word,' " she mimicked.

"That's it?"

She nodded. "He claims he doesn't know where they got their information."

"Well, neither do I."

"That's begging the question."

"No it isn't—I don't know whether the book's an exposé or not."

I was hoping she would leave it at that, but of course she didn't. "You're trying to find out, aren't you? That's why he *hired* you."

I smiled serenely. "Your husband around?"

"I'd appreciate an answer to my question."

"You know better." I started to stand up, but didn't. "How's Jane Ann?"

The shift was unexpected and her eyes widened in

something close to fear. "Why? Did something happen to her?"

"Not that I know of, I was just making conversation. Where'd she go to high school, by the way?"

Margaret frowned. "Why on earth would you want to know that?"

"Someone told me your ex-husband is the power behind the throne at the best private school in the city. I was just wondering if his problems with Jane Ann started when she enrolled in his precious school."

"If you're asking if Jane Ann went to Sebastian, the answer is yes. But as I told you before, she didn't graduate."

"What year was she?"

"The class of 'eighty-four."

"Did her friend Lloyd go there, too?"

She nodded. "To the extent he was anywhere, that is. I want to know why you're asking these questions."

"Sorry," I said. "He in there?"

I pointed to the door to Bryce's office and when Margaret didn't answer me I went over to it and knocked. When I heard a mumble I went inside.

"Marsh," Bryce exclaimed when he looked up. "Good to see you, have you found him yet?"

I shook my head. "Nice hype in the *Examiner,* though."

Bryce's voice fell to a conspiratorial level. "*He* did it, don't you see? He's *out* there somewhere, planting leaks, spreading rumors, promoting the project, remaining invisible. It's incredible, isn't it? He must be a chameleon, don't you think?"

"That's one word for it, I suppose."

Bryce was as ready for my attentions as a puppy. "So what do you have to tell me; what's been going on?"

I sat down and crossed my legs, trying to decide how to put it. "This *Hammurabi* thing may be getting close to the bone, Bryce."

"How do you mean?"

"The school in the book? St. Stephen's? I think it's a disguise for the Sebastian School here in the city."

"But that's where—"

"Your stepdaughter went. Right. And it looks like she was there when this all went down."

Bryce sighed heavily, burdened by the possibilities. "You mean it's true—there really *was* a scandal."

"It looks like it."

"So the *Examiner* was right. My God. He really *is* out there, manipulating me."

Eyes glazed and distant, Bryce was in thrall to the fantastic. "I'm giving you a second chance, Bryce," I said to interrupt the swoon. "Maybe you should put a stop to this right now, before anyone gets hurt. Maybe you should let it all stay buried."

Bryce's eyes gave off as many glints as a broken mirror. "But I *can't,* don't you see? It's too late. He's pushing it himself, he's set the thing in motion and it won't stop no matter *what* I do. The only decision left for me to make is whether I want to be on the inside or the outside—to be his audience or his publisher."

His expression left no doubt that, regardless of the consequences, the decision had already been made.

The first letter I received in prison was from a lawyer, informing me that my wife was suing me for divorce. The second was from a realtor, asking if I wanted to sell my house.

HOMAGE TO HAMMURABI, p. 173

Chapter
16

Four minutes after I got back to my apartment the doorbell rang. I wasn't expecting anyone, I didn't want to see anyone, I didn't have anything to say to anyone, but I opened the door all the same, proving that contrary to my reputation, I'm essentially gregarious.

The man facing me beneath the feeble light of the hallway bulb was big and impassive and totally unconcerned about disturbing a stranger at eleven o'clock at night. Since his somber outfit of gray jacket and slacks came complete with riding boots and a hat with a patent leather brim, I pegged him for someone's chauffeur. When I tried to think if I knew anyone who had one, I came up empty.

"Are you Mr. John Marshall Tanner?" he asked when I was finished inspecting his raiment and he had finished tucking his hat beneath his arm and finding nothing of interest in the apartment at my back.

"What can I do for you?"

"You will please accompany me to the home of Mr. Marvin Gillis."

"Except that you're both big and polite, why would I do that?"

"Because Mr. Gillis has requested it." He made the answer seem as sufficient as the theory of relativity.

"And if I don't?"

"Mr. Gillis will be annoyed."

"What does he do when that happens?"

I thought he smiled. "I wouldn't know, sir."

"You mean no one ever annoys him."

"Precisely. As Mr. Gillis would say."

"Well, hell. There's enough annoyance in the world already. I mean, the fallout from Jim and Tammy Faye alone . . . What's your name, by the way?"

"Fernandez, sir. And I'm authorized to inform you that Mr. Gillis will be happy to offer you supper if we have interrupted yours."

I looked at my watch. "How long do you figure this is going to take?"

"No more than ninety minutes."

"Where is it?"

"Baker Street, sir."

"Near the school."

He nodded. "Across the street."

"I just put a tube steak in the broiler," I said truthfully. "I'll be with you as soon as I turn it off." When I got back I flipped the light switch beside the door. "Let's roll."

Two flights of stairs and a half block later, I was snugly encapsulated in the rear of a Lincoln limousine, enjoying an eerily smooth and silent ride through the always unsmooth and unsilent city. When we came to a stop ten minutes later, the house that was visible through the tinted window at my side would have been called a mansion had it been plopped down on one of the double blocks on Drake Avenue in the small city where I spent my youth. I suppose it was a mansion under a lot of other definitions, too, but in Cow Hollow it was only *e pluribus unum*.

I was still taking in the splendor when Fernandez opened the door for me. If memory served, the last time that happened I was under arrest. "Please come this way, sir."

We left the limo in the street, something I hesitated to do in my neighborhood even with a Buick, and climbed toward the weighty edifice that looked down on our progress from a distinctly imperial loft. But the grand facade was nothing compared to the man who opened the door when Fernandez rang the bell.

He had stepped right out of the movies, one of those George Raft things that tried their best to make you envy the hell out of the rich and pretty much succeeded. His smile was adequate, no more, but his eyes were flat and business-like, taking my measure as just another chattel, another potential asset if the price wasn't out of line, another deal to be done. His clothes—white ascot, brocade smoking jacket, silk slacks, and velvet slippers—were comical or precious, I couldn't decide which, but the debate caused me to smile.

"Mr. Tanner," he proclaimed. "How kind of you to come. I'm Marvin Gillis." He absorbed my grin. "You don't seem put out about the hour. Good. Please come in."

I awaited the offer of a handshake but it wasn't extended, which let me know where I stood, which was about where I figured. After I looked at him in a way that let him know I had registered the slight, I looked at the foyer at his back, which featured a marble floor and a selection of well-aged art and half the mahogany crop of Madagascar for the year 1928. "I'm glad to see the rumors about you are true," I said. "I hate it when my prejudices prove unfounded."

His laugh was a match for his smile, which is to say it was rote. "Circumstances have been good to me, if that's what you mean. As a result, my resources allow me to live with a certain amount of style."

"Since they don't look to be scarce, I'd say they weren't the natural kind of resources."

"That depends on your perspective, Mr. Tanner. Some people feel the accumulation of wealth is the most natural urge there is."

I took another look at the foyer. "People like you, for example."

We gave each other some silent credit for being civilized enough to refrain from open warfare. "Let's go into the library, shall we? Could we interest you in some excellent brandy?"

"You already have, Mr. Gillis."

When we were halfway across the marble, Gillis paused to press a button that was hidden in the woodwork, then continued toward a door at the far end of the foyer, one that was hidden behind the staircase. The door was locked, which I found odd, but it opened easily to a key that was tied to a ribbon that was looped around a button on Gillis's jacket. As he ushered me inside, I felt like a desperate actor auditioning for a role for which I had no aptitude.

Somehow, the brandies were already waiting on the walnut end tables beside the leather club chairs that were flanking the roaring fire. Like Bryce Chatterton's office, the walls were lined with books, however these weren't a random and well-read collection but rather leather-bound and gilt-lettered icons, displayed at maximum grandiloquence. If any of them had been inscribed to Marvin Gillis, it would be proof of either forgery or reincarnation.

Gillis motioned for me to sit, so I sat. After he did the same, he grasped his snifter and waited for me to match him. We exchanged a silent toast that lacked grace on my part and sincerity on his.

"I've known several historians in my day, Mr. Tanner," Gillis began, his voice as cultured as his library, with the same touch of pretense to it. "But never one with such a provocative background."

"How do you mean, 'provocative'? Like a whore is provocative, or like Kissinger is provocative?"

Gillis chuckled dryly. "It's good of you to acknowledge the difference." The tight thin skin around his ears and eyes seemed to redden slightly, indicating he was irritated by my manner. If smart talk was all it took to shake him up, I was surprised he'd lasted this long in the law business.

"When word reached us that a self-styled writer was engaged in a muckraking campaign that could both slander innocent individuals and besmirch the reputation of the finest secondary school west of the Mississippi, we naturally became concerned. So we took steps to learn more about him."

"So we could scare him off."

"Oh, we doubted extreme measures would be necessary. We were certain a few thousand dollars—in the used bills of small denominations of which all blackmailers seem enamored—would be sufficient to persuade the gentleman to look elsewhere for his scandals. Had he been the person he claimed to be, of course."

"Of course."

"But our inquiries revealed that you are not a historian at all, popular or otherwise, you are a private eye." He raised a well-trimmed brow. "Is that the cognomen you prefer, by the way? I'm afraid I'm unfamiliar with the nuances of the profession."

"Oh, we don't have nuances anymore, Mr. Gillis. We tried a few once, but they got in the way. And just between us, the honorific I prefer is 'maestro,' but 'private eye' seems to be the one I'm stuck with."

Neither my joke nor my vocabulary merited a smile. "You have done some work for my firm," he declared brusquely.

"Yes."

"And you were formerly an attorney."

"Right again."

"Until you had a brush with my old friend Judge Hoskins."

My fist closed so tightly around the snifter I was afraid I was going to snap its stem. "You and the judge are pals, are you?"

"We were until he suffered his stroke. He's virtually an invalid, you know."

"That's swell."

He rolled his eyes. "Surely you're not still bearing grudges."

"A very nice man is dead because the judge cared more about buddies like you than about the laws he swore to uphold when he took the bench."

Gillis virtually tut-tutted. "All that happened so *long* ago. Surely you have it in your heart to forgive an old man his mistakes."

"I'm not in the forgiveness business, Mr. Gillis. If that's what the bastard wants, have him take it up with someone who is."

Gillis allowed himself a smile. "Yes, well, I'm sure he has. In his fashion. But we digress, do we not?"

"Not really."

Gillis adjusted his ascot and drained his drink. "The bottom line is, you are not what you seem."

"What I seemed to Custodian O'Shea, you mean."

Gillis bowed infinitesimally. "Arthur is a valued employee, as I'm sure you appreciate. Sometimes I feel that he's the only one other than myself who truly . . . Well. That's beside the point, which is that regardless of your true profession, you seem to be making inquiries into our past."

"Do I?"

"Come now, there's no need to fence. What are you up to, Mr. Tanner?"

I shrugged. "I'm undertaking an investigation for hire— that's almost always what I'm up to. And I thought Sebastian graduates weren't supposed to end a sentence with a preposition. Although 'to what are you up, Mr. Tanner?' does seem a bit awkward. I guess it's one of those discretionary things."

"Let's leave the grammar for another time, shall we?" He adjusted his incline, plucked at the crease in this slacks, clasped his hands atop a knee. "I want you to know that those of us who treasure Sebastian take meddlers like yourself quite seriously." His eyes were as hard as the wood in the floor.

"Is that the royal 'we' you're using?"

"It's the Sebastian 'we.' "

"Which implies what?"

"That there are a great many persons of influence in this community who do not take kindly to seeing the institution they cherish above all others being slandered by a . . . man such as yourself."

I shrugged. "If there're no skeletons in the Sebastian closets, you don't have anything to worry about."

"Sebastian is not immune to unfounded rumor, Mr. Tanner. In these days of media zealotry, few institutions are."

"I'll try to be discreet."

"I'm afraid that's not satisfactory."

"What is?"

"That you desist your prying immediately."

I smiled my friendly smile. "I'm afraid that's impossible. I'm like a bulldog, Mr. Gillis—only the client can call me off. And that's not a nuance, it's a rule."

Gillis closed his eyes and sighed. When he opened them again, they had softened to a subsistence level of civility.

"Perhaps it would help you understand my position if I amplified the Sebastian mission for you."

As I shrugged noncommittally, he got comfortable in his chair. "There are many wonderful families in this city, Mr. Tanner, the families who *built* this city, the families who *sustain* it, the families who have given San Francisco the spirit and style for which it is justly famous. Sebastian was *founded* by those families, and it has served them, it has educated them, it has in a very real sense *preserved* them. It is Sebastian's task for the future—*my* task, if you will, now that I have assumed the mantle of its chairman—to *perpetuate* the families I have spoken of, by educating their newest members, by qualifying their offspring to attend the finest institutions of higher education in this land, by making the younger generation what its forebears have been—persons of style and skill and signal accomplishment." Gillis finally paused. "And you, Mr. Tanner," he concluded with a razor's keenness, "are a threat to that tradition."

Though I was congenitally and philosophically disposed to resist everything he had just described, Marvin Gillis had succeeded in scaring me a little—for the merest moment, I was convinced that the future of civilization was in my hands.

But I can only entertain absurdities for so long. "I don't know what you're talking about, Mr. Gillis. And even if I did, I'm not nearly that powerful. And even if I was, there's nothing I can do about it. I've been hired to do a job. Unless I get called off, or unless the thing I'm looking for has disappeared or never existed in the first place, I'm going to do that job. That's *my* style, Mr. Gillis. Such as it is."

Gillis sighed dispiritedly. "Very well. If you will disclose the name of your principal, we can approach the source of the irritant directly, in order to . . ."

"Reveal the error of his ways?" I suggested.

I earned a bow. "Precisely. So? Who is it?"

I smiled. "Who's the Sebastian teacher who was jailed for molestation?"

Gillis just sat there.

"Okay, who's the student who got molested? Come on,

Gillis. *Someone's* going to talk. If you want to be sure I get it right, it might as well be you."

Gillis stood up and smoothed his jacket. "We don't seem to be getting anywhere. Perhaps we should both retire and consider what we've discussed this evening."

"Sounds good to me; brandy makes me sleepy."

I got another glimpse of the depth of Marvin Gillis's eyes. "You are excessively flip."

"I get that way whenever I ride in a car that's got more floor space than my apartment."

Gillis walked to the door of the library. "You threaten Sebastian at your peril, Mr. Tanner."

I stepped into the foyer, then turned back. "You know, Mr. Gillis, you're working so hard at keeping me from poking into the scandal at Sebastian, I'm starting to wonder if there's something involved that's even more precious to you than Sebastian's reputation."

"And what might that be?"

"Your daughter."

In the void that followed my speculation, his eyes jabbed me as tangibly as a foil. But "Fernandez will drive you home" was all he said.

I was not entirely a fool. I knew that, consciously or otherwise, young people often explore the reach of their sexuality, testing its powers first on their peers and often, if the initial reaction is buoying, transferring their attentions to the nearest adult. Since the nearest adult is often a teacher, I knew the pitfalls of being alone with a student. Any student.

To my knowledge, contrary to her assertions in the videotape, Amanda Keefer was present in my home on only one occasion—the traditional party following the fall production of the drama club. If memory serves, I had to ask her to leave, because I caught Amanda and two of her friends enjoying surreptitious sips from the bottles in my liquor cabinet when they thought neither my wife nor I were looking. Although her friends were upset by my actions, Amanda, as with virtually everything else in her life, seemed entirely unfazed.

HOMAGE TO HAMMURABI, p. 87

Chapter
17

It's not unusual for a month to pass without anything crossing my threshold but me and the morning paper, yet when I got back to my apartment I had my second visitor of the evening. When I asked her how she'd picked the lock, she shook her head with the kind of exasperation usually reserved for people who admit to preferring steak to seafood.

"Bachelors *always* stash a key near the door," she explained. "Yours was in the second place I looked. Which makes you twice as smart as most of the men I know." Christine White tossed her purse on the couch and, after looking in vain for an acceptable alternative, sat down next to it. "What have you got to drink?"

"Bourbon and scotch."

"No wine, no vodka?"

"You're lucky I have bourbon. Someone gave it to me for Christmas—someone who didn't know me very well."

"Then that's what I'll have. Ice, no water, a twist if you have it." She looked around the room once more. "Which you obviously don't. Have you at least got some munchies? All I had for dinner was take-out chow mein."

"Do you call Oreos munchies?"

"Oreos are junk food; Wheat Thins are munchies. But if Oreos is all you have, let's have a look."

I went to the kitchen to fix her drink, then fixed one of my own and took the booze and the junk food to the living room and arrayed them on the coffee table, then eased my weary bones into the chair that flanked the couch and faced the Trinitron.

Somewhere along the way, I decided I was irritated by something. By the time I was settled in my chair I decided it was Christine White's assumption that because a spark had been struck when we first met, she thought she had permission to invade my life whenever she wanted.

"Tough day in the old salt mine of estates and trusts?" The taunt was in furtherance of my pique. "Your petition for extraordinary fees get denied by some crusty probate judge?"

Her drink stopped halfway to her lips. "What do you mean by *that*?"

That I had touched a nerve made me perversely glad. "It's the only thing I could think of that would be regarded as a crisis in your line of work."

Whatever the impulse that had propelled her to my apartment in the middle of the night, its devil-may-care veneer vanished in an instant. "If you really want to know, I've been down at S.F. General, meeting with a group of lawyers I organized six months ago to help terminal AIDS patients write their wills and get their estates in order."

The apartment got as hot as her temper. "I get you wrong every time, don't I, Ms. White?"

She stuck out her tongue, which was as red as my face. "When will men realize that women are as capable and compassionate as they are?"

"When men like me are extinct." I glanced at the calendar on the wall, the one I get for Christmas from my insurance man, the one with pictures of birds with brains about the size of mine. "Which should start to happen just after the turn of the century."

I kicked off my shoes and got as comfortable in my rheumatic chair as my conscience would let me, then made a stab at business. "To what do I owe the pleasure of your company, Ms. White? And I apologize for everything I've ever said or done."

While she considered her answer, she kicked off her

high heels as well, curled her snugly skirted legs beneath her, undid the center button of her jacket, loosened the scarf at her collar, and unbuttoned the top button of her blouse. When she looked at me it was to indicate I was forgiven for yet another time.

"I just thought I'd stop by to let you know that Speedo was wonderful," she said offhandedly. "Let's see, we started with the endive salad with capers and hickory nuts, pita bread with strawberry-honey butter, then herring pickled in—"

I held up a hand. "I'm not much of a foodie. As far as I'm concerned, a pancake sandwich is as good as it gets."

"You poor man."

"That's what my accountant tells me."

Christine leaned back and undid another button, then took further inventory of the room. From her expression, she might have been touring Calcutta.

I make periodic resolutions to do something about the state of my furnishings. The resolve usually lasts until I flip over a price tag at Breuner's and discover that it will take three thousand bucks to replace my couch and chair with anything that isn't constructed from wood chips that have been hacked off Oregon logs, shipped to Japan, pressed into boards that sell for a tenth of the cost of hardwood, then returned to this country to be stapled together into a frame that will collapse the first time I flop down on it after a long night in the tavern.

Luckily, Christine's glance came to rest on the only item of quality in the room. "How about some music?"

"What flavor?"

"Something soft and stringy."

I chose some Mendelssohn, got the equipment rolling, and resumed my place. "What *really* brings you by?" I asked after a second sip at my scotch.

She gave me her lawyer's look. "The scare you threw into my roommate this morning."

"If I scared her I didn't mean to."

"A man is responsible for the reasonable and natural consequences of his acts."

"How was I supposed to know she had a history with the

man I'm looking for? At that point, I didn't even know he existed."

"You take your victims as you find them, Mr. Tanner."

"Can we lighten up on the tort maxims for a minute, Ms. White?" I took another sip. "What exactly is Emma's problem?"

Christine adjusted her legs to a more comfortable curl, then draped an arm along the crown of the tattered couch. "She thinks you're out to make more trouble for a man who's already had enough of it."

"Well, she's wrong."

She shrugged. "That's what she thinks. She also thinks you're working for Sebastian. Or Mr. Gillis, which is apparently the same thing."

"I hereby authorize you to tell her that I'm not."

"That's what I *already* told her. But she's convinced you're trying to make trouble for a man she cares for very much. So she sent me over here to convince you that if you ever manage to find him, you should let her talk to him before you do anything else."

"Why would I do that?"

"So he won't make even a bigger mistake than he did the last time."

"Last time being . . . ?"

"The time he went to jail for something he didn't do."

"According to Emma."

Christine White nodded. "Right. According to Emma."

I glanced at the sports page that was lying on the floor beside the chair. The Warriors had yet to win on the road. They should never have traded Smith. I looked up. "You know, I could wrap this thing up in an hour if someone would just tell me the guy's name."

"Wade," she said simply.

I blinked. "For real?"

She nodded.

"Did Emma tell you to tell me that?"

Christine White shook her head. "I know you're not a sleaze—Gill and Hook wouldn't use you if you were. And I know Emma's too hung up on this guy for her own good, and has been for years. She needs to resolve the situation so she can get on with her life, with him or without him." She looked at the floor. "So I did something I shouldn't have done."

"Which is what?"

"I took this out of her desk."

She reached into her purse and pulled out a small white envelope and handed it to me. The postmark was mostly blurred, but the year it was posted was 1985. Emma Drayer was the addressee; there was no return. The print was masculine, bold and basic; the writing instrument a soft lead pencil. The envelope had already been slit open, and there was a letter inside.

I looked at Christine. "You might as well," she said.

I extracted the letter and read it:

Dearest Emma,

I can't tell you how embarrassing it is to be writing you from this place. I've tried to spare you from sharing my shame by omitting my name and address from the envelope, but of course the situation is not susceptible to simple solutions, is it?

There are many aspects of your letter that I want to address, so many that I haven't sorted out my thoughts on all of them as yet (yours is the only personal letter I've received since I've been here, so I'm out of practice).

For now, suffice it to say that you're right—I probably would not have written had you not done so first, though please know that I have thought of you every day since my incarceration. You're right in another respect as well—my failure to initiate a correspondence is primarily a function of my anxiety about the questions you will ask should the relationship be continued and become meaningful, questions you would in that context have every right to ask, questions that I may not trust myself to answer for fear of loosening my tenuous grip on sanity.

But I will try. Because I owe you that much and more, and because I am in need of some answers myself. But not this time. This time I will simply

say thanks, and ask of you a gift I have no right
to—please write me again. And soon.

Love,
Wade

"Wade," I said when I had finished, my heart thumping
with the realization that I had finally found my Dennis
Worthy. "What's his last name?"

"I don't know."

"Emma never mentioned him?"

"Not that I can remember. Not by name. He was just
this man, this teacher, she said she had been fond of while
she was at Sebastian."

"So she was sweet on him."

"Let's just say he came up as proof of her theory that all
the good men were either gay or married."

"There was no actual affair with the guy?"

"I don't think so. Especially not if he was married—
Emma's not the type."

I grinned at the way she said it, as though Emma's
attitude was as outmoded as Jansenism. "As opposed to
your type, I assume."

She shrugged. "I like dating married guys—they're so
grateful for everything, particularly a little creativity between the sheets. It has its problems, of course, especially
if the wife thinks I want to take him away from her, which
of course is the furthest thing from my mind, but it's handy
when I want to break it off."

"You make romance sound a lot like liar's dice, Ms.
White."

She met my eye. "You should be so lucky, Mr. Tanner."

I drained my drink and got her glass and went to the
kitchen and fixed us both another. "Well, what am I
supposed to do?" I asked when I got back. "I can't abandon
the chase just because Emma's afraid I'll hurt her heartthrob's feelings. The funny thing is, if she would cooperate
with me, I could put her darling Wade in touch with the
person who's trying to find him and *everyone* would be
better off, Wade and Emma included."

"I don't think you can convince her of that."

"What if I promise that if she gives me his name I'll try to persuade him to see her once I track him down?"

"I don't think she'll go along; she wants to talk to him *before* you do. She's afraid if she doesn't, something awful will happen."

"Like what?"

"I think she's worried that he'll disappear from her life again. She's been dreaming about a rendezvous for a long time; now that it may be close to happening she's afraid something will spook it."

"I don't think she needs to worry about that; he's got some unfinished business to take care of."

Christine White looked at me. "You mean like vengeance? An eye for an eye, and all that?"

I blinked. "What made you think of that?"

Her shrug was casual. "Emma mentioned something about it the other day."

"It would help me to know exactly what she said."

"I don't remember. I suppose I should have asked her what she was talking about, but somehow I didn't really want to know."

As though it would redress her decision to remain ignorant of the particulars of her roommate's tribulations, Christine leered at me, broadly and bawdily. "Emma said for me to use all my wiles to convince you to help her find her friend. Since Speedo didn't turn you on, I brought something else that might." During a lurid and swollen glance, she reached for her purse.

There is a natural law that's seldom mentioned in the science texts that says that as soon as things start to get interesting with a woman, the telephone will ring. When I picked mine up I was talking to Charley Sleet.

"The vehicle's registered to something called Double L Creations," he began without preamble. "The address is on Fell, just above Masonic."

"The Panhandle," I said.

"Right. Does any of that make any sense to you?"

"I think so."

"I'm glad." He paused to light a Camel, which is Charley's signal that he wants to talk. "You want play-off tickets if I can get them?"

"Niners? Sure."

"Might cost scalpers' prices; I don't have a line on anything legit."

"In that case, I don't know; I'm not real flush of late."

"I can probably get them from the Mouse, if I can find him. If I run him down, I'll go over and—"

"The Mouse's tickets are forged, Charley."

"Not all of them."

"Most."

"I can tell the difference."

I glanced at the woman on the couch. "Can we do this another time? I'm kind of tied up right now."

"Yeah? With Peggy?" For an instant, Charley's voice became as unbridled as a child's instead of as encumbered as a lonesome cop's—Charley wants only the best for me.

"Sorry," I said, hating to disappoint him, wishing, despite the attractions sitting next to me, that he was right.

"Yeah? Well, too bad," Charley said quickly, embarrassed by his mistake and the sentiment behind it. "Have a nice night."

Charley was gone and I turned back to my guest. "Where were we?"

Her lawyer look turned sleepy. "We were talking about how I was going to persuade you to let Emma talk Wade out of becoming a vigilante."

I leaned back in my chair.

"So how?"

She pulled her purse to her side and flipped it open; it was big enough to hide a bear. "What I thought was, first I'd go in the bedroom . . ." The singsong words came slowly, as though they passed through syrup.

"That's a good way to start."

"And take off all my clothes . . ."

"That's even better."

"And then I thought I'd take some of this"—she reached in her purse and pulled out a tiny bottle, extracted the stopper, and tipped it briefly onto the tip of her index finger—"and put some of it here"—she touched behind each ear—"and here"—she touched either side of her neck—"and maybe here"—she placed her index finger between her breasts, at a point above the last buttoned button on her blouse.

"Definitely there," I voted.

She ran her tongue across her upper lip; her look was loose and languid. "And maybe here"—she swayed from side to side, so she could dab at the swells of her buttocks.

"There would be nice, too."

She met my eye. "And maybe here."

She lowered her hand to her lap, where it pressed against the skirt that was as tight as a drumhead above her pudendum, the perch of her finger as tender and intense as the weight of my excited gaze.

"That sounds like a wonderful plan," I said. "If I had to take a guess, I'd say the odds are twenty-to-one for it working."

"And then," she said, reaching for the purse again, "I thought I'd put on this."

With the flourish of an illusionist, she pulled forth a tiny teddy, silken and sheer except for a couple of lacy ornaments and two tiny yellow bows.

"That would be very nice."

"Temporarily, of course."

"Temporarily," I agreed.

"And then I thought we'd play."

"I'm always up for games."

"That will certainly be a help."

I *never thought I was perfect. But such was the spell of St. Stephen's, for a long while I was able to think my life was. When the bubble finally burst, no trace of such sanguinity remained.*

HOMAGE TO HAMMURABI, p. 223

Chapter
18

The Panhandle to Golden Gate Park is a glorified boulevard median that separates Fell Street from Oak Street along the nine-block section between Stanyan and Baker, due east of the park's main entrance. During most of its life it has functioned primarily as a pleasant place to stroll, grassy and shaded, a neat transition to the expanse of the park itself. But tranquillity vanished when the Haight-Ashbury began its bloom and the Panhandle became an important venue for the melodrama of the counterculture—a place for flower children to couple under the stars, eat free food doled out by the Diggers, and experience the visions of a drug-invaded consciousness. During those years, the Panhandle was the stage for a seemingly unending celebration, featuring free concerts by the Grateful Dead, be-ins by freshly enlightened mystics, and demonstrations in favor of everything from moral rearmament to universal fornication. Somehow, the Panhandle survived all that and more, until the sixties self-destructed. But as with most public places in our cities, no one would any longer call it lovely.

As early on Sunday morning as I could manage it, I left Christine White asleep in my apartment and my car in the garage on Masonic and walked a block down Fell, to the address of Double L Creations, the registered owner of Lily Lucerne's Toyota. As I suspected, the house was a combination home and studio that occupied one of the restored Victorians that faced the Panhandle from the Fell Street side. Because it was far too early in the day for me to have a plan of action, I passed the Double L front steps without turning in. When I got to the corner I leaned against the bus stop and tried to decide what to do.

I didn't want a run-in with the new husband, but after our confrontation at the gallery, there was no reason to suspect Lily Lucerne would be any more forthcoming on her home turf than she had been down on Post Street. Five minutes later I was still waiting for divine intervention but all I was getting were suspicious looks from the guy pruning back his hybrid teas two doors down the street. Since I didn't want to hear what Christine White would have to say to me after stumbling around my apartment all morning trying to find the makings of a bath and a breakfast, I returned to Double L and rang the bell.

It was opened by a genial lummox whose gray beard and matching sweatpants bracketed a Giants' T-shirt and a pair of half glasses dangling from a narrow leather thong. To complete the image of sporty intellectualism, he had a pencil behind his ear and grass stains on his fingers. "Yes?" It was more an admonition than a question.

In tribute to his size, if I'd been wearing a hat I'd have taken it off. "My name's Tanner," I began, then wondered if my voice sounded as meek to him as it did to me. "I'd like to see Ms. Lucerne."

He shook his head. "She's working."

"It will only take a minute. It's about some things we were discussing in the gallery the other night. I just . . ."

To put me in my place, the big guy glanced over his shoulder at a small office tucked into an anteroom off the vestibule. A computer monitor on the desk glowed with a list of something vital as a fax machine spit up an electric message, probably from someone across the street.

"If I could just peek into her studio for a second, I could—"

When he turned back to me he blocked the view. "That fax is from Lily's gallery in Los Angeles. They're mounting a retrospective next month; I'm helping them track down some early canvases. See? Over there on the Mac? That's a

list of every piece Lily's produced since we met, and the
eventual disposition of the product—purchaser, gross sales
price, gallery commission and expenses, net profit, subse-
quent sales history, plus a running record of her highest
price at auction per square inch of canvas. She's hung in
forty states," he concluded proudly. "A four-by-six just
sold in Florida for twenty-three thousand. A new P.R."

"What?"

"Personal Record."

"Impressive."

"Damn right. When I married her, she still hadn't
cleared four figures."

A bleep from the fax brought him out of his rapture. He
crossed his arms and regarded me the way he would the tax
assessor. "If you know anything at all about the artistic
process, you know the artist must remain in touch with the
product for as long as possible. Interruptions, no matter
how brief, can destroy the link. Days can be lost reestab-
lishing the creative connection. In this office, mornings are
for work—there are no exceptions."

"Even on Sunday?"

He smiled, though not in jest. "We believe God will
understand."

I was about to try a more secular line of argument when
I heard thudding sounds from somewhere down the hall that
led off the sunless vestibule. The big man turned toward the
noise and yelled, "Don't forget your lunch."

"Okay," a voice—young, male—called back.

"And be sure to be home by five."

"Do I *have* to?"

"Your mother wants you to go to the animal rights
lecture with her, and that's all there is to it."

"Okay," the hidden voice conceded grudgingly, then
punctuated his reluctance with the bang of a closing door.

The big man turned back to me. "If you call the office
after three, perhaps Lily will agree to see you. If I could
know the nature of your business, it would help—"

"Are you Paul?" I interrupted.

He frowned. "Have we met?"

I shook my head and edged to where I could see the

perpetually humming fax. "I take it you're also her manager."

"Among other things."

"Do you know anything about her former husband?"

"Wade?" He shrugged without agitation. "Not much, except that he has caused Lily a lot of pain and heartache. Why?"

"I'm trying to find him."

"And you expect Lily to help?" He grinned. "Good luck."

"I can't think of a reason for her *not* to help me."

Somewhere another door slammed. "There goes the best one right there."

"Their son?"

He nodded. "Why are you looking for Wade? Has he done something else to degrade himself?"

His tone left no doubt that sex was the adulterant he referred to. "I can't go into it," I said.

"Well, Lily knows nothing about it. She wants nothing to do with Wade. I suggest you save both your time and ours."

"Okay, I will." I glanced at the Macintosh. "I wouldn't want to put a crimp in the assembly line."

The big man's big hands became fists that looked capable of denting my chest. "Get out of here. Now. Or I'll throw you off the porch."

"Her bouncer, too," I said, admiringly. "Pretty versatile of you, Paul. A utility player, like Tony Phillips of the A's. Remember him in the Series? Should have been the MVP."

"You'll need an M.D. if you don't get off this porch."

Since it seemed a reasonable prognostication, I gave him a friendly wave, then trotted down the steps and headed for my car as I plotted an end run around Paul to get at his reclusive wife.

As I approached the corner of Fell and Masonic, I heard footsteps approaching from my rear. When I looked back I saw a young boy jogging toward me—Nikes flying high, backpack flopping at his shoulder, sweatshirt shiny with the Batman logo. He had dark hair and eyes and a slim, undeveloped physique; I guessed his age at six or seven.

He didn't say anything when he went by and a moment

later had disappeared around the corner. But when I reached the garage he was waiting for me, eyes wide, panting less from his jog than from whatever significance he thought I had to him.

"Hi," I said.

"Hi." He got right to it. "I heard you talking back there at the house."

"Talking about what?"

"About my dad."

"You're Wade's boy."

He nodded.

"What's your name?"

"Alfred."

I smiled. "From Tennyson?"

" 'The Love Song of Alfred J. Prufrock,' " he recited carefully. "Mom read it to me once. I didn't get it," he added, as though it was cause for concern.

"I didn't either," I admitted truthfully, to indicate it wasn't. I decided Mom wasn't entirely an ogre, and maybe not an ogre at all. "Do you use Lucerne as your surname, too, Alfred? Like your mom?"

He shook his head and puffed his chest. "I'm a Linton. Like my dad. Alfred Lucerne Linton."

And there it was, from the mouth of a babe—the Dennis Worthy of *Hammurabi* become the Wade Linton of Sebastian, and late of Folsom Prison.

"Do you know where your father is, Alfred?"

"Al." He shook his head again. "I did. I mean, I *used* to know where he lived, but he moved."

"Where was that?"

"Right there."

Alfred pointed to my back, at the thick strip of the Panhandle.

"What was the address?"

Alfred scowled at my obtuseness. "He didn't *have* an address—he was living in his car. It was parked right there, by that sign." He bit his lip. "Then it wasn't there anymore. I guess the cops took it with the others," he concluded simply.

Alfred was referring to the Panhandle's most recent contretemps. A year or so ago, the parking spaces along its borders were laid claim to by the homeless, specifically a subgroup of transients living in their vehicles. For several months a string of tattered rigs, sagging with rot and bulging with possessions, rimmed the Panhandle like a border of gritty and misshapen seashells.

The division of impoverished panzers made the Panhandle's lawn their home—kitchen for cooking food, yard for playing games, deck for worshiping the sun, for some even a garden to plant crops. But because the hippies who overran the neighborhood in the sixties had been for the most part displaced by more affluent and less tolerant residents, a petition was quickly mounted for the mayor to do something about the situation, without quite coming to grips with what the situation was. Naturally, the gentry had sufficient clout to get the job done, and the transients were quickly routed.

"Did your mom know your dad was living here?" I asked young Al.

He shook his head. "It was a secret. He said she'd send me away if she found out. She would, too." His nose wrinkled. "Mom hates him, pretty much."

"Did you talk to your dad very often?"

"All the time," he said proudly. "We met by the lawn bowling courts. We had a place where we'd leave messages for each other, and presents, like food and stuff. It was neat." His countenance darkened. "But I haven't seen him for a long time. Do you think something happened? There's some nice people out there—Dad introduced me to a whole bunch of them—but there's some crazy people, too. Dad always told me to be careful."

Alfred's expression indicated he was afraid his father hadn't taken his own advice. "When's the last time you saw him?"

"A long time ago. A month, maybe."

"Do you know why he left?"

He shrugged. "The cops were bothering them more and more. He probably just took off." Alfred marshaled a youthful anger. "There was no reason for it. I mean, they weren't criminals; they were just people who had bad luck."

"Like your dad."

"Yeah. People like my dad." Alfred fell silent, as

though he had delivered a eulogy and was giving me time to absorb it. "He's not like Paul said; he's a nice guy," he added as a coda.

"I'm sure he is."

Alfred looked toward the place where he'd seen his father last. A tear trickled down his cheek. "I don't care *what* they say, he's really just a dad."

I patted Al on the shoulder. When he could, he looked up at me. "What do you want to see him for?"

I had known the question was coming, but I still didn't have a good answer for him. "It's something about a book," I said finally.

"What kind of book?"

"A book your dad might have written. Did he say anything to you about it?"

"No."

"Did he ever give you anything to keep for him? Some pages he'd written out, or typed? Anything like that?"

Alfred shook his head, then fished in his pack. "Only this," he said, and handed me a sheet of paper that had been folded four times, and unfolded and refolded a dozen times that often.

"Dear Al," it said. "There is a person in the world who loves you more than any other thing on earth. Your Dad."

I handed it back. "That's nice," I said.

"Yeah."

"Do you have a picture of him?"

He sniffed and nodded. "Just an old one."

He reached in his pack again, and this time pulled out a small square, not much bigger than a postage stamp, wrapped in foil to preserve it. He unwrapped it carefully and handed it to me.

On glossy stock, its size suggesting it had been excised from a group portrait, the picture looked to have been clipped from a larger snapshot. The face in it was young, untroubled, open to the future. I could see Al in the face, and I could see a basis for Emma Drayer's years of longing in it, too.

I handed it back and Al rewrappped it. "So you're going to keep checking till he comes back again."

"Yeah. Sure."

I fished in my own pocket and handed Alfred my card. "If your dad gets in touch with you I'd appreciate it if you'd call me."

He looked up but didn't say anything.

"I think your dad would want you to. It might help him get back on his feet."

"Okay." He stuck my card in his pocket, then looked down the block. "I got to get to Jimmy's. We're going to Muir Woods."

"Okay. Good luck, Al."

"Thanks."

"And thanks for talking with me."

"Sure." He started down the street, then stopped. "Mr. Tanner?"

"What?"

"If you find my dad, tell him I'd like to see him again. Tell him we could meet by the bowling club, like we used to."

"I will."

"Promise?"

"Promise."

"See ya."

"See ya."

Alfred trotted off toward Jimmy's while I debated how much of our conversation had been a fraud and a sham, not on his part but my own.

In many ways it isn't surprising that so many people believed I had abused Amanda: She was more in need of love than any student I had ever seen.

HOMAGE TO HAMMURABI, p. 144

Chapter
19

When I called Charley and told him I'd finally come up with a name and asked him to feed it to the computer, he didn't bother to grouse. Which probably meant he was preoccupied with something foul enough to preoccupy a man who'd been a street cop for thirty years. When I told him I'd be in my office in twenty minutes, he told me he'd call if anything turned up. If something else was on his mind, I was glad he didn't bother to tell me what it was.

The phone was ringing when I walked in the door. "Wade Linton," Charley said when I picked it up. "Pleaded nolo to PC two-two-zero, assault with intent to commit rape, six years ago. Then—"

"Six?"

"Right. Released from Quentin—"

"Not Folsom?"

Charley ignored me. "Released from Quentin four months back. Outright release, no parole."

"Any current address?"

"I can tell you where he spent the last thirty days."

"Where?"

"San Bruno."

"For what?"

"Trespass. Seems he hung around the Astral Apple over on Haight, nursing a cup of coffee for about three hours.

When he asked for his seventh refill they asked him to leave. He got belligerent, so they called in the beat cop."

"Who was it?"

"The patrolman? Jerry Augustine. I talked to him—said he tried to calm everyone down and convince them to forget it, but the owner wanted to make your guy an example to the rest of the 'street slime,' as he called them, so he signed the complaint." Charley hesitated. "I guess that's the kind of example that made debtor's prison so popular a while back," he concluded in an acerbic sally.

"Is Linton still in Bruno?"

"Released three days ago."

"Any address at all?"

I heard Charley flip some papers. "When he was booked in 'eighty-four, he was living on Twenty-sixth, out in Noe Valley. When he was busted last month, he gave this one." Charley read off the address of Linton's wife and son.

"That one's bogus," I said. "He shows up there, Linton will be back in Bruno. What's the address in Noe?"

Charley read the number. "That's all I got. Help any?"

"Some, but not enough. I think he's living on the streets or maybe in his car. He was one of the guys who parked along the Panhandle till they rousted him."

"A lot of the guys from the Panhandle park in China Basin now. Of course if he's just out there on the street there's all kinds of places he could be. I'd start with the Civic Center, but there's ten thousand of them around town, so . . ." Charley refrained from fleshing out the difficulty of my task.

"Where else but the Civic Center?" I asked. "Somehow I don't see him hanging around that rowdy a group."

"They're all over, Marsh; you know that—we got homeless living in the public library, for Christ's sake. What a fucking world."

Homelessness. The scourge of the city, the shame of the nation. Charley and I had debated its causes and effects for years. Charley placed most of the blame on the assault on the poor during the Reagan years: housing subsidies cut 75 percent; eligibility for unemployment insurance, food stamps, and similar aid restricted or made so cumbersome to obtain that even the eligible couldn't take advantage; the dramatic escalation of rental costs in poor neighborhoods while welfare payments and the minimum wage remained at the same low levels, all while the rich saw their obligation to do anything about it in the way of taxes reduced by more than half.

Charley brands this new America loathsome—the America where the gap in both assets and attitudes between the rich and poor has become cavernous, the America that allows businessmen to coin money in the name of junk bonds and stock options yet requires a poor, illiterate woman to fill out a six-page form to qualify for food to feed her children, the America whose poor contribute a higher portion of their incomes to charity than its rich, the America whose best and brightest are no longer rewarded for creating things of value but for selling off our resources to foreign companies, the America whose politicians want to force everyone to pledge allegiance to the flag while hundreds of thousands of men whose allegiance to that flag included bravery and bloodshed must find shelter in doorways and subway tunnels and abandoned sewer pipes. Loathsome. I don't go quite as far as Charley does, but then I'm not the one who has to clean up the mess.

"If I was you I'd try the big food distribution outlets," Charley was saying. "Glide Memorial, Salvation Army, St. Anthony's, some of them. Hang around and see if he shows up. If he's really on the streets, sooner or later he will. The Tenderloin Self Help Center has heavy traffic, too. Or you could try the hotels on Turk and Sixth, or the Sanctuary."

"What's that?"

"You know, that place that used to be a bathhouse. It's a shelter now. He got a wife?"

"Not anymore."

"Then he's probably on his own—the men's shelters are too dangerous unless you're so strung out you can't survive anywhere else. You'll just have to try and spot him, or wait till he gets busted again."

"Can you flag his name for me? So you'll be notified if they bring him in?"

"Sure."

I was still despairing of the job of searching through a forest of homeless men to find one I'd never seen except in a tiny snapshot that was probably a decade old, when I suddenly thought of something. "If he was just busted, there'd be a mug shot, right?"

"Right."

"Do you have it?"

"No, but I can get it."

"That'll help a lot."

"I'm going to be in and out. If the machinery's not fucked up, you should be able to pick it up at the desk at Central by noon."

I thanked him. "You know, Linton has a kid living out on the Panhandle, so he has a reason to want to hang out in that area. Got any ideas where he might crash now that they don't let them sleep in their cars?"

"Over a hundred people sleep in Golden Gate Park every frigging night."

"Hard to get a line on, though."

"Damned right they are—a crafty bunch. It drives the park people crazy that they can't find their nests in all that greenery." Charley paused. "If I were you I'd show the mug to Augustine and see if he's seen the guy around, and maybe show it in some of the other joints along Haight Street, too. Hamilton Methodist and All Saints Episcopal hand out free food out there, so try them, too—I think the Episcopals do the weekends and the Methodists during the week. And Food Not Bombs passes out food at the Haight and Stanyan entrance to the park, once in a while, at least."

"I thought the city shut them down."

Charley swore. "They did but they're 'reviewing the policy.' Apparently someone suggested giving free food to starving people wasn't up there with coke cartels and child abuse in your list of crime priorities. But here's a tip."

"What?"

"You go nosing around the park and you want those guys to talk to you, you better look a lot more like them than you usually do, or they'll figure you for fuzz and stiff you. Better smell like them, too."

"Smell?"

"Yeah. Like you haven't had a bath for a while. Like for about a year."

"That'll be pleasant."

"About as pleasant as it is for them. Enjoy."

I *never saw Amanda Keefer after she assaulted me with her cinema verité accusation. But I encountered her friend Jeffrey outside school the morning I came to remove my effects. When I asked why she had done this to me, he donned an infuriating smirk and said, "Because you're expendable, you cretin."*

HOMAGE TO HAMMURABI, p. 149

Chapter
20

I had some time to kill before the mug shot would be ready at the Central Station, so I decided to drive out to Noe Valley and see what Linton's former neighbors had to say about him. Enough differences were developing between the world according to *Hammurabi* and the real events that had transpired at the Sebastian School that I needed all the information I could get to help me separate fact from fiction. Plus, if there was a way to find Linton without going undercover in Golden Gate Park disguised as a homeless transient, I wanted to be sure I found it.

Noe Valley is at once one of the more interesting and anonymous of the city's neighborhoods. Long a tranquil mix of artists and writers and intellectuals folded in among a wide spectrum of working folk, it was one of the last areas in the city to be gentrified. But its time has come as well, as it has with every other desirable neighborhood in town, with the result that Noe housing has become priced out of the reach of anyone of normal means—the last time I looked, the average price of a single-family dwelling in Noe Valley was $360,000. Still, from my observation of the steady stream of foot traffic that passed by as I sat in my car on the corner of Noe and Twenty-sixth, at least some of the old-timers had resisted the urge to sell their homes for more money than they'd earned in their lifetimes. All I had to do was find one who had known the Lintons before they were transformed by the events at Sebastian.

The address Charley had given me turned out to be a typical San Francisco duplex, a boxy structure in the middle of the block, gray stucco stuck onto the front of a wood frame, three levels, blue trim, garage on the ground floor, spindly tree fighting for its life in the middle of a concrete box out front. The numbers on the mailbox indicated the Lintons had lived on top, so I pushed the bell for the second level.

The man who answered was on the far side of middle age, his physique a waistless gourd, his expression frank and anticipatory. He was still in his robe and not ashamed of it, and in contrast to the usual reaction to my arrival on any given scene, he seemed pleased to have someone to talk to.

I told him my name and asked if he remembered some people named Linton who used to live in the flat on top. He scratched at his hair, hitched his pajama bottoms above his bulge, and tugged at the ends of his sash. "I've lived here for thirty years, and I'm not one of them that goes in for ignoring your neighbors. I remember the Lintons as well as I remember my Lotto numbers. Name's Gunderson by the way. Tiny's what they call me when they've known me for a while."

He stuck out his meaty hand and I took it. Then he chewed on a fingernail, remembering. "Don't know where they are now, though; up and gone, like that." He snapped the finger he'd just pruned. "I remember the boy the best—Allen, I think his name was. Cute little rascal. Could hear him cry all the way down here. I often wonder what happened to him."

"I saw him this morning. He's six or seven now. He turned into a nice young man."

My reference to young Al had apparently been the legitimizing sign that Tiny needed. He motioned for me to join him inside the apartment, then turned and preceded me toward the rear.

I hurried to keep up as he continued his patter. "You got any more questions you better come on back; I'm in the middle of my business and it won't get done with me out here jawing in my jammies."

"I can come back later if that would be better," I offered as I tagged along.

"No need—I can work and talk at the same time. Coffee?"

"Please."

"Good. I got a new machine I'm itching to try. Come sit in the kitchen. Don't mind the mess, but don't do anything about it. I got a *method* to my madness."

He led me through a living room so dark I could barely find my way, to the small, bright kitchen in the rear of the apartment. It was cramped but cozy, featuring a stainless steel refrigerator the size of a boxcar and an array of culinary devices that made the countertop look like the appliance aisle at K mart.

Tiny gestured toward the table in the corner. It was round, covered with yellow oilcloth, then covered again with hundreds of squares of paper, some dull as newsprint, others brightly coated stock, all of them promoting something or other.

I gestured at the piles. "What are they?"

"It's how I make my living since Trudy died."

"But what are they?"

He shook his head in disgust. "Are you rich?"

"No."

"Then you're not married."

"Right."

"And never have been."

"Nope."

"Well, if you had ever had a wife, you'd know those were coupons. Discounts and entry blanks and rebates. I got them laid out by dates and deadlines."

Tiny turned his back and poured me some coffee from a Krups machine that was issuing a steady gush of it. When he turned to present me with the cup, the look on my face provoked him.

"I feed me and Bill"—he gestured toward the cat in the corner by the stove—"on fifteen dollars a month over and above the coupons and that includes a meat dish three nights a week, plus I make two hundred extra from the rebates. So don't be looking like I'm some kind of nut."

"I wasn't—"

"And I got all *these*"—his arm swept toward the

appliances that filed across the counter like a parade of miniature war machines—"for *free*. Plus"—he looked to make sure I was paying attention—"I been to Hawaii sixteen times. All expenses paid."

"I'm impressed."

"Well, it ain't easy, let me tell you. Got to spend a lot of time in garbage cans, digging out proofs of purchase, plus you go blind trying to read the fine print they put on there to trick you into buying the product but fouling up the entry rules. But I got me a magnifying glass, so they don't get anything by me anymore. The biggest problem I got is the local librarian."

"What's the matter with her?"

"She's trying to bar me from the periodicals room—doesn't like me cutting up the magazines. I promised her there'd be nothing that amounted to anything on the other side of any of my clippings, but she won't listen to reason. She's hauling me in front of the board next week."

"Well, good luck."

He shrugged. "If they kick me out of the local branch, I'll just go back downtown. Got to be tricky to get by these days. Tricky or rich, and I'm not rich." He pulled out two chairs and we sat and sipped our coffees. "So what do you want to know about the Lintons?" he asked when he was ready.

"It's Mr. Linton I'm mostly interested in."

"What about him?"

That stumped me. "Well, what did you think of him?"

He shrugged. "Nice enough, I guess. To me."

"But not to his wife?"

"I heard a few strong words. No subflooring up there, so there's little way not to. But any marriage has strong words—I thought Trudy was going into conniptions when I started with the giveaways." He sipped more coffee, frowned, and looked back at the machine that was still evacuating a jet-black stream. "Tastes a little funny, guess I'll give that one to the Seniors Center. I got four more in the closet. He was a weak man," he added in a quick switch.

"Wade Linton?"

He nodded.

"Weak how?"

"Made that wife of his do too many things for him—come down with the rent, paint the bedroom, fix the faucet, take care of the packing and moving after he went off to his new job. Maybe not weak, maybe just different. Maybe just spoiled." He thought for a moment, then shook his head. "Can't think why they chased him for a government job. 'Course the government's full of weak men, now that I think of it. Sort of a convention of 'em, is what it amounts to. In this city, at any rate."

"What government job?" I asked, more than a little confused.

"The one that other guy was asking about. The one back East that Linton left here for."

"When did this other guy come around?"

"Way back. Just before they got the baby, as I remember it."

"You mean a man came by here asking questions about Mr. Linton?"

He nodded. "Just like you."

"And he said it was because Linton was being considered for a government job?"

"That's it exactly. Very mysterious, he was. I told him I was sure Wade'd be good at whatever it was they wanted him for, but I sort of hoped it wasn't as head of the FBI, if you know what I mean."

"Did this man give you a name?"

"If he did, I forget it."

"What kind of information was he looking for?"

"Everything I had to say about them."

"Was the man with the questions asking about anything specific?"

"Moral stuff mostly, if you know what I mean. Did they drink, did they use drugs, did they get behind on the rent. I told him no to all of it." Tiny drained his cup. "Funny how they check so hard on their morals *before* they get them jobs, then let 'em run hog wild once they're where we can't get hold of 'em."

When I tried to find a meaning in what Tiny Gunderson had told me, I couldn't do it. "So you think Wade Linton left here to take a government job back East. Did someone tell you that?"

"I don't remember, but someone must have. Or maybe I just put two and two together."

It was time to zero in. "Have you seen Wade Linton around lately?"

His response was firm and prompt. "Nope. I suppose he's still back East. One of them bury crats."

"Is there anyone else in the neighborhood who knew the Lintons well?"

He thought about it. "The Devlin woman, two doors down. Bridget and Lily were friendly. Artist types, the both of them. You figure an artist has a use for one of them?" He gestured at a collection of electric spray paint devices stacked in the corner. I told him I didn't know, it probably depended on the artist.

I thanked Mr. Gunderson for the information, but when I started to get up he reached out a hand and stopped me. "I'm pretty sure to win another trip to Hawaii this month—I can give you a deal on it."

"I'm not sure I can get away. Why don't I let you know?"

"How about a bicycle? I got three down in the garage—those knobby-wheeled ones like they use now. I'll sell you one for twenty bucks. Take your pick."

I shook my head. "But if I see the Linton boy again, maybe I'll send him by."

Tiny brightened. "You do that. My but he was a cute little thing. Me and Trudy said many a time we could have used one of those ourselves."

I let myself out the front, but not before Tiny gave me a coupon for a free can of shaving cream and a pack of disposable razors.

The Devlin place was a triplex not much different from Tiny's but for the extra floor. The woman who came to the door was tall and ungainly, with a long, thin face and limp brown hair gathered into a wispy braid which swayed with her lethargic movements. She was dressed in faded Levi's and a surgeon's smock, and both the woman and her clothes were streaked with paint, yellow and white mostly, making her look like a walking daisy.

The apartment was warm and her brow was bright with sweat, but the temperature didn't extend to my welcome. In contrast to Tiny Gunderson, Mrs. Devlin saw me as an irritant. The ease with which she assumed a hostile attitude indicated that that was the brand she put on most aspects of her life.

I gave my name and asked if I could talk with her for a moment.

"Are you selling anything?"

I shook my head. "I'm a private investigator."

"You're kidding, I hope."

"Nope."

Her eyes exploded with concern. "My God. Something happened to Carrie."

"I don't think so. Who's Carrie?"

"My daughter."

I shook my head. "I'm here about the Lintons. They used to live down—"

"I *know* where they used to live." Anxiety was trumped by enmity. "I suppose this has to do with the letter—I knew she wouldn't have the nerve to face me herself." She looked at me closely. "I figured she'd send a lawyer."

"What letter are you talking about?"

"*My* letter to Lily."

Her look was so intense and expectant it made me want more information about her communication with the former Mrs. Linton, but I didn't want to waste time getting it. "I don't know anything about a letter," I confessed. "I'm here about *Mr*. Linton."

The shift deflated her. "He's in jail," she said simply.

"Not anymore."

She rebounded. "Really? When did he get out?"

"Four months ago. Have you seen him?"

She shook her head. "But I'd like to. I'd like him to know about Carrie," she added, as though she was afraid I might misunderstand.

"I take it you liked the Lintons."

"At first. Then Lily and I had problems, but Wade was wonderful." She misinterpreted my look. "To Carrie, I mean."

"What exactly did he do for her?"

Her tone was defensive. "He got her an excellent education, for one thing. Basically, he changed her life."

"How did he manage that?"

She met my skeptic's eye. "He arranged for her to get a scholarship to Sebastian."

"You make it sound like a miracle."

"Well, *we* certainly didn't have the money for anything like that, so it was a miracle in that sense. And if you knew Carrie in those days, you'd think she was the *last* person who would succeed in such a school. But Wade saw something in her, and he took a chance and recommended her for the scholarship, and eventually he made it work."

"How?"

"Carrie was never a good student. Actually, she was pretty wild—she cared more about hanging out at Stonestown than she did about her studies. She had a tough time at Sebastian at first, but Wade turned her around. She started doing well in school and was picked as judge of the student court. She even got a boyfriend, a *rich* one. She graduated with honors and was admitted to Stanford; now she's in Spain on a fellowship."

By the time she finished, the litany had become a hymn. "You must be proud of her," I said unnecessarily.

She nodded. "She'll be everything I'm not."

"Which is what?"

Her lip lifted nastily. "Successful."

"What did Carrie think of Mr. Linton?"

"As a man or a teacher?"

"Either. Both."

"She liked him as a person. And appreciated what he'd done for her. But she thought he was a tyrant as a teacher."

"Really? Why?"

"He was too demanding. Too idealistic. Impractical and inflexible in his requirements."

"Is that what the administration thought too?"

She shrugged. "Maybe. Maybe that's why they *railroaded* him."

"You have evidence of his innocence?"

She stiffened. "Just what he did for Carrie. Which was hardly the act of the monster they tried to make him out to be."

I've been in the business long enough to know that there's no connection between sex and any other aspect of a person's life; sex is separate. It may be better or worse than the rest, but it's separate, which means anyone is capable of anything in that regard. But there was no point in lessening Wade Linton in Mrs. Devlin's eyes. "When's Carrie coming back from Spain?" I asked her.

"Nineteen ninety-two, if she gets her way. She's fallen in love." She made the condition sound both rare and terminal.

"Are any of Carrie's Sebastian friends still around?"

"Carrie didn't have many Sebastian friends. She was on scholarship," she added, as if that would explain it, and maybe it did.

"I don't suppose you've seen Linton around the neighborhood lately?"

She shook her head. "I kind of hoped . . ." She didn't complete the sentiment, but I didn't think all of it had to do with her daughter.

"Do you know anything about a man who came around several years ago, claiming he was doing a background check on Linton for a job of some sort?"

She frowned and nodded. "But he didn't *really* work for the government. He was a lawyer."

"How do you know?"

"I saw his picture in the paper later on. His name is Messenger. I don't know what he was up to, but it wasn't the government job service."

"Did you ever see this Messenger again?"

"No."

"Is there a Mr. Devlin?"

"Danny?" She crossed her arms. "He's in Stockton."

"Temporarily?"

"Permanently."

"Are you divorced?"

"What does it sound like?" She stepped back and put her hand on the door. "I have more work to do. So do you, since I don't know anything that would help you."

Like a traveling salesman, I put my foot where it would keep her from slamming the door in my face if she had a mind to do it. "Do you know the name of the student Wade Linton was supposed to have abused?"

She shook her head. "We didn't travel in those circles, so it wouldn't have come up."

"I thought your daughter might have mentioned it."

"Carrie didn't talk much about what happened to Wade. I think she was ashamed of the school for what it did to him."

A thought scratched at me and finally broke through. "Do you happen to have one of Carrie's old yearbooks around?"

"From Sebastian?"

I nodded.

"Is this important?"

"Possibly."

She thought it over. "Just a minute, I'll check. I remember Carrie tried to throw them away one time, but I rescued them."

Mrs. Devlin left me on the threshold. All I could see inside the house were some imitation Colonial furnishings, a small TV, some art on the walls, and the accumulated clutter of a person living alone. I recognized it because in the realm of clutter, my own apartment was a clone.

When she returned I was admiring the picture across the room, a colorful rendering of a potted geranium. I gestured at it. "Nice flowers."

"Thank you."

"Did you paint it?"

"Yes."

"It reminds me of Mrs. Linton's work. I guess she's Lily Lucerne now," I said by way of explanation.

Her lips tightened. "It *should* remind you of her work—she stole the technique from me. And she's made a mint from it, which is what my letter was all about. Not that it'll do any good. Here."

On a tidal wave of betrayal, Bridget Devlin thrust a heavy book into my hands, one with a padded cover, a glossy weight to the pages, and a brightly embossed title—*The Sebastian Senator*. I flipped through it till I got to the faculty section.

The teachers were grouped by subject—science teachers in the lab, history teachers by the globe, art teachers in a gallery. The English teachers were in the library, posed around a table piled with classics, except that the volume beneath *Moby Dick* was *A Fan's Notes*.

Only one of the assembled faculty was a candidate for that little bit of rebellion. He was by far the youngest, handsome enough to have fathered the tot Tiny Gunderson remembered so fondly and to have earned a lot of female faith in his rectitude. His tousled hair and mischievous blue eyes gave him the untamed look of a bookish James Dean, which was sure to have been a lure to more than one of his young students, as it had apparently been to every adult woman who had ever crossed his path. I fixed the image in my mind, then blended it with the snapshot his young son had showed me. If I was lucky, Charley Sleet had left the third panel of the triptych at the Central Station, one that would show what half a dozen years in prison had done to the unsuspecting face of one Wade Linton.

I flipped more pages and stopped at the senior section. The students appeared alphabetically. Beneath their picture, along with their nickname and activities, was a slogan thought appropriate. Some of the annotations were endearing and others were alarming—Chamber Group, Future Business Leaders, Mock Stock Exchange, Investment Club; "Judas Priest," "Road Warrior," "Mr. Macho," "Wonder Woman."

Carrie Devlin was there, her socioeconomic distance from her peers somehow obvious merely from the cut of her blouse. "Cinderella," someone had cruelly dubbed her. Her sole activity was the student court. Someone—presumably Carrie herself—had drawn a big, black *X* through her photo, as though to void her entire high school experience. If her generation was anything like mine, that impulse was close to universal.

I turned the page. A familiar face looked up at me, a young woman in a sweater with a big white *S* on her chest, the duplicate of a picture I'd first seen in Bryce Chatterton's office. Her nickname was Fishy. Her activities were soccer and the drama club and something called the Auxiliary. Her motto was "Just for Kicks." The entendre, I was sure, was at least double.

If I have learned anything from this experience, it is that no one without wealth is exempt from destruction. Intelligence, morality, decency, industry, none is sufficient to confer immunity to downfall, not unless it has been successfully subordinated to the accumulation of riches.

HOMAGE TO HAMMURABI, p. 289

Chapter
21

On my back to the office, I swung by the Central Station. There was an envelope for me at the desk, nine-by-twelve manila, with my name scrawled across the front in Charley's hand. I thanked the sergeant, tucked it under my arm, and toted it back to my office. When my shoes were off and the coffee was on, I tore it open.

It was Wade Linton all right—Al's father, Carrie's savior, Emma's heartthrob—but just barely. The once-bright eyes were vague and unplugged. The hair was sparse and graying, so long and oily it hung over his ears like a tattered scarf. The skin was sallow, the sweater torn, the mouth made comic by the loss of an eye tooth. Linton had been mugged, if not by a specific villain, then by the long misfiring of his life. I tried to imagine how badly his agile mind—the mind of *Hammurabi*—had been warped by his plunge. Then I wondered what course that mind might take at this point, and whether my invasion of his life would aid or complicate its future.

I set aside the mug shot and tried to make sense of the pieces of the puzzle I'd just uncovered, to decide whether Carrie Devlin had any part in Linton's fall, whether her mother's tiff with Lily Lucerne was anything I had to check on, whether any of the ties I'd unearthed were strong enough to make Wade Linton return to his old neighborhood and thus make that my focus.

I hadn't made much progress toward any answers when the door to the outer office buzzed. Since my current secretary is only on duty irregularly, pursuant to her whim more than my requirements, I trooped out to answer it myself.

Bryce Chatterton was in the hallway, as fidgety as a boy dating a girl whose father liked to chat. I brought him in the office, sat him down, put some coffee in him, and encouraged him to relax. The effort went for naught—Bryce was as gloomy as I'd ever seen him.

In the middle of his marvel about the imminent reopening of the Bay Bridge, he looked around the office. "What's different about this place?"

"Different from what—yours? About fifty thousand bucks' worth of interior decorating."

"I mean from before."

I thought for a minute. "Peggy took her plants home," I concluded finally.

"Oh."

"Yeah."

"Not good."

"No."

"So buy some new ones. You need greenery."

"I've got greenery."

"Where?"

"On the ceiling above my shower."

Ever fastidious, Bryce made piano movements with his hands, as though just the thought of all that mold made the air alive with spores.

"What brings you here?" I prodded. "Progress report?"

He shook his head. "I've been talking to Andy."

"Potter?"

He nodded.

"Double-checking my research? I don't blame you."

He shook his head, then reached into his jacket pocket and pulled out a thick wad of paper. "This."

He handed it to me. When I unfolded it I was looking at a notice of motion for a temporary restraining order, directed at Bryce and Margaret and Periwinkle, asking for a order "preventing the publication of a novel entitled *Homage to Hammurabi* and/or any other work of fiction or nonfiction consisting in whole or in part of a libel per se or libel per quod against the Sebastian School, its students, teachers, administrators, or alumni, individually or collectively." There were some points and authorities attached, and a statement under penalty of perjury from Marvin Gillis swearing and affirming upon information and belief that publication of the novel would mean the Decline of the West.

"How'd he find out about it?" I asked.

"I don't know."

I handed the papers back. "This is bullshit, Bryce. There are all kinds of cases that say you can't restrain speech before it's published, that the only thing you can do is collect damages afterward if you can prove them. He can't get away with it." I considered Bryce's persistent gloom. "Can he?"

Bryce wasn't cheered by my essay. "He can if I don't resist."

"Why wouldn't you resist?"

"Because resistance costs a fortune. Andy estimates fifty thousand dollars. And you know lawyers' estimates—multiply by three."

"Another example of a theoretical freedom being practically untenable."

"I guess."

"So you're giving in?"

He shrugged. "I don't know yet."

Bryce looked so miserable I picked up the phone. "Andy? Marsh Tanner. Bryce is pretty upset by this TRO thing."

"He should be," he said in a breathy voice that belied his solid sagacity.

"Why? It's a sham, isn't it?"

"Not entirely."

"Why not? Prior restraint is—"

"There are kids involved," Andy interrupted. "Kids make bad law."

"They aren't kids anymore," I said. "If they ever were."

"What do you know about it?"

"More than I want to."

Andy hesitated. "We may need you as a witness, so keep Thursday open."

I told him I would. "Tell me something that will calm Bryce down."

"Anytime a big law firm agrees to take on a lawsuit against you, you have reason to be worried. No lawyer will defend a case on a contingency; it's going to cost him some bucks."

"Can't you keep down the tab?"

"If Gillis is serious about this, keeping it down may mean keeping it under six figures. Expenses are high, Marsh; I've got partners to answer to."

"Well, do what you can."

"I always do. So how's it going with you?"

I looked at my vastly ungreen office and my vastly apprehensive friend. "Not worth a damn."

After I replaced the phone, Bryce looked at me. "So that's *my* story; what have *you* been doing?"

"Well, I've made some progress."

"Really?" He brightened by a watt. "Good." Then he remembered his predicament. "I guess."

"The author's name is Linton."

"That's wonderful. Where is he?"

"I don't know."

"Oh."

"I'm going to try a couple of leads, but . . ." I shrugged to establish my pessimism.

"I've been thinking about what you said about Jane Ann," Bryce said, as though he'd read an earlier edition of my thoughts. "If all this really happened at Sebastian, she probably *does* know something about it. I should talk to her," he concluded nervously.

"Why don't you let me do it?"

"Why?"

"Because it's my job. And because she'll have to be pushed to get her to talk, and she'll resent whoever does the pushing. There's no need to put that in your relationship."

Bryce was obviously relieved by my offer. "I suppose not."

"I'll let you know how it comes out."

"Fine."

"And Bryce?"

My tone was enough to make his nerves return post-haste. "What?"

"If someone *did* frame this poor teacher, it had to have been done with the cooperation of at least one student at Sebastian."

"The girl, you mean. The victim."

I nodded. "And my sense of kids is, they seldom go out on their own at that age. Teenage schemes and antics tend to be group things."

"So?"

"So if Jane Ann had anything at all to do with this, she could be hit with a conspiracy charge."

Bryce recoiled. "Nonsense. Jane Ann wouldn't—"

"All members of a criminal conspiracy are equally guilty, Bryce, even if only one of them did the actual deed. I just want to make sure you know what the risks are of going on with this—I don't want to bring down a bunch of grief on you and your family."

I had expressed that caution twice before, without effect, but this time he hesitated. "Maybe I should talk to Margaret. She doesn't even know about this." He waved the papers in his hand.

"Maybe you should."

"Don't do anything else until you hear from me."

"Fine."

"And, Marsh?"

"What?"

"Thanks for . . . looking out for me."

"My pleasure," I said, because it was. If it wasn't, I shouldn't be in the business.

After Bryce had gone, I cleaned up some odds and ends as I plotted my next move, assuming Bryce ultimately authorized one. When I was getting ready to go home, the phone rang. It was Margaret Chatterton.

"I've just spoken with Bryce," she announced furiously.

"And?"

"He's fouling the whole thing up."

"What thing?"

"The business, the family, everything. Now he's going to drag *Jane Ann* into this . . . this *whatever* it is. You have to put an end to it."

"How?"

"By stopping whatever you're doing."

"And if I don't?"

"I'll have to bring in Marvin."

"Marvin's already in."

"You mean the lawsuit?"

I thought back to my nocturnal meeting at the Gillis mansion. "And other ways."

"Marvin gets what he wants, Marsh. If he wants to stop you, he will. Especially if I help him."

I sighed. Bryce had talked a lot about truth in literature. Well, I deal in truth as well, and truth is often unpalatable in my business too. "I don't want to hurt you or Jane Ann, Margaret, but Bryce is still my client. Unless it involves something illegal or immoral, I have to go by what he wants."

"You find it moral to ruin a young girl's *life*?"

"No one's talking about doing that."

"That's precisely what Bryce thinks you *were* talking about."

"If it looks like that's what's happening, I'll call a halt. Unless she was mixed up in framing a man for something he didn't do. Then it might get complicated."

"Don't be ridiculous. This is my *daughter* you're referring to." She marshaled her weapons. "If I hear you're threatening her happiness, I'll take steps, Marsh. Don't think I won't. I won't let you hurt her."

"I wouldn't want you to, Margaret," I said, but I was talking through a severed thread.

When I replaced the phone and leaned back in my chair to ponder the events of the last half hour, I found myself looking into the alabaster disdain of Jane Ann's fey and furtive boyfriend.

"What brings you by—collecting for United Way?"

"Not this month." Lloyd's smile remained infuriating. "I'm here to give you a dollop of advice."

"That's great—I haven't had any advice for about thirty seconds."

Lloyd was too caught up in his persona to react. "I've been tight with Jane Ann since Country Day," he said.

"Whatever that is."

"It's a *grade* school."

"Oh."

"There are certain . . . *episodes* in her past that her stepfather is unaware of."

"I'm sure there are. I'm sure the converse is true as well. And I'm sure there are things in *your* past that would make your parents change their names."

"My parents are dead."

I reddened—even Lloyd didn't deserve that. "Sorry."

He shrugged away my sentiment. "The events I'm referring to would be very upsetting for Mr. Chatterton if they were made public. Upsetting, and perhaps expensive."

"Bryce is a big boy, Lloyd."

He raised an invisible brow. "Really? Poems about *traffic*? You could have fooled me."

Lloyd reached into his pocket and took out a cigarette—black paper, gold filter, exotic length. He made the ceremony of lighting it a dalliance with death.

"The Sebastian story is complex, Mr. Semi-private Eye. It's straight out of Kafka—nothing is as it seems; no one is unsullied; guilt and innocence are indeterminable."

"It sounds more like Ross MacDonald."

"My advice, Mr. Tanner, is to disappear. Until Wade Linton is removed from the scene." He inhaled enough smoke to fuel a bagpipe and an assessment. "You have no idea what's at risk in all this," he concluded.

"I don't even know what 'this' is."

He exhaled an insouciant cloud. "It will be pretty of you to keep it that way."

"Hemingway, for God's sake?"

But Lloyd had already closed the door.

I've spent hours choosing the first thing I'm going to do after I'm released—the first luxury I'm going to allow myself. At last I believe I know—after I get off the bus from Folsom, I'm going straight to Grace Cathedral to enjoy a minute of perfect silence, a delicacy I've been denied for a decade. Then I'm going to find a place that doesn't smell—the Alta Plaza, perhaps, high enough for the ocean breezes to sweep away the fumes of the stagnant city.

And then I'm going to Nordstrom and buy the best outfit I can afford, in any hue but blue.

HOMAGE TO HAMMURABI, p. 278

Chapter
22

I've held someone's life in my hands before, both literally and figuratively. On more than one occasion, I didn't realize it until it was too late, and the results were tragic, so on the way home I tried to decide whether Jane Ann Gillis was in danger from me or not. By the time I stuck the key in my lock I decided I didn't know whether she was or wasn't and didn't have a way to find out except to keep doing what I had been doing—looking for the author of *Hammurabi*.

I was halfway through my bowl of Campbell's Home Cookin' when the phone rang. Bryce Chatterton's voice was jacketed in steel. "Stay with it, Marsh. Do what we talked about. I'll deal with the consequences when they arise."

"Does Margaret approve of your decision?"

"Does it matter?"

"I guess not."

After Bryce hung up, I set the stage for my impersonation. I turned up the heat, though the room was comfortable without it. Then I exercised. I don't do it often, and even then reluctantly and intermittently, so it didn't take much to work up a sweat—jumping jacks, stretching, some sit-ups and push-ups, a couple of minutes of running in place, a handful of reps with the set of free weights I'd owned for twenty years and ignored for a dozen.

When I was lathered from the exertion, I put on the shirt

and cap I wear when I play softball with Charley on the Central Station team the day it takes on the self-important swells from the Washington Square Bar and Grill, then donned the pants I wear when I change the oil in the Buick. Then I performed another stunt I don't indulge in very often—I cleaned the apartment.

I cleaned places that hadn't seen the light of day for years—behind the refrigerator, behind the toilet, under the bed, beneath the TV, under the bath mat and the throw rug. Then I washed the kitchen floor—by hand, with a sponge that was soiled to its core before I was halfway through and emitted when I squeezed it a jaundiced sauce reminiscent of a mix of marmalade and pancake syrup. Then I cleaned, believe it or not, the oven, with a chemical agent that was sufficiently noxious to suggest it would kill me long before it made a dent in the crud that made the bottom of my stove a nifty diorama of the far side of the moon.

When the fumes were reduced to tolerable levels, I rounded up all the pencils I could find along with a small hand sharpener and scraped off enough ground graphite to rub into my face and hands until I looked like a Kentucky coal miner. Then I went to bed. In my clothes. Without turning down the heat, or taking a shower, or shaving, or brushing my teeth. That I actually slept, eventually, is testimony to the toil that exercise can take on a body that is preferably at rest.

When I got up the next morning, I stayed in my clothes, stayed in my beard, stayed in my fuzzy and fetid mouth while I ate a sandwich of ketchup and onions, drank half a can of beer and poured the other half over my head. After toweling off, I got in my car and headed west, and got where I was going without looking at myself in the mirror.

Golden Gate Park was established in 1870 on an expanse of some one thousand acres on a portion of the San Francisco peninsula so remote and desolate it was known in those days as the Outside Lands. A windswept expanse of dangerously shifting sand dunes, the area was thought by most experts of the day, including Frederick Law Olmsted, the architect of New York's Central Park, to be permanently incapable of supporting vegetation.

Initially a haven for thugs and thieves, over the years of

its development the park became the object of political warfare between the forces of the rich—who employed the venue as a private playground—and the poor—whose idea of diversion was more organic and elemental. More aggressive members of the latter group periodically regarded the park's undeveloped acres as a home for those without the means to afford a real one, to the extent that just prior to the turn of the century an entire village of squatters' shacks known as Mooneyville had sprung up in the outer reaches and had to be dismantled by authorities.

A more sanctioned invasion occurred in 1906, when some thirty thousand refugees from the earthquake took up residence in the park, complete with tents to live in, food to eat, and schools for displaced children. As recently as the sixties, an illegal occupation occurred once more, when a troup of flower children tried to commandeer a portion of the park known as "hippie hill." This time the invasion was stymied when park gardeners covered the entire mound with two inches of manure.

Fortunately, the wealthy did not prevail entirely, either. The more glaring sources of their entertainment, from gambling casinos to a "speed road" on which to race their horses and motorcars, were also excised over the years, despite the protests of the playboys. But the struggle over the grounds continues, and the current source of dispute is the occupation of its nether reaches by a substantial number of the city's homeless.

By the time I parked the Buick on an unobtrusive block of Beulah Street and had made an unsuccessful trip down Haight on the chance Wade Linton had revisited the scene of his most recent legal skirmish, it was after noon. On the corner of Haight and Stanyan, already reeking with sweat and embarrassment, I experienced a strange sensation. In the glade across the street, a curious ebb and flow seemed underway, as though the forest had come alive à la Shakespeare's Birnham Wood.

I blinked and looked again. What was on the move was not trees but people, a score of them or more, bedrolls on their backs, knapsacks under their arms, plastic bags over their shoulders or gripped tightly in their hands, converging from all directions. Few words were exchanged, few eyes sought peers or were raised above the ground that stretched before their ill-shod feet, but there was a sense of common purpose in the air as the migration began to coalesce and meander across from where I stood.

In the hope Wade Linton would eventually join the throng, I entered the park, found a place on a bench and sat down to wait next to a woman who was clearly one of those I sought to ape. Before I could strike up a conversation, the woman took off her socks and shoes and started rubbing her feet, which were swollen and scabbed and the color of mud. Her clothing swaddled her like bunting; her scent was reminiscent of cooked cabbage.

The massage was comforting only briefly. Shoes and socks in place, she became hyperagitated—the object of her wrath seemed to be the heavy woolen sweater which was buttoned to her neck.

With a feral curse, she tore at the garment until a button popped, then looked at me accusingly, as though I'd done it by some trick. "They're not sick, you know," she spat.

"Who's not?" She was so inflamed and active, I was afraid she was going to hit me.

"The trees."

"Oh."

"They say they're sick, but they're not." As if to prove her point, from somewhere beyond us the chatter of a chain saw tore the air. "They're just cutting them down so we won't have any place to hide."

"Oh."

"They'd rather destroy the park than give us a place to sleep. Isn't that amazing?"

I agreed it was.

The woman tugged at her sweater once again, with hands that were gnarled and chewed and blotched with blood, still agitated by the fate of the trees and her excessive warmth. I wondered why she didn't take the sweater off, until I remembered Charley Sleet had told me that homeless women wear far more clothing than they need in order to deter men from attacking them, on the theory that the rapists will give up in frustration before they make their way through the maze. It sounded like a flimsy defense. Charley had agreed, then told me about a woman named Donna who lived in a stairwell on Minna Street and wore eight pairs of panty hose and had been raped a dozen times.

"The other way they stay safe is keep awake all night," he'd continued. "Every stinking night, and most of the day as well—always on the move, keeping an eye out for the fiends. You see a woman on her own on the streets—*any* woman—you can bet she hasn't slept more than an hour in the last twelve."

The woman next to me on the bench was unquestionably such a victim—exhaustion branded her face like a birthmark. My impulse was to say something to her, to somehow acknowledge her existence, but I couldn't think of anything that would remotely touch her. In something like a panic, I reached in my pocket for Wade Linton's mug shot and held it out. "Seen this guy around lately?"

She didn't even look at it. "What you want him for?"

I thought I was ready for it. "He's my brother."

She regarded me with generic distaste. "Like shit."

She gathered her belongings and lumbered away, cursing all the while, on feet that must have made it as pleasant as a walk on coals. I hadn't noticed before, but among her effects was a baseball bat which was brandished at her side in a strong right hand. I don't think she used it for sport.

While we'd been talking, several more park people had gathered in the area, some waiting stoically, others almost slavering in anticipation, still others, like the young man in the faded yellow slicker who was seated on the bench across from mine, crying silently, from woes as invisible as the curse that spawned their suffering.

It was too depressing to continue, was what I decided as I watched my benchmate take her bat off into the trees, too much in the nature of a tease to pursue Linton in this way, too much a mocking of these people to maintain my absurd disguise. Feeling profane and craven, I abandoned the bench and started back to my car. A moment later, as I was waiting to recross the street at Stanyan, I heard a screech and a thump from somewhere to my side.

As though on cue, the multitude looked eagerly toward the sound as two young men and one young woman clambered out of a battered blue van that had just pulled to the curb. After a moment of discussion and an exchange of greetings with their audience, they started hauling tables and boxes and insulated metal canisters out of the back of the van and setting them up just inside the park. The last item put in place was a handmade sign—FOOD NOT BOMBS.

As if a Pavlovian bell had sounded, the homeless began to fall in line, silently, ineluctably, and somehow reluctantly as well, as though lining up for a wage they hadn't earned. One group in particular caught my eye—a family of three. The father was young and vibrant, his energies harnessed by his circumstances in a way he clearly resisted, his backpack bulging with the family's meager possessions and, it was somehow possible to believe, with a tuck of dignity as well. The mother was a different story—thin and harried, her surfaces pale and blank as though all vestiges of vitality had been worn away. The roll of bedding hunched high on her shoulders made her slumped and humped; the vacancy in her eyes was the look of an hysteric. And then the child, a girl of three or so, who looked toward the food tables with an expression so ecstatic it could only have had its roots in starvation.

As I watched, the little girl tugged at her father's hand, then said something to him. He smiled in reply and reached to the top of his pack and untied it. After a moment of fumbling, he found her prize—a teddy bear, its fur soiled and matted, its form and function still undamaged.

The girl clutched the bear to her chest and began to speak their private language: "They've got plenty today, Sally. See? They won't run out *this* time. But don't eat too fast; if you do it will make you sick." I closed my eyes and tried to understand why the city I lived in had determined that Food Not Bombs constituted a public nuisance.

I was still contemplating that and other travesties when I saw him, coming from the direction of Kezar Stadium, looking left and right, as alert and wary as a buck. Without question he lived in the park—his face was smeared with dirt, his hair was tangled with twigs and leaves. A grimy raincoat came to a ragged end just above the drooping cuffs that ringed his sockless ankles, which were as bright as bone above his laceless leather shoes. The yellow scarf around his neck was the only splash of color in the ensemble, but when he joined the line for food I noticed there was a number 7 stitched on its center, which made it not a scarf at all but the flag from the pin on the seventh green of the nearby golf course. It took a leap of faith to believe that this was the man that *Hammurabi* said he was.

When Wade Linton had taken his place at its dreary end, I joined the line as well. He got his food—a thick stew, a hunk of bread, a cup of coffee—three places before I did. When he wandered behind a bush to eat his feast, I marked the spot in my mind and when my own plate was full I headed that way.

I was balancing my foodstuffs carefully, trying not to trip or spill anything, so when I rounded the bush I had to swerve to keep from stepping on him. I muttered an apology, went to what I thought was a suitable distance, then sat on the sodden grass and began to eat.

A few bites later I looked up and found Linton staring at me, his eyes deep pits of consternation that deemed my presence an affront. To disturb him further, I waved affably. "Not bad today," I said, gesturing with my plate.

"Compared to what?" Linton grumbled.

"Compared to yesterday."

"They didn't come yesterday—the van broke down."

"Then compared to eating out of a dumpster."

"I wouldn't know; I don't eat out of dumpsters."

"Does that mean you got a steady source?"

"You ask too many questions."

"I been told that before; it's sort of a habit."

"Then maybe you should get another one."

"Like what?"

"Like keeping your mouth shut."

Though his plate was still half full, Linton clambered to his feet, brushed off his coat, and started to walk away from me.

"Emma Drayer says hello," I said easily to his departing back.

He took two more steps and stopped. In the interval, I had gathered my feet under me and was about to stand, but I was still crouched near the ground when he turned and rushed me. With a grunt he threw his plate and its steamy contents at my face, aimed a quick kick at my throat, then took off running for the trees.

The kick was off-line just enough to barely brush me, so the only loss was my balance. But the stew was effective as a blindfold, and by the time I cleared my eyes I had only a brief glimpse of Linton, well in the distance, as he dodged behind a tree and disappeared. I got to my feet and started after him, slipping in the puddle of food, cursing the tactic that had driven him off before I got a word in edgewise.

He reappeared a second later, still on the move, but he was younger and quicker than I and I couldn't offset either advantage. Although I pursued him as fast as I could, within seconds he had vanished once more, this time in a grove of eucalyptus that bordered Kezar Drive on the west. When I got to the street I tried to spot him beyond the honking stream of traffic, but Linton seemed long gone.

I muttered another curse and stood on the edge of the roadway trying to decide what to do next as cars raced by me at distressing speeds. My only alternative seemed to be to abandon the chase, go back to the apartment and divest myself of my ersatz homelessness, and seek out Jane Ann Gillis in the hope that she knew the Sebastian story well enough to tell me where Linton might be headed when he left his lair in search of the person who had stolen six years of his life. But as I started to do just that, something caught my ear and eye—the bark of a dog and a blur of movement.

Flushed from cover by the dog that was no doubt as ravenous as the little girl with the bear named Sally, Linton had abandoned his sanctuary in the eucalyptus and was on the move in the direction of the ocean, ever deeper into the park. I edged behind a tree, then peeked out just in time to watch him vanish yet again, this time behind a hedge of oleander.

I waited for a gap in the traffic, then crossed the road and hurried through the grove where Linton had taken temporary refuge. When I emerged in the meadow on the other side, Linton was visible again, raincoat flapping around his legs, scarf trailing down his back, trotting along the hedge that bordered the bowling fields where he used to meet his son. I stayed put until he disappeared beyond the bowlers' nifty clubhouse, then set out in hot pursuit.

He led me a merry chase, over hill and dale, through grove and meadow, past the aquarium and the Temple of Music, behind the Japanese Tea Garden and the Boathouse at Stow Lake. Eventually, he must have decided he'd ditched me, perhaps because from a distance I looked more like friend than foe, because at that point it became less a chase than an odyssey.

His mission became not flight but food—at every opportunity Linton examined the contents of trash barrels and dumpsters, picking up any empty cans he came across and sticking them in the pockets of his raincoat to redeem for the deposit pursuant to the state's inadequate recyling program. Occasionally he would sniff at a bag or bottle and, if no signs of spoilage were evident, would consume the dregs before adding the container to his stash: supper alfresco and on the run. I could only gag and watch.

I stayed some thirty yards behind, far enough to avoid detection on the few occasions he looked my way. By the time we crossed Kennedy Drive and made our way around Lloyd Lake and the Portals to the Past, I was eager to get where we were going, which I assumed to be his home. My car, I estimated from the state of my fatigue, was at least three miles at my back.

At about this point it occurred to me that if I was going to write a book about the Linton case, this would be the chase scene. A few minutes later, as I felt a blister rising on my heel, I decided that if I was going to try to interest Hollywood in the story, I would have to spice it up. Motorcycles, maybe. Or, given what was the most popular mode of conveyance through the park on summer weekends—roller skates.

The journey hadn't ended. After wending our way through the forest west of Marx Meadow, we crossed a slender bridle path, skirted the miniature boats on Spreckels Lake and the hulk of the Senior Citizens Center, crossed the deserted dog training area, then plunged into woods again. This time we proceeded north to a point where I could hear the roar of traffic from somewhere ahead of us. For a moment I thought we were going to leave the park entirely and continue the chase through the city streets, but as I was trying to guess Linton's true objective he ducked into a bulge of vegetation and disappeared from view.

I was only twenty yards behind, but in no hurry to make up the distance until I knew what he was up to. When nothing had happened two minutes later, I moved forward, using techniques I'd learned in basic training at Fort Lewis a quarter century before, lacking only a weapon and a war to make it real. But when I got to where I'd lost him, I could find no trail to follow; my way was blocked by the dense tangle of brush that flourished beneath a stand of pine and cypress.

Surprisingly, I was within spitting distance of Fulton Street, so close I could see cars flashing past gaps in the greenery. I broke through the shrubs and looked up and down on the chance that Linton had left the park, but I saw no one familiar on either Fulton or Forty-first Avenue, the nearest cross street heading north. I ducked back into the park, took off my bulky jacket, took out my knife, and descended, tentatively and reluctantly, into the thicket that was the only place left to look.

The going was tough—I could have used a bearer or a bulldozer—and the more avidly I attacked it the more impenetrable the underbrush seemed to be. But at least the way was downhill—the undergrowth masked a steep falloff of topography. Before long I formed the distinct impression that I was hacking my way into a grave.

Ten minutes later, all I could see was more of the same—vines and branches interlocked in a leafy net so tightly woven its primary purpose must have been to keep me out. Spitting bark dust from my mouth and picking thorns from my hands, I resolved to push through to the other side, more because of the challenge in the task than the prospect of finding Linton squirreled away somewhere en route.

I shoved yet another branch out of my way and ducked beneath a sweep of cypress. Then, two steps deeper into the gloom, I heard the clank of bending metal. I stopped my dig immediately but heard nothing more revealing than the labor of my tortured lungs, so I took another cautious step. As the ground gave way a trifle, a metallic burp echoed in the arbor once again, this time from beneath me.

I eased to my knees. After brushing away the leaves and bark, I discovered I was kneeling on an indeterminate expanse of blue, scratched and rusted, thick enough to hold me, apparently immobile. I crawled forward, one step and then a second, scraping away detritus as I went. Although it took only seconds for me to figure out what it was I had discovered, by the time I did so I was tumbling helplessly through space, as though I'd fallen off a cliff.

Luckily, the drop wasn't far. Shortly after impact I had caught my breath, collected my wits, and moved enough joints to know I wasn't badly hurt. From my new perch it was obvious what had happened—I'd fallen off the top of a car, Wade Linton's presumably, the one he'd inhabited at the Panhandle, then driven under cover of night into the thicket bordering Fulton Street after being ousted from the former location, the one he'd painstakingly enshrouded in leaves and branches and earth and sod in order to hide it from the legions of gardeners bent on rooting out the homeless from the park. With a mix of effort and admiration, I replaced the camouflaging canopy as best I could and then took stock.

The hollow I'd fallen into was a makeshift patio adjacent to the passenger side of the car, carved into the hillside and topped by a handmade weave of vegetation. Given the circumstances, it was furnished in high style—car seat easy chair, air filter lid frying pan, radiator barbecue grill, hubcap lazy Susan, spare tire coffee table. In contrast, the car itself was comparatively barren—little more than a bed in a steel shell, littered with linens that ranged from grimy bed sheets stolen off a nearby line to strips of roofing felt pilfered from a construction site. There were a few luxuries—portable radio, tiny reading light, several well-worn books—but when I searched for a typewriter or other tools of authorship, I didn't find any. And Linton himself was nowhere to be seen.

I wondered how long he'd lived down here—Robinson Crusoe come to San Francisco—wondered how long his idyll could survive before it was discovered and dismantled, wondered who or what it harmed that people like Wade Linton had homesteaded a corner of a public park.

Wondering at that and more, I was languishing on the

car seat, feet stretched to the spare tire, when I heard a sound from somewhere behind me, possibly a pinecone that had dislodged and plunged to earth, possibly Wade Linton returning to his lair.

I turned but saw nothing. In the next moment, as some sense told me the noise was both deliberate and human, someone clubbed me from behind and I sank into a pit far deeper than the one in which Wade had made his stand.

Some people will sacrifice anyone or anything to survive. There are others whose chief impulse in the face of adversity is to sacrifice themselves. I tend to be one of the latter, but I take no credit for it. Indeed, I have come to believe that self-sacrifice is the most basic form of cowardice.

HOMAGE TO HAMMURABI, p. 133

Chapter
23

I woke in a bog so glutinous I assumed there had been a downpour while I lay unconscious. But only my brain was clouded; as my senses revived and my aches and pains gradually laid claim to all of them, I realized the muck was a blend of the blood that was escaping from the wound in my scalp and the ground that had made my mattress after Wade Linton slugged me from behind.

I tried to get up but couldn't lift my head. Only after an agonizing collapse of time—seconds became epochs, minutes eons—did I manage to sit up, regain my equilibrium, remember where I was, locate the source of the blood and press my handkerchief to it. Still, it was another ten minutes before I felt well enough to try to stand and ten more before I tried it again, this time successfully. Somewhere in the process, I discovered I was clutching a buckle in my hand, a souvenir of the assault more weighty than the lump on my head and the blood that was leaching through the algid earthen floor.

I stuck the buckle in my pocket, leaned against the fender of the car long enough to make sure I was stable, more or less, then adjourned to the car seat sofa. In the part of my consciousness not given over to diagnosing my condition, it seemed that things were different, that Linton's personal effects were more visible, and possibly more numerous, than they had been before my fall. I should have checked it out, of course, in search of leads to where Linton might have gone, but a stronger sense was telling me that I was not yet capable of deduction, that significance and symbol were beyond me and would be until my brain had been given time to repair its wires and reroute its messages.

I looked up. The burrow seemed so well secreted as a result of the arrangement of foliage overhead and the cut of the car into the slope that there was little room for discovery unless someone plunged willy-nilly into the thicket the way I had a while before. Like MacArthur, I would leave, recover, and return.

Though not right away. My head was a balloon of blood, pulsing and throbbing, expanding and contracting, in time to my labored heartbeats. Waves of dizziness passed through me like bite-size hangovers, so that I was no longer sanguine about fighting my way out of the thicket the way I'd come in. As I endured yet another wave of nausea, I spotted what looked to be a path leading the direction opposite the way I'd come. That bit of encouragement let me stiffen my resolve. After one last look at Linton's refuge, I gathered as many of my wits as came when I called and lurched toward freedom.

It took a good version of forever for me to reach the clearing east of the thicket, and a sequel to find a path to Fulton Street. When I finally reached its open vistas and firm footing, I felt something akin to resurrection.

When I started down Fulton I had every intention of walking all the way to my car, but my head hurt so badly and my balance, jostled by the blow and befuddled by my effort to keep my handkerchief pressed against my wound, was so consistently precarious I opted for leaning against a light pole until I could flag a cab.

Several passed me by before a kind soul slowed to a stop. When he saw the bloody handkerchief he laughed. "Touch football, right?"

"Right." I wrestled with the door, fell into the rear seat, and told him where to take me.

"You know your problem, don't you?" he said when we were underway.

"What?"

"The threads. You looked like a bunch of Nixons out there, man; I mean, it's a *game*, not a negotiation, you dig? Get yourself one of those spandex jobs—knocks wind resistance to zero and there's nothing for the DBs to grab when you're cutting for the post."

I glanced at his license. The cabbie's name was Leo. He'd clearly been watching a game somewhere in the park, being played by guys like me. Though I'd convinced myself I was cleverly disguised as a transient, Leo joined the army that had seen through me right away.

When I got back to the office the phone was ringing. It took a long time to think of a reason to answer it.

"Marsh? It's Bryce," he began breathlessly. "I've been calling for hours; where have you been?"

"On a nature walk."

"I hardly think this is the time . . . oh. You're joking."

"Not really."

It didn't slow him down. "Anyway, listen; could I come down there for a minute?"

My stomach was making origami of itself. "When?"

"Now."

"Do you want me here, or do you just want to hang out in my office?"

"I want to see you, of course; I . . . You sound strange, Marsh. Has something happened?"

"Nothing helpful. What's the problem?"

"The rest of the book came in."

"Hammurabi?"

"Of course."

"Can't you give me the highlights over the phone? Or send it over by messenger? There are some things I need to—"

"I need a place to *keep* it. I'm afraid to leave it at Periwinkle, in case there's another break-in."

I leaned back in my chair to see if I could get my blood to flow in the other direction. "What break-in?"

"The one we had last night."

"Anything taken?"

"Not that I could tell, but I'm sure they were looking for

Hammurabi. You still *have* it, don't you?" he asked in a sudden burst of panic. "It's the only copy, you know."

"I have it," I reassured him, then pulled out the bottom drawer of my desk to make sure, then decided to hide it in a safer place.

"We need to talk about this, Marsh. It won't take long. Please?"

I sat up and waited for my brain to right itself as well. "Come on over. But do me a favor and get some aspirin on the way. The biggest bottle they've got. If they're having a sale on skulls, pick one of those up, too."

I hung up in the middle of his question.

By the time Bryce buzzed in the outer office I'd washed my face and hands, rinsed most of the mud and blood out of my hair, and changed into the spare set of clothes I keep at the office for times like this. The only additional remedy at my disposal was scotch, and when I opened the door I was holding a juice glass full of it in each hand.

I guess I hadn't done as good a restoration job as I thought, because when he saw me Bryce quailed. "My God. What on earth *happened*?"

"I finally found your author."

"Dennis Worthy?"

I laughed or tried to. "Dennis Worthy is a figment of the imagination, remember? The author's name is Linton."

He pointed. "And *he* did that to you?"

I handed Bryce his drink. "I think he wants to remain anonymous—you'll have a tough time getting him on *Oprah*."

Bryce followed me into the inner office and sat on the couch next to a box of pistol rounds and the bloody handkerchief I'd rinsed in the sink and spread to dry. His shirt and slacks were rumpled, his hair was a tangled mess, his eyes were bloodshot and bleary. Food Not Bombs would have fed him without a qualm.

"You should see a doctor," he advised as I was about to issue the same suggestion.

I nodded. "Friday night."

"But this is only . . . oh. Poker night. Is Goldsberry still taking your money?"

"Along with everyone else's."

"I miss those nights."

"They miss you. Charley was saying just the other day how much he'd like to see you back in the game."

"Maybe when all this is over . . ."

We shared some wistful silence. "So tell me about *Hammurabi*," I said finally. "What's the thrilling climax? Who did the dirty deed?"

Bryce closed his eyes and leaned back until his head found refuge with the wall. "You won't believe it."

"Sure I will. I believe anything—I even believe George Bush when he says he has personal qualms about abortion."

Bryce waved away my joke. "Her father."

"Whose father?"

"Amanda Keefer's. When Dennis Worthy gets out of jail and goes looking for the guy who framed him, what he finds out is, the girl was sexually abused by her father."

It hurt even to frown. "I don't get it. Who was her father? How did he get the school to go along with the frame-up?"

Bryce opened his eyes. "The headmaster."

"Bullshit. Rufus Finner's too old to . . ." I stopped and shook my head. "Now *I'm* doing it."

Bryce looked as pained as I felt. "You still think this happened at Sebastian, don't you?"

"Don't you?"

"I don't know."

"I don't either. But *something* happened there, and it's close enough to the stuff in the book to upset Marvin Gillis. How's the litigation going, by the way?"

"We go to court on Thursday. Andy says I'll have to testify. He also says the chances of defeating the motion are only fifty-fifty." Bryce shook his head helplessly. "So what do we do now?"

"We find Amanda Keefer."

"How?"

"There are two people I can think of who might know who she is; one of them's your stepdaughter." I raised a brow. "You still want me to handle it?"

Bryce fidgeted. "Jane Ann gets upset if she thinks I'm prying." His abdication ended with a sigh.

"Prying is my profession," I said, my brain's effort at

evolution apparently stuck somewhere in the nineteen thirties. "Where can I find her?"

"She lives in one of those lofts by the wharf."

He gave me the address and I noted it in my book. "I'll let you know how it comes out."

Bryce stood up. "I'm going to publish, Marsh. Now that I have the entire manuscript, I'm bringing it out as soon as I can."

I raised a brow. "Without talking to Linton?"

"I'm counting on you to find him. And when you do, I'll give him what he wants—I'm sure he'll be reasonable." When he looked at me he sagged, as though I was proof to the contrary. "But like I said—I need the book."

"I know you do. I just hope it doesn't—"

Bryce shook his head. "I mean *literally*. I need to get the first part of the manuscript back from you so I can get a copy editor on it. I've got a free-lancer all lined up."

I had a sudden impulse, the kind you get in this business, the kind that either makes you feel smarter than you are or inclined to turn in your license. "I don't have it. Not here, I mean. I'll pick it up this evening and bring it by."

Bryce frowned. "There's not a problem, is there? I mean, Hemingway left the only copy of some stories and a novel on a train and never found them again."

"I've got it, Bryce. It's in my most secret place; I'll bring it to Periwinkle tonight. But I think you should wait before putting it into production."

"Why?"

"If there *is* a real Amanda Keefer, and if she really was abused, her father isn't going to appreciate reading a book that accuses him of doing it."

"This is *fiction*, I keep telling you."

"And I keep telling you that it doesn't matter to the courts *what* you say it is."

Bryce paused. "I guess I'll deal with that problem when I come to it."

"I think you're going to come to it pretty soon."

"What do you mean?"

"I think I'm starting to figure this thing out. But I need more time to put the pieces together."

When he saw the look on my face, he said, "What?"

"It doesn't add up, you know."

"What doesn't?"

"The plot. Of *Hammurabi*."

"How do you mean?"

"For one thing, why would an up-and-coming young man allow them to put him in jail for something he didn't do?"

"Worthy talks about that in the book, remember? He didn't want Amanda to have to reveal herself in court as an abuse victim, and he didn't want his family to have to hear those kinds of things being said about *him*."

"But he didn't put up a fight. He didn't hire a lawyer, he didn't hire an investigator to look into her story to find her motive for lying—hell, if we can believe the book, he didn't even confront her himself. He just sat back and let them lock him up."

"It seems curious, I know, but . . . Maybe it *is* just fiction, Marsh. Maybe *none* of it really happened."

"Even fiction needs a better plot than that," I said, and picked up the phone.

Bryce reached out to stop me before I could dial a number. "There's one more thing, Marsh."

"What?"

"You didn't ask what Dennis Worthy did when he learned Amanda's father was the one who actually assaulted her."

"Okay, what did he do?"

"He hunted him down and killed him."

"*Hammurabi* again."

"Right."

"The plot seems to be getting thicker."

"My advice is to do what's right," the lawyer advised me.

"If I knew what's right, I would have already done it."

"Then perhaps I can point the way."

"Are you saying there's a solution that's best for all concerned?"

"From a certain perspective."

"What about from my perspective?"

"Your perspective is that there is no perspective," he said.

HOMAGE TO HAMMURABI, p. 156

Chapter
24

I didn't want to, and I tried very hard to find a reason not to, but in the end I placed a call to Charley Sleet. "You know that manuscript I had you check for prints?"

"Don't even ask; I got no more time for fairy tales."

"This tale just turned real."

"Yeah? How?"

"You remember I told you the guy who wrote the book might be out to avenge a frame laid on him some years back?"

"The innocent con. Right. Like I said, a fairy tale."

"The fairy just committed a battery."

"Against who?"

"Me."

Charley sighed an old cop's sigh. "Talk."

I talked, about *Hammurabi*, about learning the name of the author, about trailing him through the park, about the car and the cave and the blow to my head, about the threat in the final section of the book.

"So who's he got it in for?" Charley asked when I was done, cutting to the quick.

"I don't know yet," I admitted. "The only real-life name I have is Linton's."

"It might be nice if someone warned the guy this Linton's out to get him."

"I know, but I haven't identified the girl so I don't know her father. But I think I can get a name later today."

"What am I supposed to do in the meantime?"

"I thought you could go out to the park and put a scare into Linton, so he doesn't do anything dumb."

"Cons tend not to scare too easy, especially cons who don't have parole hanging over their heads."

"So ride herd on him for twenty-four hours. By then I should have this book thing figured out."

"And maybe by then Captain Harris will have me back on the beat."

"You never *left* the beat."

He relented. "Where'd you say this playhouse was?"

I described the route to Linton's hideaway. "And Charley?"

"Yeah?"

"Make it solo, huh? And make sure he knows you're not there to blow the whistle on him to the park police."

"How about busting him for the fungo on your noggin?"

"Don't do that, either."

"Any other laws you want me to ignore?"

"The speed limits."

Charley cursed me and hung up. I pried my Buick out of the lot and drove down to the wharf.

Jane Ann Gillis had the top-floor loft in a former warehouse that had been refurbished without regard to expense. The security system included a video camera focused on my nose and an audio system that was sufficiently sophisticated for me to carry on a polite conversation with Jane Ann while overhearing the frantic scrapings and straightenings as she tried to make the place presentable before she let me in. I guessed the commotion had a lot to do with the disposal of illegal drugs.

The buzzer finally got me through the thick steel door and into an airy lobby topped by a skylight three floors up and dominated by a delicate staircase that was a monument to an ironworker's art. Since I was still feeling the effects of my mugging, I bypassed the stairway in favor of the elevator. When it came to a stop three flights up, it opened into Jane Ann's bathroom.

The elevator retreated at my back as Jane Ann appeared

in the doorway, weary and unfocused. Beneath her gray shirt, red shorts, and black suspenders, her boots were white this time, knee-high, decorated with silver studs and turkey feathers. Given the site of our encounter, I was thankful she wasn't wearing a towel.

As she grasped her suspenders just below her clavicles, her smile was as kinetic and uncertain as my own mixed sentiments. "Rather a new concept in entryways, isn't it?" I said, gesturing to the primarily porcelain surroundings.

She raised a brow. "Foyers are such a waste of space—I thought I'd do something with mine."

"What happens when someone's using it?"

"Then someone else gets a big surprise."

She turned on a heel and led me into the core of the loft. It was vast, close to two thousand square feet, I guessed, entirely high-gloss white but for the vinyl that made the floor a horizontal vein of coal, so brightly lit by its skylights and spotlights it sparked a pain behind my eyes. The art on the walls was sadistic, blood-red shafts piercing puffy gray protuberances that were humanistic if not quite human. The furnishings were so simple—metal and white leather, stone and chrome and glass—they must have cost a fortune.

The guy on the couch was Lloyd, wearing nothing but black bikinis and a headset, his own flesh so concordant with the hide of the couch his body seemed possessed of only a curl and a crotch. On the table next to him was a photo of Jane Ann, incongruous in a gym suit, foot atop a soccer ball. If I could believe the CD jacket that leaned against the speakers, Lloyd's lullaby was the output of something called The Butthole Surfers. Next to the speakers, a pit bull was chained to a ring in the floor, but he didn't seem to mind.

I gestured toward the picture. "Were you on the Sebastian varsity?"

Jane Ann looked momentarily puzzled.

"You play in the infamous Balboa game?"

"How'd you know about that?"

"Emma Drayer told me."

My knowledge of Jane Ann's sporting career seemed to disturb her. "I don't know why you're here," she said. "Am I supposed to?"

I shook my head. "Not yet."

"Then why *are* you here?"

"It's time to talk."

"What about?"

I glanced at the couch, where Lloyd still lounged in headset seclusion. "Can we do this in private?"

She looked around the room. "This is a loft. Privacy's not included."

"Maybe Lloyd would like to go out for a doughnut."

"Lloyd never goes out in the daytime."

"If we tied a bag over his head, he'd never know."

She wanted to laugh but wouldn't let herself. I reached for her hand and tugged her back the way we'd come, then closed the door behind us. "Which do you want, toilet or tub?"

She hesitated, then turned down the toilet lid and sat on it. I kicked off my shoes, climbed in the tub and stretched out as fully as its chilly dimensions would allow.

"Is this about Bryce?" Jane Ann asked as I was still getting comfortable.

"This is about a lot of people. Including you."

"But—"

I held up a hand. "Hear me out a minute." I rolled to my side to relieve the pressure on my coccyx. "Ordinarily I don't reveal a client's confidences to anyone. Not even a daughter."

"Stepdaughter."

"Right. But I'm going to make an exception in this case, because I think you know most of it already."

"Most of what?"

"First of all, you know about the book."

"What book?"

I met her eye. "Your fingerprints were on the title page, Jane Ann. This is going to take all day if we spend the first two hours dancing with each other."

"I . . . okay. I know about the book."

"Thank you. I thought for a while you might have written it, actually, and I still think it's a possibility." I waited for a denial or a confirmation but she didn't give me either. "But let's just say you were prowling around Bryce's desk, the way kids do with their parents' papers, and this time you found a prize. And you told Lloyd, and he told your father."

When I looked at her, her eyes were closed. "You don't know anything about this," she said, so softly I almost didn't hear her, the admonition so similar to the one Lloyd had brought to my office they must have been rehearsed. "You don't know what's at stake."

"What did you think when you read it?" I went on cavalierly, deliberately ignoring her comment, trying to inject emotion into the situation. "Kind of a Russian tone to it, I thought. Dostoyevski, maybe—he was a prisoner like Linton, wasn't he? Or maybe Kafka. That was Lloyd's suggestion, but I haven't read much Kafka except for the story about the guy who turned into a cockroach. So what do *you* think? Critically, I mean. Is *Hammurabi* a great book or not?"

"I thought it was derivative and sentimental."

I continued to tease, trying to make her angry, on the theory that anger spurs paroxysm and encourages revelation. "There was some of that, all right," I said. "But what about the plot? The sexual thing? That's certainly topical these days—old men taking advantage of young girls?—it's apparently as common as colds. So the commercial possibilities are exciting, wouldn't you say? And the frame-up. Vengeance *always* sells, they tell me. Those Charles Bronson movies? *Very* big. Plus it was true to life, didn't you think? Bryce says its attention to detail reminds him of Capote."

I looked at her till she was forced to answer. "I didn't think it was *any* of that."

"Really? How did you find it flawed?"

"This is America. No one gets put in jail for something they didn't do."

"You sound like the Republican I know. And the cop I know also, come to think of it."

Although her face was red and her eyes were hot, she didn't take the bait.

"Come on, Jane Ann, let's cut the lit chat. A lot of people are hooked into this book already, to the point that someone's life may be in danger."

She blinked. "What did you say?"

"The rest of the manuscript turned up. What happens is, the schoolteacher gets out of jail and hunts down the person who framed him. You might want to know what happens then."

"What?"

"He puts a bullet in his brain."

"*Whose* brain?"

"The man who really molested the girl. It's an eye-for-an-eye type thing."

"The Code of Hammurabi."

"Babylonia. Right. Eighteenth century. B.C."

"That's crazy."

"Maybe. And maybe it's fantasy, fiction, fable, whatever. But I can't afford to take the chance. And neither can Bryce."

She tugged at one of her suspenders, stretched it to its limit, then let it snap back. "What do you want from me?"

"Just a name."

"What name?"

"The real name of the Amanda Keefer character in the book."

She looked perplexed. "Amanda who?"

"The girl who was assaulted at Sebastian." It was time to press her. "You know what I'm talking about—who was it, Jane Ann?"

She shook her head and clasped her knees.

"I need to know. Right now."

"Why?"

"Because her father could be in danger."

Her eyes were vacant and unknowning. "Why?"

"According to the book, her father's the one who molested her, then put the frame on Linton."

Jane Ann stood up, the back of her hand pressed against her lips, as though another word would cause her world to shatter. "I . . . How can this be *happening*? Who's *doing* this to me?"

Her panic was real and surprising. Despite her mother's fears, I hadn't expected Jane Ann to be personally involved in the Linton business, though I did expect her to know something about it. I'd expected to learn that something— the names of the players, if nothing else—without much trouble, because why would she resist telling me if she knew her silence could be jeopardizing someone's safety?

"Was it you, Jane Ann?" I asked softly.

She shook her head.

"Were you the student who was molested?"

Her eyes were wet and wretched. "There wasn't anything *like* that, I . . . Please stop, Mr. Tanner."

"I don't know that much about this, Jane Ann. But I do know if you make a man spend six years in jail for something he didn't do, he's likely to lose focus on the distinction between right and wrong. I don't know what Linton's going to do, but if I was his lawyer I'd plead temporary insanity to any crime he commits from this point on." I got out of the tub and stood before her with what I hoped was compassion. "Was it Gillis? Did your father abuse you sexually, Jane Ann? . . . What did he have on Linton that let him stick Linton with the blame?"

Jane Ann curled forward in a convulsion of denial. I was still trying to come up with an effective approach when the bathroom door opened and Lloyd stood outlined by the back light of the loft, headset loose about his neck, skin as bloodless as the tiles that surrounded us. "Tell him, Jane Ann," he ordered.

We waited for her to speak, but she didn't move a muscle beyond the one that loosed her tears. Lloyd's sneer turned her way, branded her with its verdict, then returned to me. "Carrie," he said, as though he were identifying a corpse. "Carrie Devlin's the one he nailed."

When I looked at Jane Ann, her eyes were locked on a square of tile, as black as doom beneath her feet.

"*Tell* him," Lloyd insisted again.

As slowly as a sunrise, Jane Ann raised her head and nodded. Satisfied, Lloyd plugged the headset into his ears and returned to the couch. As Jane Ann began to sob, I climbed out of the tub and headed for the elevator.

When it was on its way to get me, I looked back. "Why did they call you Fishy?"

She sniffed. "Gillis . . . gills . . . get it?"

"Do you like the name?"

"I hate it."

"Was Lloyd around the loft this morning?"

"Probably, but I was at my art lesson. Why?"

"I thought maybe he went for a walk in the park."

"It doesn't sound like him," she said. "But then what does?"

"Fingernails on a blackboard," I suggested, then entered the elevator and pressed button number one.

When I found her, finally, Amanda Keefer was alternately brazen and apologetic, braggart and penitent. Her changeableness was such that I began to fear for her sanity, and indeed she advised me that she had been getting therapeutic help.

It was hours before she began to talk truthfully, and hours more before I got it all. After I had it, I went out and bought a gun, the type recommended by my cell mate. "No way they walk away," he promised.

Then I went looking for her father.

HOMAGE TO HAMMURABI, p. 289

Chapter
25

After I left Jane Ann and Lloyd, I found the nearest telephone. If *Hammurabi* was actually autobiographical, and if Carrie Devlin was the real-life counterpart of the fictional Amanda Keefer, then Wade Linton could be on his way to Stockton to find her father. But when I called Noe Valley I didn't get an answer. Since I didn't know Bridget Devlin well enough to try to track her down, I recycled my quarter and called the clerk of the Superior Court in the person of one of his assistants, my old friend Sadie.

"Well, well," Sadie commented after they'd managed to track her down. "We don't see you around this way much anymore."

"I'm hanging out with a better class of person."

"No more criminals?"

"They're criminals, all right; but they're not the kind that get caught."

I got a sour reproof instead of the laugh I sought. "That's nice to hear; I was afraid it was something personal."

"You're still my favorite female in the Civic Center."

"Okay, Marsh." She sighed resignedly. "What can I do for you this time?"

She'd succeeded in making me feel like what I'd aspired to only hours before—a tramp. "I need a peek at a file."

"Well, come on down to City Hall and—"

"Not an active file, a closed one. Criminal case—docketed in 'eighty-three or maybe 'four. *People versus Linton.*"

"I don't suppose you have a number."

"Sorry."

"It's probably in storage, and you know our vault—people have gone down there and never been seen again."

"If there was another way, I'd use it, Sadie."

"If there was another way, I'd *make* you use it."

"All I want is the best you've got."

"I don't bring that to the office." Her tone thickened with intimacy. "How come when you had it three years ago, you decided it wasn't enough?"

"That's not the way it was," I protested, though I couldn't remember if she was right or not. The recent reappearance of both Betty and Sadie in my life was making me feel like Scrooge, haunted by the ghosts of romance past. "The breakup was mutual and you know it."

"Breakups are *never* mutual," she ventured, then scurried back to business. "I'll check the index and give you a call."

After I'd chewed over Sadie's outburst long enough to establish my blamelessness in the matter of our parting, I tried the Devlin number a second time. There was still no answer. I thought there might be a Stockton phone book among my collection back at the office; if so, it might let me bypass the intermediary, which is always a good idea when the intermediary is an ex-wife.

I was counting the Devlin listings in the Stockton book and gnawing on a day-old bagel when the phone rang. "I been after you for an hour; it would help if you'd go cellular." Charley was sufficiently irascible to indicate he had a problem. "You better get out here."

"The park?"

"The school."

"Sebastian?"

"That's the one. I found your buddy Linton."

"And?"

"He's dead."

I swore. "How?"

"Some janitor clubbed him."

"O'Shea?"

"You know him?"

"Some. How did it happen?"

"Apparently your guy Linton was trying to break into the school earlier this evening and O'Shea had to club him to stop him. Clubbed him hard, clubbed him often."

"What do you mean 'apparently'? What does O'Shea say about it?"

"He's not around. The stiff just turned up a while ago—it was in a light well by the gym; some kid found it chasing a Frisbee."

"Shit."

"That's what I said when I ripped my goddamned sportcoat climbing in there. Which was mild compared to what I said when I saw him—his skull looks like frigging aspic. You got any idea what he was up to?"

"Not for sure."

"I better not find out that's a lie, Tanner; my stomach's too delicate for gore."

"I'm sorry," I said, and meant it. "I'll be there in twenty minutes." I dug my car out of the lot and drove out to Cow Hollow.

Whatever else he had done in life, for good or ill, Wade Linton had touched me with *Hammurabi,* had become both kindred spirit and inspiration, so I was feeling something akin to the loss I felt when other friends, more of them than I cared to think about, had died unexpectedly. Linton's demise seemed particularly tragic—the wasted years in jail, the achievement with the book, the obsession with a wrong whose rectification would likely return him to prison, all while living homeless and alone and separated from his son. If you see life as essentially ironic, it could easily seem inevitable that Linton would be found dead in a bludgeoned heap back where it had all begun.

A part of my mood was reserved for Arthur O'Shea, whose itchy sparring with his militaristic past would not let him live easily with what he'd had to do to Linton. But my sympathy was reserved for J. Alfred Prufrock's young namesake. I could still hear the way he had spoken about his dad—the reverence and warmth in his tone, the longing for reconciliation—and I wondered who would break the news to him. I hoped it was someone more magnanimous than his mother seemed to be.

Yellow police lines stretched across the playground like the trappings of a school yard game—Red Rover, maybe, or Flag Tag—but the faces within the boundaries were anything but playful. The investigation was still active, so no one paid much attention when I ducked into the square of officialdom. I saw a couple of detectives I knew slightly, along with a uniformed patrolman and the assistant ME. I was about to ask if Charley Sleet was around when he came around the corner of the building.

"I love the hell out of finding dead people, Tanner. That must be why I look forward to doing your work for you."

"Sorry, Charley. I didn't envision this." I reached in my pocket. "But I can save you some time with the evidence."

I pulled out the buckle I'd torn off Linton's coat as I'd gone under. "Don't waste time looking for this puppy—I'm the one who took it off him, not the killer."

Charley took the buckle and examined it. "You got this how?"

"Like I told you—when I trailed Linton to his place in the park he was lying in wait for me. He clubbed me from behind, but just before I checked out I made a grab for him. This was all I came up with."

"And this was when?"

I looked at my watch. "About six hours ago."

Charley shook his head. "I examined him myself. There was no buckle missing from anything he's wearing now, and from the look of him he didn't have a wardrobe that let him change outfits twice a day." My expression spurred Charley to defend himself. "If you don't believe me, ask Savin. He's catching the case for Homicide."

"I believe you, Charley," I said, and shook my head. Every time I reached a conclusion in the case, it turned out to be wrong. I said as much to Charley, then tried to readjust the facts. "Someone must have been lying in wait for Linton; I may have chased him into the trap. Any chance he was killed in the park and then dumped here?"

Charley shook his head. "All the ingredients were over in that frigging light well." He pulled a plastic bag out of his coat and dropped the buckle in it and took it over to a technician, muttered some words of advice, then came back to where I was standing.

This time when he saw my look Charley patted me on the shoulder. "It happens that way sometimes. I could have saved a thousand lives over the last thirty years, except I'm not psychic. My guess is, neither are you."

"Good guess." I looked at the school building. It was as oppressive as ever, unfazed by what had transpired beneath its aristocratic gaze. "What was Linton trying to do, did anyone know?"

Charley shrugged. "Get in the building is all I know so far."

"Who have you talked to?"

"Just the only teacher who was around when the kid found the corpse. Plus I called the headmaster."

"Finner."

"That's the one."

"What's he say about it?"

"He chose to reserve comment till his boss showed up."

"Marvin Gillis," I said.

Charley looked at me. "So that's no surprise to you, either."

"Nope."

"What does a heavy hitter like Gillis have to do with this joint?"

"He's chairman of the board of the Sebastian trustees. He loves it like a son—he lights up like a freebaser every time he talks about the place."

"Think he knows anything about this Linton thing?"

I never lie to Charley; well, hardly ever. But sometimes I tell him less than unexpurgated truth. "If he does, he won't tell you about it."

"I'd like to have a reason to press him. You got one?"

I shook my head. "Not yet." I took a look around, and Charley knew why.

"If you're thinking you want to see the body, I suggest you change your mind," he said. "It'll stay with you."

"I have to, Charley."

It was worse than he'd said, of course—violent death is always worse than the words that describe it, even the words of writers like Wade Linton. It's why war didn't disappear with the *Iliad*; why murder didn't end with Raskolnikov. As I leaned against the wall of the light well, I tried to tell myself that in a larger sense Linton had been dead already, that his disgrace at Sebastian, justified or not, had put a meaningful life beyond him, that his future would be as alien and ostracized as his present. But then I remembered Alfred, and the rationale fell apart.

I sensed a shift in my professional perspective as well. Although I'd been hired to find the author of a book, ever since I'd pasted a face and a name and a history onto my objective, my focus had become an effort to find Linton before he accomplished his quest for retribution and added a real crime to his fabricated one. Well, Wade Linton wasn't going to kill anyone now, but as I climbed out of the light well and returned to Charley's side, I asked myself why Linton had been skulking around Sebastian instead of on his way to Stockton to hunt down Danny Devlin.

"Did he have anything on him?" I asked when Charley raised a brow.

"Just this." Charley reached in his pocket and pulled out another plastic bag. In it was a small snapshot of Wade Linton's young son.

"His name is Al," I said. "He lives on Fell, at that DMV address you got for me. He's a nice kid. Go easy when you tell him."

"Maybe you'd like to do it yourself."

Although it was a burden I should have taken on, I didn't. "Sorry, Charley. I've got things to do."

I hurried to my car and drove west. This time I parked on Fulton, half a block from where I'd flagged the cab that afternoon. I got some things from my trunk—flashlight, gloves, gun—then slipped through the hedge into the suddenly sinister reaches of the park.

The only light was from the streetlamp, which wasn't enough to illumine the way. The thicket was as forbidding as when I'd left it, the going difficult even with a periodic assist from my flashlight. With senses more useful than eyesight, I crept back to the cave by the easier route, wary of detection by the park police, equally wary of another assault. After listening to be sure no one had been trailing me, I used the flashlight to inspect the area as closely as I'd intended to before the meteor had landed on my skull that afternoon.

It was a kid's idea of a perfect hideout, snug, secret, soothing, the stuff of *Tom Sawyer* and *The Hardy Boys*, but my blood was on its ground and its creator was a corpse so the image didn't last. On the way down, I'd decided to start with the trunk of the car, but after I worked my way to the rear of the vehicle I discovered someone had beaten me to it—the lid had been pried open and the contents were as scattered as if the woman with the bat had been looking for her breakfast. As far as I could tell, there was nothing left but junk.

I crawled back to the patio and sat on the car seat and pondered the situation. Wade Linton must have been on a mission when he was killed, but the place of his demise indicated it was something other than the one suggested by the concluding chapters of *Hammurabi*. The person who'd slugged me must have known what it was and was bent on keeping Linton from accomplishing his task, which meant it was probably someone I'd encountered during my investigation, someone I'd alerted to the threat Linton constituted, the threat I still couldn't fathom. It's disconcerting when you know you've been close to a killer without knowing it, and it's more so when someone might still be alive if you'd done something different. I got rid of such thoughts the way I always do—I convinced myself I'd done the best I could. Also like always, it wasn't quite enough.

I kicked idly at the tire and heard a muffled thud. It made me think of hidden, hollow places, which made me think of drugs and where the couriers hide them, which made me think of rocker panels and car doors. I returned to the Datsun, opened the only door that would, tapped around its interior circumference, and decided it was worth a look. Conscious that I was disturbing evidence, I got out my knife and put on my gloves and sliced into the plastic that formed the inside panel of the door.

It was a treasure trove of sorts—dozens of items had been stuffed into the narrow cavity and they all spilled out

over the ground after they were liberated by my knife. At
first I didn't see anything of interest—they were personal
effects primarily, from Linton's time at Sebastian—some
pens and pencils, a ruler and compass, a photo of Linton's
wife and son with little Alfred a doughy lump in his
mother's arms. Of more interest was a Sebastian *Senator,*
the same edition I'd examined at Mrs. Devlin's. There were
some college catalogs for that year as well—Stanford and
Cal, Occidental and Pomona—and one more item—a file
folder bound in rubber bands, crisp and official and provocative.

I tugged off my gloves and picked up the yearbook.
There was nothing remarkable about it until I came to the
senior section. There, beside the pictures of at least a dozen
students, Linton or someone had written a series of numbers, one above the other, in blue-black rows. The numbers
next to Carrie Devlin were 2.7, 938, 3.6 and 1215. Jane
Ann Gillis had a different set—2.4, 1016, 3.4 and 1332.
Her friend Lloyd's were 2.2, 888, 3.5 and 1382. Several
other pictures, of kids I had never heard of, were similarly
annotated. I thumbed through the rest of the book but found
no further scribblings.

I replaced the yearbook and picked up the file folder.
The rubber bands slid off with a twang and the folder fell
open in my hands. Its contents were obvious—a set of
course transcripts from Sebastian, at least fifty of them,
photocopied and arranged alphabetically. There seemed to
be no pattern—both boys and girls, a variety of courses
taken, a spectrum of grade averages. The transcripts were
not complete—they failed to include the last semester of the
senior year—and the only thing they seemed to have in
common was the name of the academic adviser—someone
named Brian Finney. I put the material back in the folder
and it and the other materials back in the door cavity, then
left the park and found a phone.

Bridget Devlin was finally at home. "Are you going to
be there for the next hour?"

"I'm going to be here for eternity."

"I'll see you in fifteen minutes."

"It's pretty late," she parried quickly, then changed her
mind. "Not that I've got anything better to do. And who

knows? You might do something that will make me laugh."
The prospect cheered her for two seconds. "Is it a social
call, or more about Wade?"

My impulse to tell her about Linton's death was auto-
matically subordinated to the possibility that it might be
more productive if I sprang it on her later. As I held my
tongue, I decided I was meaner than I used to be.

I dug out another quarter and got Sadie's number from
my little black book. She answered on the seventh ring. As
I told her who it was, I heard "All the Way" in the background.

I laughed. "Sinatra's still the mood of choice, I hear."

"This is not a good time, Tanner," Sadie observed in a
whisper.

"Sorry, but things are happening and I need to get in
front of the curve. Did you come up with anything on that
file I asked you to check?"

"That's the easiest job you ever gave me."

"Why?"

"The file's under seal. Court order—Judge Hoskins. No
way I can get at it."

"Hoskins. That son of a bitch."

"That seems to be the consensus."

"You didn't happen to come across the name of the
defense counsel, did you?"

"As it happens, I did. The defendant was represented by
Julius Messenger, Esquire."

"Why is that name familiar?"

"Julius is known as Mercury in certain circles."

"Why?"

"Because he's the Messenger to the Gods. His specialty
is defending the embarrassingly delinquent offspring of the
extravagantly rich and famous. On suitably remunerative
occasions he disposes of their inconvenient issue as well."

"What does that mean?"

"Mercury is legendary for arranging private adoptions
for the progeny of pregnant little rich girls who forget to get
abortions."

When Amanda told me her story, I asked the question that was so often asked of me before I went to jail: "How could he do such a thing?"

A decade ago, I had no glimmerings of an answer. Today, I am able to suggest, "Perhaps he was very lonely."

HOMAGE TO HAMMURABI, p. 289

Chapter
26

Bridget Devlin was still pouty and paint-spattered and at war with the world. She made me stand in the doorway while she took an elongated look at her watch that suggested the hour was unspeakably uncivilized, though it was only ten o'clock. When I apologized again for the intrusion, it seemed to provoke her further. "Why are you here?" she demanded. "I have nothing to *do* with the Lintons. I don't *want* anything to do with the Lintons."

"I'm here about your daughter."

"We already *talked* about my daughter," she protested, but by now the plaint was frail and resigned. "What kind of trouble is she in? Please don't lie to me; I know something's happened—I haven't heard from Carrie in weeks. What is it, did she steal something? Or get caught with drugs? Is she in some Andalusian jail? What *is* it?"

I was shaking my head before she finished the projected rap sheet. "If she's in trouble at all, it's for something she did six years ago."

"Six years ago." She sighed. "Sebastian."

I didn't say anything.

"God." She folded her arms across her chest and leaned against the doorjamb. "Even after Wade arranged the scholarship, Carrie begged me not to send her. But I insisted. I told her it was the chance of a lifetime, the chance to really *make* something of herself, to have the same opportunities the *rich* kids had." She paused, remembering and regretting. "What I *really* meant was that it was a chance to prove I wasn't a failure, at least not as a parent, to show that I could do good things for my child even if I never managed to do much for myself."

She took a step back. "I guess you might as well come in. I've got some burgundy left, I think. It's just Gallo, but . . ."

"Gallo's fine."

Her smile was bleak. "I don't even know if we're supposed to drink Gallo anymore. For a while there we weren't, but I don't remember why."

"The farm workers, I think."

"Right. The farm workers. How are they doing these days? I've kind of lost track."

"Better. But not as good as the rest of us."

Her eyes were damp with sadness. "Are you sure?"

"Not really," I admitted.

She turned her back on me and my notion and walked toward the rear of the house. I hurried after her. When we got to the kitchen she pointed toward the cupboards. "Wine's in there, glasses to the left. I'll be in the studio, finishing up an outline so I can get into the guts of it first thing in the morning. Bring me a glass, too. We'll celebrate something."

"What?" I asked, conscious that given what I'd seen that evening at Sebastian, the most appropriate ceremony was a wake.

"Keeping ahead of the farmworkers. It's the door at the end of the hall."

Bridget Devlin left me in her kitchen and padded down the hallway, soundlessly, as though my presence had made her insubstantial. I rummaged in the cupboards until I'd found everything but a corkscrew, then made a second tour in search of that. The dishware and utensils indicated my hostess was living an overused life, without the systematic replacement of worn-out goods, without the injection of luxury or whim, without a trace of self-indulgence. I lived such a life myself, but I didn't regard it as an achievement.

It took me so long to find the corkscrew she came back

to see what I was up to. When I told her my problem she pulled out a drawer and rummaged brusquely through its unkempt contents until she came up with it.

"I was afraid if I did that I'd cut a finger off."

She shook her head. "Not in this house. I've never owned a sharp knife in my life. I suspect they don't exist."

I followed her down the hall to a door with a colorful quilt painted over its entire surface, in a geometry of bright enamels. When she opened it we confronted an eerie darkness that seemed to ooze out of the studio and envelope us like the Blob. She told me to wait where I was, then vanished into the gloom.

A moment later two rays of white light split the darkness, twin beams that were focused on two large rectangles that loomed like mainsails halfway across the room. The intensity of the light and the brilliance of its impact with the targets made me squint and shield my eyes. Suddenly a switch was flipped and the beams became multicolored, softer, inviting. A moment later, Bridget Devlin's shadow moved across the rectangle on the right, through the projection of what seemed to be a picture of a flower. In the clinging elastic of the blue-green light, she seemed to be wearing a rose tattoo. I thought for a moment she was going to stage a shadow play, but I finally realized she was working.

The light came from two side-by-side projectors containing matching slides of a yellow rose lying on a marble table next to a pewter goblet. Though the slides were identical, their targets were not. The square on the left was a movie screen, the one on the right a canvas, stretched tight, gessoed white. Standing in front of the latter, Bridget Devlin was tracing the outline of the rose onto the canvas, working carefully and quickly, with a craft she'd obviously mastered. From time to time she glanced at the adjacent screen for guidance, when her view of the canvas was blocked by her shadow, and from time to time she backed out of the light entirely to inspect her work.

Ignored and uninvited, I lingered in the doorway. The sensible thing to do seemed to be to pour some wine and let her finish, so I did. It took ten minutes for her to render the still life in outline in the exact proportions of the template slide. After drawing a final inch of line, she walked to the wall and turned on the overhead, then switched the projectors to the fan setting to allow the bulbs to cool.

"So much for that," she said as she joined me by the door.

I filled the second glass and gave it to her, then looked at the array of finished pieces leaning against the walls—precise renderings of everything from onions to apples and rag dolls to beach balls. "There are nice."

"Thanks."

"What gallery shows your stuff?"

Eyes on the canvas she had just been working with, she laughed bitterly. "The gallery to be named later."

She returned to the canvas and drew two lines near the top of the rose stem, making the outline of a leaf, then stepped back. "No gallery, no museum, no ever-so-supportive patron for Ms. Devlin." She stepped forward and drew another line, this time on the stem of the goblet. "Would you like to know where these end up?" Her gesture encompassed the entire collection.

"Where?"

"On postcards." With reluctance, her eyes left the canvas and locked with mine. "I take them to a photographer downtown; he snaps their picture, reduces them in size, and sends them to a company in Oakland that prints them up as postcards. I make fifty dollars per painting. The cards are distributed from here to Seattle. I'm so very proud." The final phrase was poisonous.

"Does it bother you that they're not accepted as real art?"

She looked at me. "It's a blister on my heart. But there's not much I can do about it."

"Why did Lily Lucerne get famous and you didn't? I can't tell much difference between your work and hers."

Her lips cracked and wrinkled. "The *difference* is, *my* work has *blood* in it."

"Blood?"

"Feeling. Soul. Humanity. Butter wouldn't melt in Lily's mouth, as I discovered all too late, but she had *Sebastian* behind her—all those wealthy alumni—so doors opened for her. If you bring along your own collectors, any gallery in the *world* will hang you."

She took one last look at the canvas, then walked to the shelf where she'd set her wine and took a deep sip. "So much for wine and roses," she said, and gestured toward an overstuffed and oversized couch that sat in between some canvases that were leaning against a nearby wall.

"Why are you so interested in Carrie?" she asked as we sank a foot into its innards and she curled against an arm and faced me.

"Because I've been told Carrie was involved in a messy incident while she was at Sebastian."

Her face carried no hint of deeper knowledge but no doubt that it was true. "What incident?"

"The one that got Wade Linton sent to jail."

The wineglass stopped halfway to her mouth. "Are you telling me you think Wade had sex with my daughter?"

"To put it bluntly."

"That's absurd." From her tone, I got the impression she'd expected me to suggest something worse.

"I know it's not pleasant to contemplate, but how can you be certain it didn't happen?"

"I just . . . know."

"The sex urge is—"

She gripped her glass with both hands; wine spilled down her fists. "Don't sit there and tell me about the *sex* urge, Mr. Tanner. I know all *about* the sex urge. I know about *my* sex urge and my *daughter's* sex urge. And she didn't play house with Wade."

Her outburst told me more about her own sexuality than her daughter's, so I approached from a new angle. "You said Carrie felt out of place at Sebastian. Since Linton was responsible for her being there, he—"

"*I* was responsible for her being there."

"But Linton made it possible, so he'd naturally have given Carrie extra help when she needed it, both to be sure she survived academically and to be sure she justified his recommendation for the scholarship."

"So?"

"Carrie was attractive—I saw her picture in the yearbook. And you and her father were evidently having some troubles—when was the divorce, by the way?"

"August of 'eighty-one."

"So Carrie could have been searching for a new father figure, subconsciously at least."

Her sneer was reminiscent of Lloyd's. "I didn't know you were also a *psychiatrist*, Mr. Tanner. What an interesting combination, the Shamus and the Shrink. Someone should write a book about you."

I didn't let either the sarcasm or the irony slow me down. "It adds up, Mrs. Devlin. That's all I'm saying."

"And I'm saying you're wrong."

"Do you mind if I talk to her?"

"She's in Spain."

"By phone, I mean."

"No. I won't have you"—her glare slid into a smug rebuff. "She's traveling, so you can't. She's in Morocco—she won't be back in Madrid till December."

"She's on a graduate fellowship?"

"Yes."

"What department?"

"International Policy Studies. It's a very exclusive program. She'd had French at Sebastian, so she spent her junior year at Stanford in Paris, and now she's learning Spanish. She's already been offered a position with the State Department, but she's not sure she's going to take it." The pride of a parent was evident, the peculiar pride that suggested refusing a job offer from the government was more exalted than accepting one.

I was sorry to bring her back to earth. "Did Carrie ever mention Wade Linton after she graduated from Sebastian?"

"No."

"They never corresponded while he was in jail?"

"Why would they?"

"Did the Sebastion people ever contact you about Linton?"

"No."

"How about the District Attorney? Did that office ever speak to you about him?"

"Why would they do that?"

"Because if my information is correct, Linton was

indicted for a felony against your child. The DA should have talked to you about it. If it happened."

"*He* didn't because *it* didn't."

The possibility that she was right confused me. I stood up and strolled about the room, looking at Bridget Devlin's obsessive intensification of reality, trying to solve the mystery of Wade Linton's similarly large preoccupation. "Would you do me a favor?" I asked her.

"What?"

"Write me a note, addressed to the registrar at Stanford, authorizing me to see Carrie's college records. We'd have to get it notarized, but I can dig up someone and get back here in an hour or so. I can draft it for you if you like, it won't take—"

"No."

I looked at her until I had her full attention. "Wade Linton is dead, Mrs. Devlin."

She frowned, not comprehending. "What did you say?"

"Wade Linton is dead. He was murdered earlier tonight."

Tears made her eyes as bright and varicolored as the enamels on the studio door. "But I thought he was *out* of jail, that the bad times were behind him."

"I'm sure he thought that, too."

"I don't understand."

"I don't either. But the note to Stanford could help change that."

She shook her head wearily. "What difference does it make, if he's dead?"

"It could tell me why he died."

"What gives you the right to know that?"

"I was a fan," I said, surprising both of us. I hurried to keep from explaining. "I should warn you that the police are going to want to talk to your ex-husband. And probably to you as well."

"Why on earth would they want to talk to Danny?"

"There's a possibility Linton had a grudge against him. Or vice versa."

We were drifting away from the world as she knew it and she grasped for safety. "Am I crazy or are you? Wade and Danny barely *knew* each other. And why would they want to talk to me?"

I answered her question with one of my own. "How would your husband react if he thought Wade Linton had molested Carrie?"

She puckered with distaste. "He'd take communion and declare it the will of God."

I looked away, reluctant to take the next step. "Was one of the reasons for your divorce your suspicion that your husband might have made improper advances on your daughter?"

She stood and confronted me, as animated as she'd ever been. "You *bastard*. What right do you have to come in here making suggestions about Carrie that are untrue, then saying something like *that*? I divorced Danny for damned good reasons, but he doesn't deserve to be called a *child* molester. My God. You think you can say anything, don't you? Just let your mouth run until someone fesses up to *something*. Well, not in *this* house, mister. Get the hell out of here, Mr. . . . whatever your name is. Now."

"I'm sorry if you're offended, Mrs. Devlin," I said, a trifle timidly. "But a man's been killed and it may not be over yet. I had to—"

"Just leave," she interrupted, a tear in her eye, her lips stretched tight across her teeth.

I decided there was no reason not to. "I'd appreciate that authorization for Stanford," I said when we reached the door. "It could answer a lot of questions."

She shook her head. "I won't do that without Carrie's permission."

"But she's unavailable."

"That's your problem."

I turned to go, then stopped. "Two more things."

"What?"

"Did Carrie play soccer? On the Sebastian team?"

She shook her head. "She never did *anything* at Sebastian, except punish people on the student court."

"But she did have a boyfriend."

Bridget Devlin nodded. "Her senior year she went with a boy named Lloyd. He was very strange and very rich. He dumped her the night of the Winter Ball."

"It's not the killing that's hard," my cell mate told me one morning. "If you've got a reason and a weapon, killing's as easy as wiping your ass. The problem is, as soon as he's dead you see your life isn't all that different, so you start thinking maybe it wasn't important after all, that maybe you fucked up."

"Not me," I told him.

HOMAGE TO HAMMURABI, p. 301

Chapter
27

It was close enough to midnight to make calling someone a breach of etiquette, but my work wasn't done and it doesn't traffic a lot in etiquette anyway.

"Do you know what *time* it is?" Emma Drayer complained when she answered.

"This is Tanner. I need to talk to you. Christine, also. I'll be there in ten minutes."

"Tomorrow, Tanner."

She was about to hang up. "I found Linton," I said quickly.

Her breath sizzled. "Where?"

"The park."

"*What* park?"

"Golden Gate."

"What was he doing?"

"He was camping out."

She was skeptical. "You're telling me Wade Linton's been living in the park?"

"Yes."

"Since he got out of prison?"

"Mostly. Except when he was back in jail for trespassing."

She hesitated again, working with the picture I'd just painted. "He graduated from Princeton, you know."

The *non sequitur* was so startling I made a wisecrack: "Which means he probably wasn't as good at camping as the rest of the guys."

Emma errupted. "How can you *joke* about this? Homelessness is *horrible*. And Wade is one of them? I can't believe it. What does he eat? Where does he sleep?"

"I imagine he ate what he could scavenge from the dumpster behind the Eight Avenue Safeway—my cop friend tells me it's a veritable cornucopia. And he slept in the back of a buried Datsun."

Her focus was on my attitude and not my information. "What's *wrong* with you? How can you make *light* of him like that?"

"I'm not making light of him, I'm making light of the rest of us."

Though insufficient, the justification seemed to mollify her. "Well, what did he say? How is he? Did he mention my name? When can I see him?"

Despite the cascade of questions, I was reluctant to issue truth through the telephone. "I'm coming over," I said. "We'll talk when I get there."

But she wouldn't let it go. "Did he say anything about me when you saw him? Just tell me that."

"I didn't get a chance to talk to him. He was a little jumpy. But the thing is, Emma, he's—"

"Why *wouldn't* he be jumpy, for God's sake? Framed for something he didn't do, jailed for no reason, living like an animal, it just—"

"I agree," I concurred quickly. "I'm just saying I didn't get a chance to talk to him."

"Are you going to see him again?"

"I don't think so."

"Then tell me how I can reach him."

"It's not that simple. I—"

"*Please*. I have to talk to him."

I hesitated, then opted for assistance. "Is your roommate there?"

Emma's tone turned brittle. "That's *really* why you called, isn't it?"

"The reason I called was to ask if I could come talk to

you. *Both* of you." When she didn't resist, I went on. "So how's Christine?"

"Fine."

"She still awake?"

"We keep different schedules—she has her alone time in the morning; I have mine at night."

"Tell her I'm a morning person, too; we have something in common."

Emma Drayer paused, then found a new inflection, one that implied a reassessment. "She seemed to have a good time the other night."

"You sound surprised."

"Only because she usually gets all contrite and remorseful after those types of things."

"What types of things?"

"You know—one-night stands."

"If it's only one night, it'll be her choice, not mine."

"I think I'll tell her that."

I grabbed at the opening. "Why don't I come over and tell her myself?"

She stiffened. "No. Now that your love life is taken care of, we can both get some sleep. But I'll be at your office first thing in the morning and I won't leave till you tell me about Wade."

"It can't wait that long, Emma."

"It'll have to."

I took in enough air to do my damage. "Linton was killed tonight."

"I . . . He's *dead*?"

"I'm afraid so. I'm sorry."

Her gasp became a reedy wail. "He *can't* be. You just said—"

"I was trying to postpone things till I could give you the news in person."

"Oh, my God." The sobs accumulated into a chorus of thick grief. "After all these years. After I waited and waited for another letter, for something, anything, that would—"

"There are things I need to know," I interrupted, cruelly, under the rationale that she needed a diversion. "Wake up your roommate. Make some coffee. I'll be there as soon as I can. Did you hear me? Go get Christine. Let her help you through this."

"How did he die? He didn't starve, did he? I mean, if he *starved*, that means he didn't even think enough of me to—"

"He was beaten to death."

She paused. "Robbed, you mean?"

"He was caught breaking into the school. If I let them, the police will call it a justifiable homicide."

"Is that what it was?"

"I don't think so. Can I come over? Please?"

Emma was so silent it was impossible to know what she was thinking. Then I heard noises in the background. What I hoped was that Christine had been awakened by her roommate's outburst and had gotten up to find out what was going on. I listened for a minute more. In the middle of a murmur of what sounded like condolence, I hung up the phone and drove across the city.

The air was cold and damp; in its gritty gleam the world had become as icy as my self-regard. When Emma opened the door she seconded the motion. "If you were lying about Wade, I'll kill you."

I shook my head. "They found him a few hours ago."

"At Sebastian?"

I nodded.

"God. All he went through at that fucking school, and now that."

"Misery is not evenly distributed. I first noticed it when I was nine. It's why I stopped going to church."

She stepped back to let me in. The single lamp was low, but there was enough light for me to see Christine White standing in the kitchen with her back to me, wearing yellow pajamas and matching fuzzy slippers, pouring hot water over freshly ground beans. When she heard my voice she turned my way and tried to smile. Under the circumstances, it was the most intimate moment I'd shared with a woman in years.

I waited for Christine to distribute the coffee before I launched my spiel. "First of all," I looked at Emma, "I want you to give Christine a dollar."

"What are you talking about?"

"Just do as I ask, please."

Eventually she walked to the counter and dug in her purse. "All I've got is a five."

"Give it to her."

She glowered, but crossed the room and held out the bill. "Here."

Christine took it, then looked for instructions. "What am *I* supposed to do with it?"

"Take it to the office tomorrow and put it in the trust account."

"Why?"

"Because now you're Emma's lawyer."

Christine blinked. "Why does she need a lawyer?"

I looked to my left. "Emma knows. Don't you?"

Emma didn't move.

I looked back at Christine. "What her lawyer needs to do at this point is advise Emma not to talk to anyone about anything having to do with the Sebastian School. Anyone but me, that is."

"Why?"

I looked at Emma. "Do you believe I know what happened?"

She bowed her head.

"Maybe it will help if I make some findings of fact."

Emma stayed silent. "Will someone please tell me what this is all about?" her roommate asked, but it was one of the few meetings in history when a lawyer wasn't in charge.

I kept my eyes on Emma. "It was supposed to be about abusive sex, but that wasn't exactly it, was it? What it was about was a baby."

Emma's smile turned as soft as Christine's silly slippers.

"Alfred," I said. "From 'The Lovesong of J. Alfred Prufrock.'" I looked at Christine. "That's a poem by T. S. Eliot."

She stuck out her tongue. "I had a liberal arts education; I know who Prufrock is. What I *don't* know is where this is going or whether I'm supposed to do anything about it."

When I looked at Emma again, she was looking back at her. "How did you know about his name?"

"Alfred told me. I talked to him yesterday."

"Truly?"

I nodded.

"I'd love to see him." She blinked. "You must be good at what you do."

"Good enough to learn more than I want to know, sometimes. He prefers Al, by the way. And he didn't understand the poem when his mother read it to him." I paused for effect. "But of course she's not his mother."

Emma glanced at her roommate. "I think he's right—I'd better keep quiet and I'd better have a lawyer. Can you do it?"

Christine shrugged. "For now, I guess. But if you're seriously in trouble—criminal trouble—I should bring in someone else."

Emma looked at me. "Is that all you have?"

I shook my head.

"I don't see how you could know everything if you didn't talk to Wade."

"As you said, I'm good at what I do."

She sat there, frozen in time and consequence, until her roommate went to her side and took her hand.

"The key to it all, of course," I went on with a touch of pride, "is that Al wasn't the Lintons' natural child." I looked again at Emma. "Have you got any more money?"

Her grin was weak and mordant. "This is the most expensive conversation I've had since I was audited." Nevertheless, she dug in her purse until she found a coin.

"Give it to me."

She held out a palm; I plucked up the coin and stuffed it in my pocket. "Now I'm your lawyer, too. So when you tell me Al Linton was adopted, no one can pry the information out of me."

Emma didn't respond to the implicit invitation.

"I can find out elsewhere, you know. I can hound the boy's birth mother until she relents and tells me about it, or I can work on Mr. Messenger. All lawyers have skeletons in their past; it won't take long for me to dig up Messenger's and trade it for what I need."

"He was adopted," Emma confirmed grudgingly.

"I don't know what you're talking about, you know," Christine chimed in uneasily.

"You don't have to."

I turned back to Emma. "I want you to know that I wasn't hired to bring this out—the reason I got into the Sebastian stuff was essentially trivial. If it wasn't for what happened to Linton, I'd probably leave it alone. But Linton's dead; I have to find out whether I'm responsible for that and the only way I can is to find out why he died." A tear traveled down her cheek. "From what I know now, I don't think you'll be prosecuted, but if you're vulnerable in ways I don't realize, you should tell your lawyer about them."

Emma walked to the window and looked into the gloom and glisten to the night. "I've been hurt so much already, the rest of it won't make any difference."

She was talking about time and love and unrequited aspects of them both, talking about the past, which meant there was nothing I could do to make it other than it was.

I looked at Christine. "I'd like you to invite your boss to meet me in your office at noon tomorrow."

"Which boss?—I've got a dozen of them."

"Gillis."

She frowned. "What do you want with him?"

"I want to warn him that I'm about to tell the cops that he's a killer."

Did I launch a surprise attack? Of course not. Like any sportsman I made quite sure he knew that I was coming.

HOMAGE TO HAMMURABI, p. 311

Chapter
28

I slept the sleep of the just and was on the freeway by nine the next morning—truth can be adequately communicated by telephone, but lies are most effectively transmitted face-to-face.

The trip was slow going—a trip anywhere in the Bay Area was slow going these days, though the bridge was due to be reopened in a week and most people were hoping the situation would instantly return to normal. A few of us were hoping the situation would be *better* than normal—that the staggered work schedules would be continued and the people who had reduced their contact with the home office to the fax machine and the modem would decide to keep doing it that way.

I abandoned the Bayshore at the University Avenue exit, which had apparently suffered some quake damage itself, and drove through Palo Alto toward the tree-lined drive that is the gateway to the Leland Stanford Junior University. Eucalyptus gave way to palms and the palms yielded to the carefully tended gardens and shrubs and lawns that served as the welcome mat to the tile and sandstone facades of Stanford's timeless quad—The Romanesque rectangle of the original campus.

It is a special place, one of the handful of excellent universities in the country, perhaps even the best of them, but as I parked my car in the visitors' lot and headed toward the quad on foot I remembered Betty Fontaine's charge that the most prestigious schools lacked a sufficient commitment to eliminating the crush of inequality that has overwhelmed the country, that the elite colleges and universities were not part of the solution but part of the problem. I didn't know if her assessment was fair, though I did know the percentage of blacks and Hispanics who went on to college had dropped dramatically over the past decade. And I had no answer to offer—the issue is complex, and without a child to raise, my need to confront higher education on a personal or emotional level had vanished when I got my own sheepskin a quarter century ago. The only thing I knew for certain was that problems of the sort Betty spoke of will *never* be solved unless places like Harvard and Stanford come to grips with them.

My original objective was the registrar, but halfway to the administration building I took a different tack. Three questions and a pointed finger later, I pushed through the heavy wooden door to the International Relations Department.

The chairman's office was on the second floor, secreted behind a walnut door and an even more formidable barrier in the form of a stiff-backed secretary and her outsized breasts. I approached her desk with the trepidation of the marginal student I had been at every level of my ill-used education.

"Hi," I began.

"Good morning."

Once again I summoned a twang and syntax from my youth. "I'm not real sure I'm in the right place." I hoped I looked hapless and displaced, in need of some mothering.

Her smile was off the cover of McGuffey's. "In what place *should* you be?"

"International Studies or some such."

"Graduate or undergraduate?"

"Graduate."

"If it's the International Policy Studies program you're seeking, then you are there." She became officially prim and personally antiseptic. "How may I help you?"

"Well, this girl—my niece—is out of the country on

some sort of . . . what do you call it? It's like winning the lottery."

"A sabbatical, perhaps? But then she's not a professor, is she?"

I shook my head. "She's a student. A damned good one."

"Not uncommon at Stanford." Her smile was leaking patience. "You'll have to do better."

"She's in Spain. That's all I know."

"Then perhaps she's on a fellowship."

I snapped my fingers. "That's the one. A fellowship to Spain. That's what she has."

"A Fulbright?"

"Oh, she's fully bright, all right. As bright as they come. What I need to know is how to *reach* her. On the telephone, I mean."

"I'm afraid you should more properly take that up with the registrar."

I tried to look befuddled; I accomplished it by thinking about the instructions to my VCR. "I believe that's the folks that sent me over here."

She gave her head a quick shake. "I'm sorry, but I don't have the authorization to—"

I switched to my somber look—the one that comes more naturally. "I'm not here for fun, ma'am. Her mother—that's my sister—was visiting us at our place south of Kingsburg when she took sick. The local hospital sent her to the one up here at the school—they say it's the best around and I hope they're right because Sissy don't look real good—and, well, I thought Carrie ought to know the situation. In case she wants to come home."

My story merited empathy and a pitying pucker. "How unfortunate. But the registrar, or perhaps the dean of students—"

I manufactured righteousness. "I've come as far as I'm going. My wife's half crazy with the commotion and I should be over there with her instead of bouncing around like a billiard ball trying to find out how I can tell some poor little gal her mother may be about to join her maker." I pointed a finger. "I believe there's someone behind that door that knows where Carrie is, and there's nothing I see from where I sit that's going to keep me from asking about it."

I started toward the door, hoping it didn't lead to the rest room.

"There's no need to disturb the chairman," the receptionist said quickly. "You seem distraught and, well . . . What was her name? Carol?"

"Carrie. Carrie Devlin."

"I'll just be a moment. Now you sit right there and wait for me."

I followed instructions and she disappeared behind a thick partition. A moment later I heard a file drawer roll open. Some moments after that I heard some keyboard keys click rapidly, then again, and then once more. When she returned she was perspiring and perplexed.

"I'm not sure what's going on here. What did you say your name was?"

"Tanner."

"Well, Mr. Tanner, I have no record of a Carrie Devlin, or any other Devlin for that matter, currently enrolled in International Policy Studies. Nor has a Carrie Devlin *ever* been enrolled in *any* aspect of International Relations as far as I can tell."

Now I was the one who was confused. "Are you sure about that?"

"Of course. I checked the electronic and paper files, both." Her nose wrinkled above the nostrils. "I'd better consult the registrar. This is becoming *very* irregular."

"I'm on my way there now," I said to head her off, then hurried out the door. Along the way I stopped long enough to make a call.

"Anything more on Linton?"

"Not much," Charley said. "We think the weapon was a forty-five automatic, GI issue."

"O'Shea was ex-army."

"I know."

"Find him yet?"

"Nope. Got any suggestions where to look?"

"Afraid not."

"Then why are we talking?"

"I was wondering what office Linton was trying to break into when O'Shea smacked him."

"I don't know, let me look." The line fell silent. "Someone called Finney. Mean anything?"

"I'm about to find out."

The minions of the registrar were not excited to see me, either. The inquiry by the young man at the front counter was pro forma because he and the rest of the staff had their ears tuned to a conversation taking place in the rear of the room, among a group of four men and a woman. Unless clothing styles were different at Stanford from anywhere else I had ever been, one of the men was a cop.

"I need to see the boss." I had interrupted the young man's eavesdropping and he didn't appreciate it.

"Why is that?"

"Why don't you let me tell him about it?"

He looked at me long enough to decide I was out of his league, then joined his peers in the rear. He had to wait his turn to get a word in edgewise, but when he did, all eyes turned my way. I bowed to my audience and waited while the man in the whitest shirt and reddest tie detached himself and approached me. "Your name, please?"

"Tanner."

The young man who'd helped me was standing right behind him. When he heard the name he piped up. "Spittle at Int Stud just called about him. He's looking for his niece, or so he says. He claims he's her uncle but Spittle says she looked him up and he's really a private eye." The young man couldn't help himself. "*Are* you?" He would have been less surprised to encounter a swami.

"Guilty as charged."

The white shirt retook control. "Of what student are you making inquiries?"

"Of Carrie Devlin."

"What is the purpose of your questions?"

"To learn her status at the university."

"Do you have proper authorization?"

"No."

"Then that takes care of it, I'm afraid. I'm sure you understand—we can hardly give out information in our files willy-nilly. Even if we were so inclined, the Education

Code is very strict about student confidentiality—we are subject to both civil and punitive damages. When you have obtained the necessary enabling documents, we will be happy to speak with you again." He started to turn away.

"I can offer you a deal," I said quietly.

He lingered. "What kind of deal could Stanford possibly need from you?"

"If that's a cop back there, and if the reason you folks are a little tense this morning is you've been warned your records may have been breached, I think I can be of help."

His face was trying to match his tie. "How do you know about these matters?"

I smiled. "It will cost you a quid pro quo to find out."

The white shirt glanced back at the clan from which he'd come. "Perhaps you should talk with Sergeant Pinckney of the campus police."

"If you bring the sergeant in on this I'll be tied up for hours. I can't afford the time and neither can you. Give me what I need, and I'll give you some peace of mind."

He still couldn't decide, so I had to help him.

"You were warned about admissions records. The man who warned you is Marvin Gillis, the chief mucky-muck at the Sebastian School."

He was a Stanford man, so he was trained to be conservative. "Even if that's true, I still don't see what you can do for me."

"I can name the man who's after your files and I can tell you where you can find him."

At least he was decisive. "Agreed."

"First, give me whatever you have on Carrie Devlin."

"But I don't—"

"I just want to know where she is. What she's studying. And how I can get in touch with her."

He glanced at the cop again. I was afraid he was going to dillydally so long even a campus cop would smell a rat, but Stanford cops aren't Stanford grads and the white shirt had time to make his move. "I'll be right back," he said, and went through a door in the rear of the office.

When he returned he was relaxed, even affable. "Where is she?" I asked him.

"You haven't completed your part of the bargain."

"The man's name is Wade Linton."

"Is he an alumnus?"

I shook my head. "Princeton, as I understand."

"Then what does he want from Stanford?"

"Evidence of a crime."

"What kind of crime?"

"Fraud."

"I don't understand."

"You will if you read the morning paper."

"Where is Linton now?" His brow narrowed. "You're not him, are you?"

I shook my head. "Linton's dead."

"What?"

"Wade Linton is dead, as of last night. He won't cause trouble for you, with records or anything else. Check with Gillis if you need to, though you should do it before noon. Now tell me about Carrie Devlin."

The white shirt had gone tentative on me again. "This is all quite astonishing. I should—"

"We have a deal, Mr. Registrar."

Apparently Stanford men are men of honor. "Ms. Devlin is not currently enrolled," he recited formally. "She is not on fellowship, either, at least not under the auspices of Stanford. She left this institution in the spring of 1986."

"Why?"

"For academic deficiencies."

"She flunked out."

"Yes."

"Her sophomore year."

"Correct."

"No junior year at Stanford in Paris?"

"Hardly."

"No transfer to another school?"

"There's no request for transcripts in the file."

"Speaking of which, could I see it?"

He stiffened. "I'm sorry. I've told you too much already."

He was right, but I wanted one thing more. "Do you admit many Sebastian students to Stanford?"

"Of course. It's the best secondary school in Northern California."

"Have you ever made a study of how many of them flunk out?"

"No. Why should we?"

"Because if you don't, some assistant DA is going to do it for you."

He did not do nearly enough to elude me. In fact, as I pulled the trigger, it occurred to me that I might be doing him a favor.

HOMAGE TO HAMMURABI, p. 327

Chapter
29

The senior partner resides in the bowels of a law firm the way a pearl nestles within the clammy flesh of an oyster, and Marvin Gillis was no exception. As I made my way through the law offices of Gillis and Hookstratten, I wondered if the message I'd delivered by way of Christine White had been enough to flush him out, but as I rounded a final corner my question was quickly answered—the number of secretaries and file clerks and paralegals lingering within earshot of Christine's office was proof that something strange was up. The something strange was me.

I tapped on the door and went inside. Appropriately, the setting was out of Sayers and Christie—elegantly appointed office, brocade drapes that cast the assembled faces in sinister shadow, nervous glances arcing across the room in furtive looks of dread, anxious sighs leaking like bursts of steam through aspects of assiduously injured innocence. As I crossed the room and took the only available seat, which was the one behind the desk, I began to have doubts that I made a respectable Poirot.

I bowed to the multitude and greeted Christine White by name. "Are you still representing Ms. Drayer?"

Christine nodded. I looked at her client and tried to indicate my support and sympathy, but since she still wasn't convinced I was on her side, she was having none of it. Then I looked at the rest of them.

Marvin Gillis—three pieces of pin-striped armor cinched in place, flawlessly groomed from head to toe—followed my every move, his outrage was barely in check. Like a bull in his private pasture, he was snarling and snorting in readiness to do what he was bred for—charge the intruder and keep charging until he reestablished his supremacy or expired in the effort. There is a certain nobility in that, of course, but I couldn't let it interfere with what I hoped was my own.

Seated next to Gillis was my old friend Jake Hattie, preeminent criminal counsel in San Francisco. "Are you representing Mr. Gillis, Jake, or did you just drop by to revise your will?"

"I never drop by, Tanner—I occur, something like a thunderstorm. Lightning included."

I bowed. "Nice image."

I'd worked for Jake, and drunk with him, had even lounged around the pool at his horse ranch in Sonoma County among the opulent charms of Jake's usual entourage of bathing beauties, but now I was on the other side. As with all great lawyers, that made me his blood enemy until the job was done.

Jake fired the opening round. "You may assume Mr. Gillis is apprised of the rights he need be apprised of in *this* exceedingly specious matter." Jake pulled out a stogie and lit it. "Frankly, you surprise me, Marshall." Jake's the only one who calls me that. "I'm afraid those rights may include defamation proceedings." He paused and puffed. "If you're not careful."

"I'm seldom careful, Jake. But I'm often right."

As Jake shook his head with what I was supposed to regard as paternal concern, I looked at the other men in the room. The elder of the two had a tumultuous mane of silver hair that was the most luxuriant object in sight, but that was the only thing about him that glowed—seated in a weary slump he was bent and asthmatic, his age draping him like a shawl. He was Rufus Finner, I presumed, Sebastian's titular headmaster, but the tables were clearly turned. He was so frightened I began to feel sorry for him, until I remembered he had no doubt spent forty years instilling the same degree of terror in Sebastian students summoned to his office for discipline.

The man next to Finner was a lawyer who, from the pinch to his mouth and the cut of his clothes, was not used to the rough-and-tumble of criminal litigation. I expected him to defer to Jake in everything but his taste in cuffs.

After one last survey of my audience, I plunged ahead. "This whole thing started with a book," I began, mouth dry, pulse rapid. "It was a manuscript, more precisely. A manuscript that will become a book in a week or so."

"Who will publish?" Jake asked.

"Periwinkle Press."

"Mr. Chatterton."

"Right." I glanced at Gillis, then back to Jake. "Your client evidently forgot to tell you that he's trying for an injunction against publication. In my judgment, he doesn't have a prayer for a TRO, but here's an irony you'll like—without your client's property settlement with his ex-wife, Periwinkle would be dead in a day."

I swallowed to clear my throat, but had to try it again before I got it right.

"Let's dispense with the editorials," Gillis grumbled.

"Fine," I said as Jake whispered a piece of advice to his client. 'Keep your fucking mouth shut' was what I thought he said.

"The book was purportedly written in prison by a man who'd been falsely accused of a crime. According to the manuscript, the man was a teacher, the crime was sexual abuse, the victim was his student, and the date was nine years back."

"According to the *book*," Jake mimicked.

I nodded. "I got into this because Bryce Chatterton hired me to find the author—the manuscript showed up at Periwinkle unaccredited. Kind of a weird assignment, I thought, and after I read the book it seemed even more bizarre, because what I decided was that what was purportedly fiction was most probably a roman à clef that described a set of historical circumstances and the fallout therefrom." I paused and looked around the room. "I apologize for the lawyerese—the fumes off the Commercial Code are warping my brain."

Jake took advantage of the interruption. "Who else knows this story you're telling?"

"No one but me knows the whole truth, I don't think, not even your client. The police know some of it and when I'm through here they'll know enough more to make an arrest." I looked at Gillis. "A friend of mine has a letter that lays it all out in the event something untoward befalls me on my way back to the office."

I leaned back in the chair and put my feet on the desk. "The assumption that the author had been in prison for the reason set out in the book seemed legitimate at first. I found a school—Sebastian—where a sex scandal had apparently occurred, though not nine years ago but six. Then I got the name of a teacher—Wade Linton—who had gone to jail for a similar crime even though the people who knew him best said he was incapable of such an act and suggested he'd been framed. Finally, I got what purported to be the name of the victim—a former Sebastian student named Carrie Devlin."

"Who?" Emma Drayer asked sharply.

"Carrie Devlin. Scholarship girl from Noe Valley. Kind of a loner at Sebastian; she didn't even play soccer."

"You're saying *she's* the one Wade made love to?"

"I'm saying that's what someone told me."

"Who?"

"It doesn't matter."

My attentions started to return to Jake, who was the only audience I cared about, but I thought of something that needed nailing down so I kept my eyes on Emma. "The day we met, Christine mentioned that you'd taken one of the soccer players to Europe, to attend a special camp."

Emma frowned. "So?"

"I was wondering which one it was."

Her glance flicked toward Marvin Gillis, then retreated from his lordly stare. When she looked at her lawyer, she got only a puzzled shrug. In the resulting vacuum, Emma Drayer decided to say nothing.

"This is about *soccer*?" Jake's sarcasm was in full bloom.

"This is about fraud and murder."

"Not so far."

I glanced at Gillis, who was careful to meet my eye, but his bluster had begun to wilt. "At this point my theory started to fall apart," I went on. "For one thing, the victim's mother was certain her daughter had never been molested, plus she had never been advised by the DA that such a charge had been made, rather a strange omission. Also, the actual perpetrator of the crime, according to the book—Carrie Devlin's father—doesn't seem to have had an opportunity to do it, since he was divorced and out of the household by that time. And finally, the manuscript contains some text that indicates it wasn't written by a person who'd been locked away for the last six years."

"What kind of text?" Jake asked.

"The kind that talks about establishments that didn't exist when the author went off to Folsom."

Gillis couldn't contain either himself or his image any longer. "What's this crap about a father?"

"Lloyd didn't tell you? The last section of the manuscript showed up at Periwinkle a few days ago, the part where the protagonist is released from jail and hunts down the person who actually *did* abuse his student. According to the book, the real bad guy was the father."

"That's preposterous," Gillis growled.

"That's the book."

"Get on with it, Tanner," Jake Hattie demanded again. "Where the hell's the crime?"

"The crime is that your client killed Wade Linton."

Jake fought my accusation and my look. "That's absurd."

"Or, rather, had him killed," I amended, "by a man named Arthur O'Shea. The cops are looking for him now."

I turned to Gillis. "I don't say it's going to be easy to pin it on you—you didn't do the deed, after all, you were just behind the scenes pulling the puppet strings, the way you always have at Sebastian. But somehow you lured Linton into thinking the evidence he was looking for was still in the counselor's office at Sebastian. Then you warned Arthur O'Shea he was coming. O'Shea's a sanctimonious automaton, probably battle-fatigued as well—he thinks he owes his soul to Sebastian and you had him primed to defend it with every ounce of his well-trained strength. When Linton showed up, sneaking around the way you had said he would, the mix was made and the end inevitable."

Gillis was poised to rebut me, but Jake held up a hand. "You say nothing," he instructed darkly. "This man has accused you of staging a murder. That's slander per se. We'll have a complaint on file by Monday."

"A waste of time, Jake."

"Just stick to the narrative, Tanner." He looked at his client. "Does this O'Shea person have a lawyer?"

Gillis shrugged.

"Everyone sit still." Jake walked across the room, picked up the telephone beside me, dialed, whispered some instructions, and hung up. "He's got one now," he said on the way back to his chair. "Go on, Tanner. And let me say I'm shocked at what you're doing."

"Not as shocked as that poor kid was when he found Wade Linton's body in the light well."

Next to me, Emma Drayer began to cry.

Jake whispered something and Gillis shook his head. The distress in the air was palpable. I waited for one of them to say something more, but they left the lead with me.

"What I finally figured out was that the book—*Homage to Hammurabi* is the title, by the way—was both right and wrong. There was a frame, all right, and Linton really was imprisoned for something he didn't do. But it wasn't because Carrie Devlin was sexually abused, it was because of what happened to another student at Sebastian."

"Who?" Jake asked.

"Jane Ann Gillis."

Gillis exploded. "How *dare* you tar my child with your slur. Bad enough that you make scurrilous allegations against me, but to inject Jane Ann into your perverted fantasy is criminal. I'll see that your license is—"

"I know what happened, Gillis," I interrupted. "I know how Jane Ann was involved, and how you used her mistake to further your own purposes. If you think I don't, ask Emma. That's why she's here."

When Gillis looked at her he was greeted by a perfect

mask of loathing. In its acrid glare, Marvin Gillis chose to opt for silence.

"The question you have to decide is whether I go into Jane Ann's part in all this," I went on. "Or do I keep it quiet for as long as I can? It's up to you. If you're as concerned about your daughter as you say, you'll go along with my proposal."

"Which is what?"

Jake started to say something to him, but Gillis shook his head. Bluff and bluster dropped from him like leaves. "Go ahead," he added softly.

I made my pitch. "If you go along with me, I'll do my best to keep Jane Ann's situation confidential. No guarantees, but I'll try." I looked around. "And so will everyone else in this room. In return, you and Jake have to get together with the people downtown and come up with a plea bargain I can live with. Between the two of you, you've got enough clout to cut any deal you want, but I want a real plea—no nolo, no dismissal. The deal has to include jail time for Gillis—one year, minimum. If I hear you're denying involvement in Linton's death, I'm going to the DA and tell all." I smiled. "In other words, Mr. Gillis, I'm doing to you what you did to Wade Linton back in 'eighty-three—I'm sending you off to prison without a trial by a jury of your peers."

Gillis sagged. "No," he said softly. "I can't. Not that." His plea was elemental, the entreaty of a frightened old man.

"Are you saying Marvin molested his child?" Jake demanded. "If you are, I have to warn you that—"

"No," I said quickly. "I should make that clear. I'm not saying that at all. It's the book that said that."

"Then what *are* you saying?"

"I'm saying Marvin Gillis had Wade Linton killed to save the Sebastian School."

There was a long lost moment before Jake Hattie asked, "How could this Linton character be a threat to an institution like Sebastian?"

"Because Gillis and his henchman Finner had a little scam going."

"Which was?"

"Falsifying grade transcripts and test scores to get Sebastian kids admitted to colleges for which they didn't qualify."

"You must be mad," Finner rasped in the hush that followed, but the effort was meek and tepid, in keeping with surrender.

"Linton was framed to keep him from getting enough evidence together to blow the whistle," I elaborated, for the first time certain I was right.

Jake thought it over. "More," he said simply.

"It was pretty basic, actually. Over the years, Sebastian had justified its existence by getting its graduates admitted to the most prestigious colleges in the country. That kept the parents happy, which kept the endowment flush. But in the eighties, the job got tougher. On one hand, the student body contained an increasing number of pampered kids who spent more time hanging out in SoMa and Stinson Beach than hitting the books at Sebastian. On the other, because of what was going on at the colleges, there were far fewer places left over for the Sebastian grads. When the number of Sebastian admissions to the good schools started dropping precipitously, Gillis and Finner came up with a way to cheat."

"This is kid stuff, Tanner," Jake groused. "Literally."

"Talk to people, Jake, people with teenagers. What you'll hear is that they're in a panic these days. They want their little darlings to go to Cal and Stanford and Harvard and Yale like they did, but getting admitted to those schools has become almost impossible. Berkeley is twenty-five percent Oriental because so many Asians have top grades and test scores. Stanford's reputation is as good as Harvard's, so it gets a dozen applications for every available slot. Because things have tightened up so much, kids are applying to ten or twelve schools instead of one or two which makes the whole admissions process haphazard. I'll tell you how bad it is—last year, Cal turned down two thousand applicants who came out of high school with *four-point averages*. How do Jason and Jennifer McWealthy compete with all that? They don't, unless they come out of Sebastian with almost perfect records. And if you think I'm exaggerating about the panic, you've been spending too much time with your bimbos."

"You're saying the colleges are corrupt, too?"

I shook my head. "I'm saying when the child of a mover and shaker is involved, maybe they don't look real hard at the student's stats. But they're no more corrupt than the admissions system in general; it's Sebastian that fudged. The grades were upped and the test scores were inflated as well."

"How?"

"The grades were just a double set of books. Linton got his hands on a set of the real transcripts just before he went to jail. What he needed were the applications that showed the phony numbers Sebastian sent to the colleges."

"What about the scores?" Jake asked. "Those are national testing companies. Are you saying they were in on it, too?"

I shook my head. "Those companies rely on local institutions to administer the tests, and I'll bet Sebastian administered a lot of them. Once Gillis and Finner decided to cheat, my guess is they used ringers to take the tests for the poor performers. I'm told kids take the SATs half a dozen times these days, starting as early as eighth grade. There are courses that do nothing but teach kids how to beat the stupid things. As a result, scores can hop by hundreds of points. If the first results of a Sebastian student were poor, I figure Finner sent in a reliever."

"Aren't they fingerprinted or something?" Jake asked.

I shook my head. "A teacher I know tells me the only thing they do is check the admission slips the kids receive from the testing service against their driver's license or other ID. You know as well as I do that if money and honesty aren't drawbacks, you can beat any security system there is, and Sebastian could certainly beat that one." I laughed. "I suppose it's progress, in a way. It used to be the athletic departments were the ones trying to beat the tests—back when I was a lawyer I had some cases of ringers taking SATs for jocks or jocks taking the test themselves but copying every answer from the person sitting next to them, with the cooperation of that student in return for a payoff from the athletic department. The bottom line is, if no one questions a given result, the system can be beaten, and no one was raising questions about the Sebastian kids till Wade Linton came along."

"This is the reason you're claiming Gillis had Linton sent to jail?" Jake asked.

I nodded. "And ultimately killed."

"You have evidence of this scam, as you call it?"

"It's around. The police are at Sebastian now, impounding records. The admissions files at Stanford and Cal are being screened to compare with what they find at Sebastian, and they've issued a subpoena duces tecum to the testing company in New Jersey. Also, somehow or other, Linton got hold of the double numbers for about a dozen students, from talking to the kids, or maybe because he had friends in some college admissions departments. The notations of grade and test score discrepancies he made in a yearbook are in the hands of the police as well. What he was after when he died was documentary proof to take to the cops. I suppose as an ex-con, he figured he had to nail it down before he could get anyone to do anything." I looked at Gillis. "He was probably right."

"Where did they find the yearbook?" Gillis blurted.

"In Golden Gate Park. That was a break—I figure you sent your flunky Lloyd out to track down Linton after the manuscript showed up. Lloyd must have located his hideout just before I did, but he got scared off before he searched the place well enough to find Linton's stash." I grinned. "Next time you need a surrogate, pick one with some guts."

"Is this true?" Emma Drayer blurted. I thought the question was addressed to me, but her eyes were fixed on Gillis.

"Of course not," Gillis said stiffly.

"You killed Wade Linton to save that obnoxious *school*?"

Gillis flared. "That school is the most important institution in this city. It has done more for San Francisco than any of you will *ever* do. Sebastian *is* San Francisco. *Sebastian must never die.*"

"That's enough," Jake Hattie said, regarding his client with what looked a bit like disappointment. Then he looked at me. "There's more to this, Tanner. And you know me well enough to know I'm going to find out what it is."

"And you know me well enough to know you can't keep me from doing what I have to do."

"Which is what?"

"Make sure no one else suffers because of what went on at that silly school."

When I was certain he was dying, I knelt at his side and asked if he had anything to tell me. His eyes would barely open; his voice was barely audible.

Instead of the apology I expected, I heard only this: "At least I have accomplished something—now you truly are a criminal."

HOMAGE TO HAMMURABI, p. 331

Chapter
30

Gillis and Finner and their lawyers stomped out of the office and down the hall, no doubt bent on further consultation, leaving Emma Drayer looking out the window at the pigeons and the rooftops while her lawyer looked at me, her feelings mixed, her stylish suit a natty barrier between us. I preferred her in a headband, so I told her so.

She waved away the observation. "You know this finishes us with the firm, don't you? Even if he survives all this, the last people Marvin's going to want to see around here are Christine and me."

"He's not going to survive this—not as a lawyer, at any rate."

"I suppose not," Christine concluded after a lengthy moment. "Clients get nervous when their attorney is the main subject of gossip at the Pacific Union Club." She looked at her friend. "Guess we'd better get our résumés up to speed, huh, Em?"

Motionless and morose, Emma didn't answer. In a dark corner of the room, she seemed as bewildered as a recent widow, receding into shadow and stupor.

Her lawyer shook her head with compassion. "There's one thing that bothers me."

"What's that?"

"I didn't hear Emma's role mentioned during all of that."

"That's because Gillis was smart enough not to take me on."

"She hasn't been real candid about all this," Christine continued, as if Emma had just stepped out. "If I'm going to be her lawyer, I think I should know what her exposure is."

I looked at Emma. "Do you have any problem with that?"

It took a while, but Emma finally shook her head.

"Do you tell her, or do I?"

Slumped against the wall, eyes still on the out-of-doors, doubtlessly wishing she was a referee rather than a participant, she told me to go ahead.

I swiveled toward Christine. "Emma didn't have anything to do with the phony records. What Emma had to do with was helping Gillis prevent Wade Linton from exposing the admissions scam back when Linton first suspected it."

"How did she do that?"

"Remember back in 'eighty-three, when Emma was in trouble for challenging Gillis over the edict following the Balboa game? She was afraid Gillis was going to fire her as an insubordinate, so she looked into the possibility of getting a new job. But when she did, she found she'd been blacklisted. She was pretty desperate at that point, quite naturally. Then Gillis came along and offered her a deal."

"What deal?"

"A trip to Europe."

Christine licked her lips. "A better deal than *I've* ever made."

"But this one had strings. One of them was, she had to take someone with her."

"The soccer player."

"Right. Only the trip didn't have anything to do with soccer, it had to do with sex."

Christine sniffed and squinted, as though I'd started speaking in another language.

"The soccer player was pregnant," I went on. "My hunch is, the main reason she played soccer was the hope that she would spontaneously abort. But whatever the reason, when she hurt her ankle in the Balboa game, her doctor recognized her condition right away. As doctors to rich men tend to do, he told her father about the pregnancy. And Daddy used the situation to his advantage."

"How?"

"The girl had waited too long to get an abortion, so there was no alternative but to have the child, then put it up for adoption. But first things first—under the circumstances, Gillis didn't want the pregnancy to take place under the eyes of the Sebastian people."

"*What* circumstances?"

"The pregnant girl was his daughter. Gillis wanted her out of sight and out of mind during the last stages of her pregnancy, so she wouldn't undercut the moral authority he saw himself as providing to Sebastian. If not the universe."

"What happened to the baby?" Christine asked. "Was it adopted?"

I nodded. "Through a private placement arranged by a lawyer named Julius Messenger."

"Who were the new parents?"

I met her eye. "Mr. and Mrs. Wade Linton."

"But . . ." Christine sputtered to a halt struggling to make sense of it the way I had tussled with it the night before. "Why would Gillis let his grandchild be raised by the man he was trying to get rid of?"

"Because that was the way to shut Linton up. I'm sure Gillis had already tried to *scare* Linton into backing off, and buy him off as well, but it didn't work. Then the pregnancy fell into his hands, and Gillis used it not only to get Linton to go to jail as punishment for impregnating Jane Ann, but also to persuade Linton to keep quiet about the phony records, in Linton's own self-interest."

"Which was?"

"To keep Gillis from having Messenger throw a monkey wrench into the adoption. As you probably know, there are all kinds of formalities in those things—notice requirements and releases and waivers and the like. I'm betting Messenger purposely left a few of the statutory steps defective, in case Gillis wanted the whole thing voided later on."

Christine thought over what I'd said. "You're telling me Wade Linton went to jail for six years, for something he didn't do, just so an *adoption* would hold up? Isn't that a little extreme?"

I played my trump. "Not if Wade Linton was the father of the child."

Beyond us, Emma Drayer gasped as though I had summoned the supernatural. Her features became a tumble of doubt and debate. "That can't be *true*," she managed finally.

"I'm afraid it is, and it can be proved if it needs to be. The biologists have got paternity down to a science these days—they run seven serologic tests and a leukocyte antigen test and afterward they can exclude ninety percent of the nonfathers." I looked at the women in turn. "One of the reasons I'm going through all this—with Gillis and with you—is that I'm hoping it won't *need* to be proved. If Gillis takes his medicine, maybe the rest of it can stay the way it is."

"So it really *did* happen," Emma Drayer mused with pained amazement. "Wade really did molest a student. Like a fool I believed him when he told me it was a lie."

"It was a lie."

"But Wade and Jane Ann . . ."

"Wade and Jane Ann fell in love. And nature took its course."

Emma sagged, then straightened, then moved out of the shadows toward the center of the room. "She consented? It wasn't rape or anything?"

I shook my head.

The new version wasn't much easier for her to deal with than the old, but finally she processed it. "At least I wasn't wrong about him." She sighed, then met my eye. "Not totally, at least."

Christine White was struggling. "Linton was trying to expose Gillis when he got killed, right? He was looking for more evidence, which means he wasn't keeping *quiet* anymore."

"Right."

"What happened to change his mind?"

"His wife divorced him."

"But what does that—?"

"It meant he wasn't able to live with his son even after

he served his time. At that point he figured he didn't have anything to lose, so he decided to drag the whole thing out in the open and hope he'd end up with custody of the boy when it got sorted out."

"And he was going to expose it through this *book* you were talking about?" Christine asked.

I shook my head. "Wade Linton didn't write that book."

Christine frowned. "Who did?"

I shrugged. "If I'm lucky I'll find out tonight."

Emma spoke from beneath the halo of the ceiling light. "I still don't understand. The crime. The molestation. Did that happen or not?"

"Not."

"But *someone* at Sebastian claimed Wade abused her. Didn't they?"

I nodded. "Her name was Carrie Devlin."

"Why did she lie about it?"

"I'm saving the answer to that for the only person in the world who needs to know," I said, then kissed Christine good-bye and headed for Noe Valley.

I got there just after one. Bridget Devlin was making lunch—the air was full of toasted cheese and tomato soup. I was as welcome as a wasp.

"Can't you let me *alone*?" she begged after she opened the door. "Every time I think I've climbed *out* of it, you come along and shove me back."

"This is the last time. I promise."

She didn't seem as cheered by the prospect as her plaint projected; lonely people never are. "Well? What is it? Carrie again, I suppose."

"Remember I told you she might be in trouble?"

"At Sebastian, you mean."

I nodded.

"God. I wish I'd never *heard* of that place." She backed into the hallway and beckoned for me to follow. When I was sitting at the small round table with a checkered cloth on the top, she asked if I wanted some soup.

I shook my head, then waited for her to finish eating, trying to decide how much I needed to tell her.

"Carrie," she reminded as she licked the mustache off her upper lip. "I hope you're not going to claim she slept with Wade Linton like you did the last time you were here."

"She didn't sleep with him," I agreed.

Her smile was pat. "I'm glad you've figured that out."

"But she *said* she did."

The smile turned upside down. "What are you talking about?"

"Carrie got mixed up in a blackmail scheme while she was at Sebastian. If it comes out in court, she could face a perjury charge. And maybe worse."

"Who did she supposedly blackmail?"

"Wade Linton."

Mrs. Devlin licked her lips again, this time out of nervousness. "Why on earth would she do that?"

"The powers that be wanted to make sure Linton kept quiet about some skulduggery at Sebastian. They used Carrie to accomplish their purpose."

"Who *are* these creatures you keep talking about?"

"You don't have to know, and it's better if you don't. Some powerful people are going to try to keep the Sebastian story a secret. If they get a glimmer that you know more than you should, you could be in trouble. If you're lucky, they'll succeed in burying it. If you're not, you'll read it in the papers. If you do, you should get in touch with me."

"I've never been lucky," she observed laconically. For some reason I thought of Tiny Gunderson, the little man down the block who had Bridget's share of luck and more.

"You haven't asked me why Carrie would go along with such a scheme," I said after a minute.

Her lips twisted. "That's because I already *know* why; it was that horrid school. Carrie was completely out of her element—lonely, insecure, feeling inferior and impoverished. Of course the rich kids made relentless fun of her—what she wore, the way she looked, where she lived—she told me once they made her feel like an immigrant. And basically that's what she was—there's an *ocean* between here and Cow Hollow. She'd have done anything to get out from under that pressure. And I guess that's what she did. Blackmail. My God."

"I'm afraid you're right," I said. "They saw a vulnerable girl with some street smarts they could use, so they made her an offer she couldn't refuse. Money was part of it, so was status—good grades, the student court, even the boyfriend was part of the deal."

Bridget Devlin nodded slowly. "There were so many changes that last year. I should have asked about them, but I let myself think she was just adjusting marvelously. The money was the key—she had much more of it than before, far more than her job at the mall could generate." Her smile was disdainful of only herself. "It occurred to me that she might be stealing. Or selling drugs. But it wouldn't have mattered *what* it was—I closed my eyes to all of it. I persuaded myself that even drugs were a good trade-off for what Sebastian would do for her."

She began to cry, deeply and convulsively. I took her hand in mine. "Motherhood's the toughest job there is," I said, partly because I thought it might help, partly because I believed it. "It's a lot like umpiring—the better it's done, the less it's noticed."

She tried to grin but couldn't manage it. "Is Carrie going to be arrested?" she mumbled between sniffs. "Should I go to Spain to be with her? Or Morocco? Or wherever the hell she is?"

"I don't know what's going to happen—it depends how quickly a deal can be cut by the bad guys. But if I were you I'd tell Carrie to stay in Morocco for as long as she can."

"But she has to go to *school*. She gets her master's next year. From *Stanford*. She can't—" Bridget Devlin stopped in midsentence. "I'm doing it again, aren't I?" she asked sheepishly.

I didn't have the heart to tell her the truth, about herself or about the status of her daughter's education. "Tell her to stay in Morocco," I repeated. "Stanford will be there when she gets back."

I left Carrie's mother the way I leave a lot of people— with too much on her mind. To ease my burden and maybe someone else's, before leaving Noe Valley I stopped by Tiny Gunderson's and bought a share of his luck myself.

What do I do now? Become a fugitive for as long as my wits will sustain me? Confess, and guarantee my return to prison? Commit suicide?

But perhaps that's premature.

I have written a book.

I think I'll get an agent.

HOMAGE TO HAMMURABI, p. 342

Chapter
31

In the nighttime mist the neon light above the Periwinkle portals was as fluffy as goose feathers. Street people looking much like Wade Linton had looked on the day he died eddied through the area in search of sustenance. I was in need of sustenance myself, in the form of putting Bryce and the book behind me, but although I sensed I had begun the final chapter, I hesitated to go inside.

In most of my cases, I consider it a job well done if I uncover one story—*the* story that has caused someone to pay me money to go out into the world and return with its message. But in this case I'd uncovered not one story but three—the real story of the academic fraud and the blackmail of Wade Linton; the story Marvin Gillis concocted to cover up his crime, using Carrie Devlin's false accusations against Linton and her implied threat to tell her tale in open court; and the story according to *Hammurabi,* which was a blend of those two stories plus a large injection of imagination and surmise.

Actually, I wasn't certain I had the three versions entirely separated out in my mind quite yet, and maybe I never would. All I knew was that each of the stories was hazardous in its own way, potentially wounding to one or another of the people who had been ensnared by the lure of the Sebastian School. Technically, the only job that re-

mained was for me to tell Bryce the name of *Hammurabi*'s
creator. In fact, the larger task was to keep as much of the
story to myself as I could, the way I always tried to do, to
minimize the pain of revelation. I pressed the buzzer next to
Periwinkle's heavy door.

Bryce had promised to have his wife and step-daughter
on hand for our meeting, but since neither of them was
enamored with my behavior of late, I was relieved when I
entered the conference room and found the entire Chatterton
clan waiting for me, if not eagerly then at least demurely.

"Thanks for coming," I said to all concerned. "This
won't take long."

"Charley Sleet wants you to call him, Marsh," Bryce
interjected. "He's still at the station. You can use the phone
in the office."

I closed the door behind me.

"We caught up to O'Shea," Charley said.

"What happened?"

"He tried to hold us off."

"I was afraid of that."

"Why?"

"He had a problem with authority and violence, left
over from his army days. It had to be weighing on him,
what he did to Linton. He was probably afraid he'd be jailed
for it."

"Well, we had to take him out."

"Dead."

"Yep."

"Damn."

"Looks like this thing is going to get political, too—the
DA's boys stopped by, then the captain called me in and told
me to lie low on anything to do with Gillis."

"So do it."

"You sure there's nothing I need to know?"

"Not at this point."

"Some day it's going to be a mistake to trust you,
Tanner."

"That'll be the day I don't ask."

When I got back to the conference room, a fire was
blazing brightly but the Chatterton family looked as though

they'd rather be freezing in Siberia than warm with me in SoMa.

Bryce was wan and pensive. "What's happening, Marsh? Jane Ann said the police came to her apartment, looking for Lloyd."

I looked at Jane Ann. "Did they find him?"

She shook her head. "Not there."

"Did they take anything?"

She shrugged. "Some of his clothes."

"Did they grill you?"

"Not much. But they said they might be back."

"You can count on it. Did they tell you what it's about?"

Her shoulders rose and fell again, even words were too much trouble. "Some drug thing, probably. Lloyd's not real discreet."

"It's not about drugs, Jane Ann." I looked at Bryce, then her mother. "The police think Lloyd had a hand in murder."

Margaret was the first to take the bait. "Well? Who was killed?"

"Wade Linton."

Since I was groping for some final strands of truth, I was watching Jane Ann as I said the name. And she was good—her eyes widened, her hand flew to her mouth, but the groan that escaped her core was barely audible. But she couldn't maintain the pose. Leaning forward in her chair, her arms crossed on the belly that once had been swollen with her child, she began shaking her head in a rhythmic denial. "No . . . no . . . no . . ."

When her mother reached her side she tried her best to comfort her. Since there was nothing I could contribute to the effort, I looked at my friend and client, who seemed less disconsolate than disconnected. "Linton's the teacher at Sebastian who was jailed for assaulting one of his students," I explained easily, as though we were starting from scratch.

Bryce nodded abstractly. "The one who wrote *Hammurabi*. I wonder if he has an executor who could authorize Periwinkle to publish and—"

"Linton didn't write the book," I countered, angrier than I should have been that Bryce's focus remained so steadfast. "That was just the way it was supposed to look."

The heat from the fire was making him sweat. "Then who did?"

"That's why I'm here." I looked at Margaret and Jane Ann, still joined in a rough embrace. "I'm not sure I know. At first, I thought Jane Ann had written it."

The women had no reaction, but Bryce frowned. "Why would she? I mean write a book about that?"

I phrased it carefully. "Because she knew Wade Linton was innocent. Because she wanted to change the public perception of the kind of person he was. Because she wanted to exculpate him, if only retroactively."

"Why would she want to do that?"

I kept my eyes away but made certain Jane Ann could hear me. "Because she liked him, I guess; he was a good teacher. But it's not important. Whatever the reason, I don't think Jane Ann would have helped Linton by accusing her father of molestation unless he really did abuse her." I looked at the object of my care, still convulsing in the arms of her mother. "Your father was mean, maybe even heartless, and he made you make a sacrifice you didn't want to make, but he didn't molest you. Not sexually, at least. Am I right, Jane Ann?"

Jane Ann shook her head. Her mental state was such that I had no idea if it was an answer to my question or a rejection of my message.

From behind her daughter's shoulder, Margaret's eyes sought mine. "Are you saying this Linton person forced himself on my daughter?"

As I shook my head, Jane Ann groaned with the burden of our private knowledge.

"Then what *are* you saying—that Lloyd killed Linton?" There was a hint of hope in Bryce's voice, as though he'd finally found the way to rid himself of a contagion.

I shook my head. "He was just a puppet; the real criminal was the puppeteer."

Bryce frowned. "Who was?"

I looked at Margaret. "Your ex-husband."

She ceased her ministrations. "Marvin?"

I nodded. "He'll be arrested in the morning, after he gets his affairs in order." Then I remembered Charley's caution. "Unless the politicians are able to shut down the investigation entirely."

"But what will happen to . . . ?" Margaret's question was too egotistical to complete. "I mean, why would Marvin *murder* someone? Good Lord. He's no angel, heaven knows, but Marvin is . . . Marvin."

"That was the problem. Linton was going to show the world that Marvin wasn't Marvin after all."

"What do you mean?"

"There were some shenanigans at Sebastian. Pretty serious, enough to destroy the school. There's no point in going into them, but if you have any more trouble with your property settlement, have your lawyer get in touch with me. Suffice it to say, Linton threatened to expose the scheme, so Marvin had him killed."

Bryce coughed. "I hate to sound like a broken record, but if Linton didn't write the book, and Jane Ann didn't, then who did?"

I smiled. "My next candidate was Margaret."

Margaret stiffened. "What would make you consider that for even an instant?"

"Because you're intelligent enough to have done it. Because you knew more than any of the other candidates about what really happened at the school. And because you had a powerful motive to punish your ex-husband and a good way to do it was make a thinly disguised allegation that Gillis was a sex pervert." I paused. "But I don't think you would have done it the way it was done in *Hammurabi,* because you had to know that if you did, your daughter would get dragged into it."

"Is there something I'm missing?" Bryce asked earnestly. "I don't understand why Jane Ann is involved in this at all."

I looked at him. "As Jane Ann relentlessly points out, you're her stepfather. Which means you didn't know what she was going through back then. Which means the *real* author of *Homage to Hammurabi* is one Bryce Chatterton."

Face red, fingers clenched, he looked for a minute like he might resort to violence. Luckily, he opted for rhetoric. "I *hired* you, Marsh. Why would I do that if I was the one who wrote the book?"

"Because it was part of the process that let you get the word out in publishing circles and the media that there was a mysterious manuscript at Periwinkle that could blow the whistle on some of the city's upper crust. The hype machine has kept pace with me all along, Bryce. And you're the one who would know how to make that happen."

"But—"

"Except you didn't get it right. Oh, it was right that Wade Linton wasn't a criminal, but it wasn't right that the father was the bad guy and it wasn't right that Linton was out for vengeance for the frame-up. There were lots of things you missed, and since you had to rely on gossip and eavesdropping instead of truth, you're the only one in the room who would have missed them."

Bryce rubbed his eyes. "I didn't *write* it, Marsh. You have to believe me."

I walked to the table beside him, placed my briefcase on its middle, and flicked open the hinges. "I brought it back," I said as I lifted out the manuscript. "The only copy."

He nodded miserably.

I looked at the roaring fire at the end of the room, then glanced at Margaret and Jane Ann. "Under the circumstances, I think it's best for all concerned if this doesn't see the light of day."

I marched toward the blaze, manuscript in my hands, my purpose clear and catastrophic. When the heat was enough to stop me, I looked one more time at Bryce, then prepared to pitch my burden into the greedy flames.

"Don't, Marsh. Please. It's all I have."

I still owed him. So I didn't.

And then I didn't owe him anymore.

It looks like the book deal isn't going to work out.

HOMAGE TO HAMMURABI, p. 345

Chapter
32

She answered the bell herself, still tiny, still garbed in black, still fearful of every living thing that coiled beyond her doorway. "Is Alfred still up?" I asked.

She shook her head. "He's been asleep for hours."

"I'll come back tomorrow. What would be a good time?"

A lip and eyelid quivered. "There wouldn't be one."

"I'll get to him one way or another, Ms. Lucerne. You'll both be better off if you make it easy for me."

Her eyes sought safety in the distance, which was gray with fog, impenetrable and uninviting. "What do you want him for?"

"I just want to tell him something. About his father."

"Paul?"

The word surprised me. "Wade."

She stiffened as though I had struck her. "I can't imagine what."

"Linton wasn't a ghost, Ms. Lucerne, as much as you might wish it. He was out of jail and living in a car parked along the Panhandle and he saw Al almost every day. They got along quite well, till the cops drove him off."

She closed her eyes and shook her head. "I don't believe you. I *can't* believe you."

"I'm sorry, but it's true."

Her eyes flamed as bright as the fire that had almost claimed the book that had started it all. "Where's Wade now? I want to put a stop to this. He can't waltz in here and—"

It was my turn to be surprised. "They didn't tell you?"

"Tell me what?"

"He's dead."

"Wade?"

I nodded. "He was killed by a custodian at Sebastian. They found his body earlier today."

Even before she absorbed its entirety, the news was already lifting the strain off her features, leaving them rounded and alive, as though she'd just unmasked. "Who would murder Wade? Was it something to do with that girl?"

I assumed it was Jane Ann she was talking about, until I realized it must be Carrie Devlin. "It wasn't about that, but it did have to do with Sebastian."

"That awful place."

I nodded. "Records were being altered so the Sebastian kids could get into the best colleges. Your husband suspected something of the sort and was going to put a stop to it, so they framed him."

Her voice grew throaty and reminiscent. "Wade was always a do-gooder. The students hated him for it."

"Not all of them," I said, then wished I hadn't. "The bottom line is, he didn't do what they said he did. He didn't touch a hair on Carrie Devlin's head."

"I wish I could believe you."

"Take a chance, Ms. Lucerne. Give him the benefit of the doubt. For Alfred's sake."

Her voice rose. "But don't you know what that would mean? About me, I mean?"

I nodded. It would mean that once upon a time she'd been mistaken and unfair. Just like all the rest of us.

She worked with it for so long I thought she was going to stick to the Gillis script, even though the show had finally been canceled. When she looked at me, her eyes were small but curious. "Was that what you wanted to tell my son? That his father was dead?"

I shook my head. "Though if you want me to, I will. I assumed he already knew."

"I should do it," she said, trying to be valiant. "Shouldn't I?"

I agreed with her. "I just want to make sure Al knows that his father didn't do what he was imprisoned for—that he wasn't a criminal, he was a nice guy."

"I still have a hard time believing that."

"What matters is that Al believes it."

When she didn't react, I began my final message. "There's a bike out in the yard, a pretty good one. Tell Al his father got it for him. Tell him it was the last thing he did before he died."

"Is that true?"

"Does it matter?"

Some cases close, other linger. This one is still around, even after all these months, the epilogue still being written in little scribblings all over town. It's one of the cases I cling to, with the idea that what I accomplished will seem significant enough to keep me going till the next one comes along. It's a nice enough concept, crucial even, but it almost never works.

Homage to Hammurabi was published in December. Although it was enthusiastically though ineptly reviewed by Colt Harrison, as partial consideration of the resolution of his wife's property settlement, Bryce agreed not to promote it or print more than 1000 copies, so it was ignored by the retail chains and the national media. It sold fewer than half the printing.

Not long afterward, the DA dismissed all charges against Marvin Gillis and Rufus Finner in return for a plea of guilty to one count of conspiracy to defraud. The jail sentences were suspended in lieu of a program of community service that Charley Sleet managed to require be performed at a storefront mission in the Tenderloin.

I had wanted Gillis to do time, but it had always been more a prayer than a possibility, and with Arthur O'Shea out of the picture there was no chance to make it happen, especially not with Jake Hattie as his lawyer. But I dropped by the mission one day, to make sure Gillis was doing his duty. And he was. He even seemed to be proud of it.

Carrie Devlin remains in Morocco, as a stringer for *Le Monde*. Just before Christmas, her mother had a show at a small gallery on Geary. Darryl Dromedy proclaimed it a commercial triumph and an artistic nightmare.

The Periwinkle Press is thriving, not because of *Hammurabi* but because of *Gridlock*, which became a cult icon, the best-selling book of its kind since *Fup*. Ironically, Bryce's model for Periwinkle, the North Point Press, was recently put up for sale by its owners, who denied the company was overextended.

Jane Ann Gillis is taking art lessons from Lily Lucerne. I saw her one day, walking along Clement Street with her son, sharing her ice cream with him. Al was pushing his bike. Jane Ann was laughing, as far as I know for the first time. Her friend Lloyd has been missing since the day Wade Linton died so I haven't returned his buckle.

My own version of the case, written in fits and snatches during televised ball games and sleepless nights, tentatively entitled *Book Case,* was abandoned on page eighty-two. At about that time, Christine White informed me that she and Emma had made a lateral transfer to a bigger firm for bigger money, and that she was about to marry a pharmacist. Since then, I've been seeing a lot of Betty Fontaine. I never did buy a computer.

Charley Sleet's friend Homer was found dead in an alley within sight of City Hall. Charley thinks it was foul play, but no one else thinks about it at all.

I still haven't heard from Peggy.